THE WIDOW'S CHOICE

BOOKS BY GILBERT MORRIS

THE HOUSE OF WINSLOW SERIES

CHENEY DUVALL, M.D.[1]

CHENEY AND SHILOH: THE INHERITANCE[1]

THE SPIRIT OF APPALACHIA[2]

LIONS OF JUDAH

[1]with Lynn Morris   [2]with Aaron McCarver

06B

GILBERT MORRIS

the WIDOW'S CHOICE

BETHANYHOUSE
Minneapolis, Minnesota

The Widow's Choice
Copyright © 2006
Gilbert Morris

Cover illustration by William Graf
Cover design by Josh Madison

Scripture quotations are from the King James Version of the Bible.

Published by Bethany House Publishers
11400 Hampshire Avenue South
Bloomington, Minnesota 55438

Bethany House Publishers is a division of
Baker Publishing Group, Grand Rapids, Michigan.

Printed in the United States of America

ISBN-13: 978-0-7642-0027-4
ISBN-10: 0-7642-0027-5

Library of Congress Cataloging-in-Publication Data

Morris, Gilbert.
    The widow's choice / Gilbert Morris.
        p.   cm. — (The house of Winslow : 1941)
    ISBN-13: 978-0-7642-0027-4 (pbk.)
    ISBN-10: 0-7642-0027-5 (pbk.)
        1. Winslow family (Fictitious characters)—Fiction. 2. Depressions—
Fiction. 3. Widows—Fiction. 4. Mothers and sons—Fiction.
5. Marriage—Fiction. 6. Brothers—Fiction. 7. Air pilots, Military—
Fiction. 8. United States—History—1933–1945—Fiction. 9. World War,
1939–1945—United States—Fiction. I. Title. II. Series: Morris, Gilbert.
House of Winslow.
    PS3563.O8742W52   2006
    813'.54—dc22   2006017662

I dedicate this book to Ginger Conlon,
my beloved daughter.
You are exactly what a woman of God should be!

GILBERT MORRIS spent ten years as a pastor before becoming Professor of English at Ouachita Baptist University in Arkansas and earning a Ph.D. at the University of Arkansas. A prolific writer, he has had over 25 scholarly articles and 200 poems published in various periodicals and over the past years has had more than 180 novels published. His family includes three grown children, and he and his wife live in Gulf Shores, Alabama.

CONTENTS

PART FOUR
December 1941–December 1942

THE HOUSE OF WINSLOW

★ ★ ★ ★

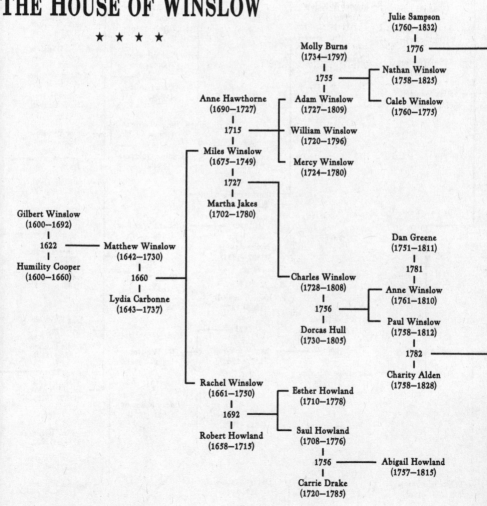

Julie Sampson
(1760—1832)
|
1776 ————————

Molly Burns
(1734—1797)
|
1755 ———————— Nathan Winslow
(1758—1825)

Anne Hawthorne   Adam Winslow
(1690—1727)   (1727—1809)   Caleb Winslow
| (1760—1775)
1715 ———————— William Winslow
| (1720—1796)
Miles Winslow
(1675—1749)   Mercy Winslow
| (1724—1780)
1727 ————————
|
Martha Jakes
(1702—1780)   Dan Greene
                                              (1751—1811)
Gilbert Winslow |
(1600—1692)   1781
| |
1622 ———————— Matthew Winslow   Anne Winslow
| (1642—1730)   (1761—1810)
Humility Cooper   Charles Winslow
(1600—1660) | (1728—1808)
1660 ————————   Paul Winslow
| (1758—1812)
Lydia Carbonne   1756 ————————
(1643—1737) | 1782 ————————
                          Dorcas Hull |
                          (1730—1805)   Charity Alden
                                              (1758—1828)
Rachel Winslow
(1661—1750)   Esther Howland
| (1710—1778)
1692 ————————
|
Robert Howland   Saul Howland
(1658—1715)   (1708—1776)
                          |
                          1756 ———————— Abigail Howland
                          | (1757—1815)
                          Carrie Drake
                          (1720—1785)

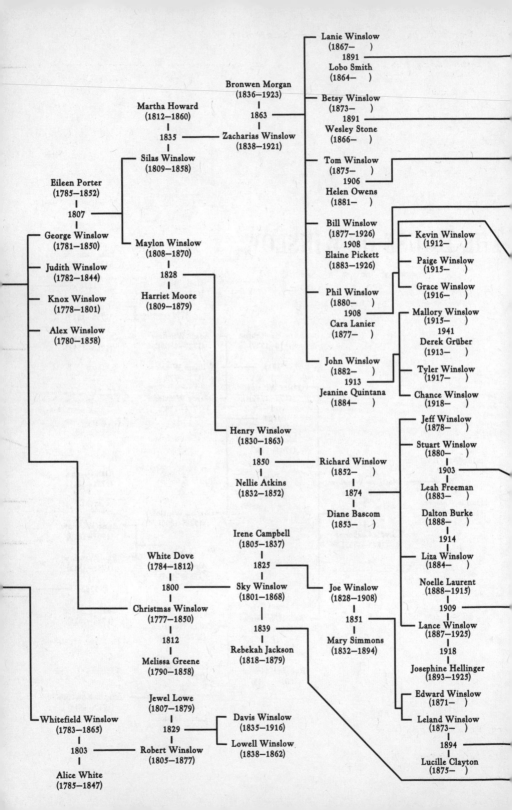

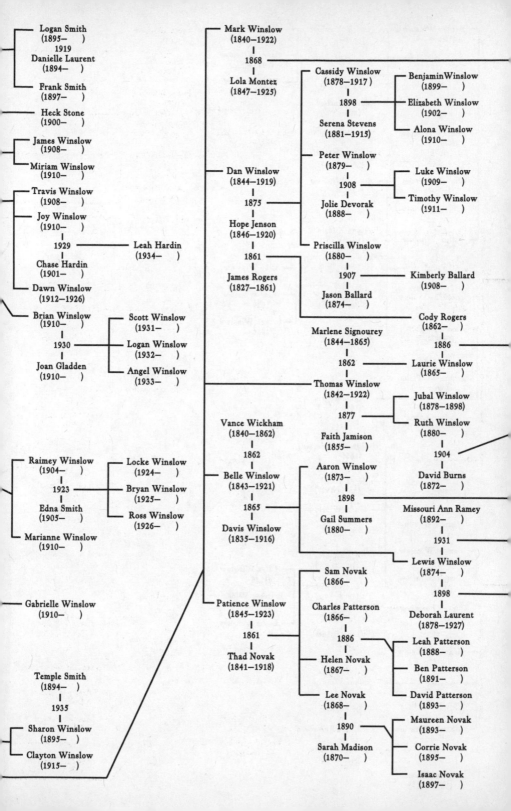

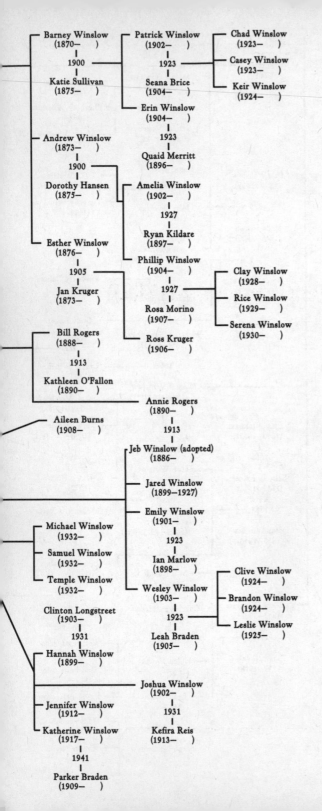

Barney Winslow
(1870–)
|
1900
|
Katie Sullivan
(1875–)

Patrick Winslow
(1902–)
|
1923
|
Seana Brice
(1904–)

Chad Winslow
(1923–)

Casey Winslow
(1923–)

Keir Winslow
(1924–)

Erin Winslow
(1904–)
|
1923
|
Quaid Merritt
(1896–)

Andrew Winslow
(1873–)
|
1900
|
Dorothy Hansen
(1875–)

Amelia Winslow
(1902–)
|
1927
|
Ryan Kildare
(1897–)

Esther Winslow
(1876–)
|
1905
|
Jan Kruger
(1873–)

Phillip Winslow
(1904–)
|
1927
|
Rosa Morino
(1907–)

Clay Winslow
(1928–)

Rice Winslow
(1929–)

Serena Winslow
(1930–)

Ross Kruger
(1906–)

Bill Rogers
(1888–)
|
1913
|
Kathleen O'Fallon
(1890–)

Annie Rogers
(1890–)
|
1913
|

Aileen Burns
(1908–)

Jeb Winslow (adopted)
(1886–)

Jared Winslow
(1899–1927)

Emily Winslow
(1901–)
|
1923
|
Ian Marlow
(1898–)

Michael Winslow
(1932–)

Samuel Winslow
(1932–)

Temple Winslow
(1932–)

Wesley Winslow
(1903–)
|
1923
|
Leah Braden
(1905–)

Clive Winslow
(1924–)

Brandon Winslow
(1924–)

Leslie Winslow
(1925–)

Clinton Longstreet
(1903–)
|
1931
|
Hannah Winslow
(1899–)

Joshua Winslow
(1902–)
|
1931
|
Kefira Reis
(1913–)

Jennifer Winslow
(1912–)

Katherine Winslow
(1917–)
|
1941
|
Parker Braden
(1909–)

PART ONE

July 1938–December 1940

★ ★ ★

CHAPTER ONE

A PERFECT DAY

★ ★ ★

Alona Jennings stared at the calendar that hung on her kitchen wall, irritated by the cheap painting of an English fox hunt. Shaking her head, she muttered, "I ought to just tear that dumb picture out. Whoever painted it sure couldn't paint worth a flip." She often wondered why she didn't throw the whole thing away and get a calendar that pleased her more, but Alona's life was busy, and money was precious. Sighing with frustration, she plucked a pencil out of her apron pocket and drew a circle around July the Fourth.

Turning from the calendar, she focused on her good feelings on this very special day. The whole family was going to a Fourth of July celebration with games and then a free lunch furnished by the politicians, if you cared to listen to their speeches long enough to wait. Truman would then be pitching for the Mountaineers, and after he won his ball game, as the boys vowed he would, they were all going to go out to eat and then take in a movie.

The sun shone brightly through the window, lighting

up the old linoleum on the kitchen floor that was worn through all the way down to the black tar underneath in a couple of places. Opening the icebox door, Alona saw that the last chunk of ice had melted down to about a five-pound lump. Closing the door to the oak icebox, she went to the living room and pulled the iceman's sign off a nail on the wall, considering how much ice to order. The sign was marked on the four corners: twenty-five, fifty, seventy-five, a hundred. For a moment she was tempted to put up the number one hundred, but money was so scarce that she settled for the fifty-pound chunk. *But we're going to have ice cream,* she told herself, changing her mind again and firmly putting the hundred-pound number at the top instead and placing the sign in the window, where the iceman could see it. She only hoped that he ran on the holiday.

Going back to the kitchen, she quickly built a fire in the stove so she could cook breakfast. Ten minutes later the fire was burning smoothly. She was about to start breakfast when a knock at the back door caught her attention. "Who could that be?" She put the skillet down on the stove and went to the door. Through the screen she saw a tall, spindly looking man with a pale, cadaverous face. He was dressed practically in rags, and he pulled off his weather-beaten hat and held it with both hands.

"Ma'am, could I chop some wood or do some work for a meal?"

Alona hesitated. This had become such a common occurrence that she had been forced to turn many men away, but something poignant in the hobo's face urged her to help him, and she said, "Yes, come on in. I'll fix you something to eat."

"I can eat out here on the porch, ma'am."

"Nonsense. Come on in and sit down at the table. The coffee's about ready. I'll cook some bacon and eggs."

The man stepped inside, looking around apprehensively and saying nothing.

"Sit over there," Alona said, pointing to the table and pouring him a cup of coffee. "Do you use sugar or cream?"

"If it ain't too much trouble, ma'am."

Alona set the glass sugar bowl on the table, opened the storage side of the icebox, and pulled out a mason jar half full of cream. As the man drank his coffee, she began fixing the meal. "Have you come far?"

"Yes, ma'am, all the way from Ohio."

"Ohio! How in the world did you get from Ohio down to Georgia?"

"Well, ma'am, the factory I worked at for twelve years closed, and work was hard to find." The man's voice was rusty, as if from lack of use. "I just drifted south lookin' for work. Do you know of anything?"

Alona had broken two eggs into a pan with some bacon but hesitated before breaking a third. "You want your eggs scrambled or over easy?"

"Any way, ma'am."

She turned the eggs over with a spatula, then put the bacon and eggs on a plate. She opened the storage compartment over the top of the stove, took out two biscuits, and added them to the plate. "There you are." She poured herself a cup of coffee and sat down across from the man, studying him as she sipped her drink. "Work is scarce around here," she finally said.

"Scarce everywhere. I don't know what we're gonna do if things don't get better."

"We'll just have to trust the Lord, I guess. What's your name?"

"Nick Saban. This is mighty good food, ma'am. I reckon I was hungrier than I knew. Please excuse my manners."

"Don't mind that. Oh, I've got some strawberry jam

that'll go good with those biscuits." She went to the cupboard and pulled out a jar of jam, opened it, and set it on the table. She watched as he very neatly layered half of one of the biscuits, then took a small bite. He had better manners than most, and she could tell that he had come from a better position in life than many of the hobos that came by. "I wish I did know of a job," she said.

"This depression. Everybody says it's Hoover's fault."

"I doubt if one man could have brought it all on."

"You're probably right."

She waited until the man had finished and said, "I'll make some sandwiches for you to take with you."

"Thank you, ma'am, but I'll need to work for this meal."

"That's all right. I've got three boys and a strong husband to do the heavy work around here." She got up, fixed three thick sandwiches of bologna with cheese, wrapped them in wax paper, and put them in a bag. She put an apple in also and handed him the package. He stood before her uncertainly, and without thinking, she said, "Would it be all right if I prayed for you before you go?"

"Pray for me? Well, ma'am, ain't nobody prayed for me since I was just a boy. My mama prayed for me, but she died when I was only twelve."

"I'd like to pray for you if you don't mind."

Saban bent his head, but she saw the glitter of tears in his eyes. "Yes, ma'am, you go right ahead."

"Lord, we ask that you go with Mr. Saban. Provide work for him. Give him health and strength. May he learn to look to you, the Lord Jesus, for every need. Father, I ask this in the name of Jesus. Amen."

Saban looked up and something had changed in his face. "That . . . that was mighty fine, ma'am. A good prayer. It reminds me of my mother."

"Let me ask you something," she said. "I've always been curious—how do you decide which town to go to, or which house?"

He smiled briefly but with a flash of humor. "I follow the signs."

"What kind of signs?"

"Signs that us hobos leave. You see, we put marks and drawings of different kinds on curbs, posts, buildings—even houses. They tell us if the people in that town will help us out. Give us work or food. I seen the mark on your house."

"I never saw anything."

"If you've got a piece of paper, I can show you."

Alona got up and found a paper and pencil, handing them to Nick. He drew for a minute and then showed her the paper.

"This sign here," he said, pointing to a group of intersecting lines, "means hobos ain't welcome. But this one here means this is a great place to stop." He was pointing to a group of three small *u*'s drawn inside a rectangle. "And three little circles like that means keep on moving—the police are out to get ya."

He picked up his small bundle of personal belongs and the sack of food. "I'll be going, ma'am, but I won't forget you."

"God bless you." Alona watched as he left and made his way down the street. She thought of the thousands of men like Nick Saban wandering the streets and countryside of America and sighed.

Abruptly, she shook off her thoughts and walked down the hall to the boys' bedroom door. Opening it, she said, "Get up, boys! Get up and wash."

The only response was a groan.

"It's the Fourth of July! We're going to have a fun day today."

She went down the hall to the other bedroom of the

small house. She tiptoed to the bed and looked down into the face of her sleeping husband. With a smile she remembered how she had felt the first time she had seen him when she was seventeen. She had gone to a ball game and seen him pitch, and although she didn't much believe in romantic tales of love at first sight, something had indeed happened to her at that game. Now, looking down at his tawny hair and the clean-cut lines of his strong body, lean as a leopard, she wanted to reach out and put her hands on him. For just a moment she felt somewhat abashed that after a dozen years of marriage she could still be so in love with her husband. Quick to cover her emotions, she gently shook his shoulder. "Wake up, Truman. Time for breakfast."

As always, he woke up suddenly—wide-eyed like a cat. Before she could move, he grabbed her and pulled her down on the bed. He began to kiss her neck, ignoring her protests and squeals.

A laugh bubbled up out of his throat, and as he held her pinioned with his face inches from hers, he winked playfully and said, "I've got great plans for you, beautiful."

"Save your strength for the ball game," she teased, scrambling out of his grasp and to her feet.

Truman swung his legs out of the bed with an easy motion. "Hey," he said, grabbing her again. "Come back here. I don't need to pitch till this afternoon."

Alona laughed and ruffled his hair. "If you win, I may have a reward for you tonight." She winked. "Now, hurry up and get down to breakfast."

She went back to the kitchen, where she found Buddy, their six-month-old collie, waiting for her at the screen door. "Hello, Buddy. Come on in." She opened the door, and he came in, jumped up on her, and tried to lick her face. "Get down, Buddy! I don't have time to fool with you." The dog whined, as he always did when he didn't get his way. His coloring was a beautiful mahogany on white. Truman had bought him for her birthday, and they had all spoiled him to distraction. The boys often stopped by the butcher to beg bones for him, and Alona put an egg in his food once in a while to keep his coat glossy. Buddy still hadn't gotten down, so she reached out and tapped his hind foot with the toe of her shoe. "Get down now."

Buddy yelped, dropped to all fours, and looked up at her with a comical, reproachful look. He whirled and went over to his corner, where he lay down, facing the wall. It was something he did every time his feelings got hurt. "You're too sensitive, Buddy." He refused to look around at her, so she tore a fragment of the roast from the night before and took it over to him. "If you'll be sweet, I'll give you this meat." Instantly Buddy turned around, sat up, and begged as they had taught him. She gave him the meat, patted his silky hair, and said, "Now, I've got work to do."

★　★　★

Truman chewed a huge mouthful of scrambled eggs mixed with bacon and winked across at the boys. "Your ma is a terrible cook, but no matter, boys, just try your best to keep it down."

"Ah, Dad, Mom isn't a terrible cook!" Tim protested. He was ten, the oldest of the boys, with light brown hair and blue eyes. His face was quite thin and sensitive. It was not for nothing he was called a mama's boy, for he worshiped his mother.

Zachary, who sat next to him, was two years younger. He had brown hair and brown eyes, and was already showing signs of the same rangy strength that his father had. He was good at sports and good with his hands, and if he was afraid of anything, nobody ever found out about it. "Dad's just kidding, Tim. Don't you know anything?"

"I think you're a good cook!" Six-year-old Carl had blond hair, bright blue eyes, and an insatiable curiosity. He had an imaginary friend named Hootie that was very real to Carl. Even now he turned and said, "Hootie, you'd better have some of these eggs."

"Too late! I'm havin' the rest of 'em myself," Truman spouted, spooning out the last of the eggs. "You'll have to give Hootie a biscuit."

"There's no such person as Hootie!" Zac told his younger brother.

"There is too!" Carl insisted.

"Well, why can't I see him?"

"Because he doesn't want you to."

The two boys argued until Zac finally intervened. "Pa, when you asked the blessing, you prayed for everything, but you forgot to ask God to let you win the ball game today."

Tim was puzzled by this. "Dad, you don't think God cares about who wins baseball games, do you?"

"Why, He does too care!" Carl said argumentatively. "You think God doesn't know about baseball?"

The two argued back and forth, and finally Alona spoke up. "Children, stop arguing. I'm not sure that the Lord is really concerned about the score of some baseball game."

"Why, of course he is," Truman said, his eyes dancing. "I don't want you teachin' these boys bad theology, wife."

Alona was accustomed to Truman's teasing. He was a fine Christian man, although his Christianity was somewhat unconventional. Sometimes he would even tease during the blessing, thanking God for every item on the table, including the salt and pepper shakers and the plates they were eating from. It was a side of him that she loved, although she pretended to dislike it.

"What kind of stuff will they be havin' at the celebration, Dad?" Tim asked.

"Well, let's see. I guess there are going to be all kinds of races and contests later this morning—three-legged race, shoe-kicking contest, watermelon-spitting contest—and then there'll be lots of boring patriotic speeches about how great the politicians are." Truman shrugged.

"Don't you talk like that, Truman. We live in a great country, and I want our family to always be proud of our heritage." She turned to the boys. "You know that before I married your father I was a Winslow, and the first Winslow in this country was a man named Gilbert who came all the way over from England. And ever since then there have been Winslows in the Revolutionary War, in the War of 1812, in the Civil War. Why, one of our family was an ace in the Great War! You need to be proud of the men and women who bore that name." She felt strongly about this, proud of being a Winslow. It was one of the griefs of her life that she lived far away from the other members of the family and had never been able to be close to her relatives—or Truman's, for that matter.

Truman winked at the boys. "Well, I've been afraid to look back and see who my ancestors were. I'd prob'ly find a bunch of horse thieves. If you boys are done, why don't you go out and play. I'm gonna show your mama how to wash the dishes."

The boys carried their dishes to the sink and then ran outside, their sounds of gleeful yelling barely muted inside the kitchen.

"You don't have to help with the dishes, Truman."

"Why, shoot—I do it so much better'n you do," he said solemnly. "I've been meanin' to talk to you about your dish washin'. It's such a shame. Here, let me show you how a real dish washer operates."

Alona laughed at his teasing. She was glad that Truman had never been afraid to help her with housework or to change diapers when the boys were babies. She didn't know of too many other men like that. It was her opinion that men who were afraid of such things were in grave doubt about their own masculinity.

As they washed the dishes, Truman became serious. "I forgot to tell you yesterday I got a promotion at work. We'll be makin' more money now. We'll be able to buy some things for the house."

Alona stopped washing and looked at him. "What will you be doing? Not handling explosives?"

"Why, sure. That's what you do in a quarry. It pays more."

"I wish you wouldn't do it, Truman. It's such dangerous work."

"Now, Alona, it's all I can find, and we need the money. Don't worry. I won't get hurt."

She did not answer, but her brow was wrinkled as they finished washing the dishes.

After the last dish was dried, Truman hugged his wife tightly and kissed her. "I'll go out and play with those no-account sons of yours. We should leave about quarter to eleven, I guess. I think the games start at eleven."

He went outside, whistling as he went, and she watched through the screen door as he ran toward his three sons, grabbed Zachary, and fell to the ground. The other boys plunged into the fray, yelling and screaming, and as Alona watched them, she felt a warm glow. She was proud of her family, but she was worried about Truman working at such a dangerous occupation.

She stepped outside and sat down on the back stoop. As she did, a raucous sound came from the sky, and she looked up and saw an enormous flock of crows passing overhead, filling the sky. Truman pulled himself away from his sons and came over to sit down beside her. "I've never seen so many crows," she commented. "There must be thousands of them."

"Yeah, it's gonna be a raincrow summer."

"A raincrow summer? What kind of a summer is that?"

"You've never heard of a raincrow summer? Shucks, I thought everyone knew about that." He looked up at the sky for a moment, then shrugged. "When you get big flocks of crows like that bunch it means the winter is gonna be bad—lots of rain and cold. My grandma Jewell always said it was a bad sign. She claimed that a rain-crow summer meant something really bad was comin'— not just bad weather."

"Oh, that's foolish!"

"I reckon so—but the old folks had wisdom that we ain't got these days." He turned to face her and saw that she was worried. "Aw, shoot, Alona, you're right. A bunch of crows, that's all they are." He sprang to his feet, pulled her up, and hugged her. "Don't forget about that reward for winning this ball game."

Alona smiled, but she looked up at the sky, which was still filled with crows. She didn't believe in such things, but there seemed to be something evil about the birds as they fled across the sky. *It doesn't mean anything—just superstition!* she told herself sternly.

★   ★   ★

The boys sat beside Alona in the stands, cheering and screaming every time Truman pitched. She had learned a little about baseball herself and had come to admire the lazy grace with which Truman threw the ball. He had a deceptive windup that made it look as if he were just going to toss the ball. No matter how lazy his windup looked, when the ball left his hand, it seemed to explode. He had struck out nine men already, and the Mountaineers were leading three to nothing.

All during the game a large boy and a big man, apparently the boy's father, sat on the front bench, directly in front of Alona and the boys. They were rooting for the other team, and the man's language was so bad Alona finally had to speak to him. "Would you mind not using such language, sir?"

"If you don't like my language, sit somewhere else," the man grunted. The red-faced man with veins in his nose and inflamed eyes had obviously been drinking. His son, who looked to be about thirteen, was keeping up a running stream of invectives against Truman, and finally Zac had had enough.

"You shut up about my father!"

"Your old man ain't worth spit!" the boy said and turned around. He had small piggish eyes and was fat but muscular too.

Zac, with his hair-trigger temper, threw himself at the bigger boy. It seemed a hopeless contest, but Zac managed to overturn the boy, and the two fell in the dust.

"Beat his head in, son!" The big man laughed.

The boy struck Zac directly in the face, knocking him over backward. The big boy went after him, fists flailing, but as he did, Tim jumped into the fight, and Zac managed to get up, and now he and his brother were both pounding on the boy.

With a curse the big man jumped down and grabbed Tim by the arm, slapped him in the face, and then made a grab at Zac.

"Truman!" Alona yelled, and she saw Truman break from the mound and come flying across the field just as the big man caught Zac in the chest with his fist and knocked him down.

Truman seized the big man and shouted, "You keep your hands off my boys!"

"I'll break your face!" the man yelled. He drew back his fist, but Truman was ready. With the same motion he used on the pitcher's mound—one that looked almost lazy but was deceitful in its power—Truman delivered a punch to the man's midsection. It sounded like a bass drum being hit, and the man fell over backward, his mouth opening as he gasped for breath. Truman looked down at him and grinned. "When you get up, I'll do it to you again."

By this time the umpire was over there too, shouting, "You're out of the game, Jennings!"

"Fine with me," Truman said cheerfully. He stood looking down at the fallen man and then reached over and helped him up. "Let's shake hands. No sense spoilin' the Fourth of July."

The big man was finally regaining his breath in hoarse, agonizing gasps. He pulled his arm away roughly and muttered, "Come on, son," and lumbered off.

"Well, he didn't have to be so rude about it," Truman remarked. "Are you okay, boys?" he asked his sons as he inspected a reddening spot on Zac's face.

"I'm fine, Dad," he said.

"Me too," Tim added.

"All right then. Let's go get somethin' to eat."

"This here restaurant's a good one," Truman said. The family was seated at a table, waiting to order. "You can tell this is a good restaurant by the calendars."

The boys all looked around. "How can you tell what the food's like by looking at calendars, Dad?" Carl inquired.

"The more calendars, the better the food in a restaurant. I've been meanin' to teach you boys that. Now, you take a restaurant with no calendar at all on the wall, and you might as well forget that one. The food will probably make you sick. If you got one calendar, it'll be so-so. But look at this place. They got four calendars. The food's gonna be great here. It never fails." He opened the menu, then shook his head. "Sure is expensive to eat in here," he remarked. "Look at these prices!"

The boys all wanted hamburgers. Truman ordered a barbecued pork sandwich, and Alona ordered a bacon, lettuce, and tomato sandwich. The hamburgers were big and juicy, and the French fries, which they baptized in plenty of ketchup, were hot and crunchy. They washed them down with red Nehi sodas, and Truman left a quarter tip for the waitress. "We're livin' high, honey." He winked at Alona. "Now, let's go see about that movie."

They walked down the block to the Majestic Theater, where *Flash Gordon Conquers Mars* was playing. Truman paid for the tickets—ten cents for the boys, twenty-three cents for the adults—and they marched inside. After buying popcorn, they went in and found seats. For the next hour they watched Flash Gordon battle the Merciless Ming, and Alona smiled every time the boys cheered, Truman cheering right along with them. They watched a newsreel showing a man with a silly-looking mustache and Babe Ruth hitting three home runs in one game and then cartoons.

As they left the theater, they could hear that the fireworks were starting. They hurried to find a good place to watch and oohed and ahhed with the crowds of people watching. After the grand finale was over, Tim took his mother's hand and said, "This was the best Fourth of July ever!"

"I wish every day was the Fourth of July," Zachary said.

"Well, it won't be. Back to work tomorrow for me." Truman laughed and ruffled Zac's hair.

As usual, after the boys were in bed and had quieted down, Truman and Alona lay side by side in their own bed, discussing the events of the day. The windows were open, admitting what little hot breeze there was.

"I think the boys are right," Truman said. "It'd be nice if every day was a vacation day like this, but tomorrow it's back to work."

Alona wanted to beg him to forget about the higher-paying explosives job, to tell him that they could do without the money, but she knew he took great pride in providing for his family, so she held her tongue. Nonetheless, she couldn't shake her fears for his safety.

For a long time they lay there talking quietly, and finally he rolled over and asked, "What about that reward you promised me this morning?" He reached over and pulled her against him.

She felt the strength of his long, lean body. "That was if you won," she teased, playfully pushing him away.

But Truman Jennings held her tightly. "Come on, now. Don't be mean."

"Well, all right. I suppose you deserve a consolation prize at least." She put her arms around his neck and kissed him firmly on the lips. His arms closed strongly around her, and she clung to him tightly, praying that he'd be with her forever.

CHAPTER TWO

WISH ON A STAR

★ ★ ★

The glow of the Fourth of July celebration was still on the Jennings family as they arrived at church the following Sunday. True enough, although Truman's team had lost the game, the boys had been thrilled and never ceased talking about how easily their dad had disposed of the big man with the obnoxious boy. Zachary had told the story multiple times, each retelling more dramatic than the last. Even now as they approached the entrance to the church, he was telling his friend Dave the story. ". . . and *bam*! My dad popped that big sucker right in the bread basket! You should've seen him, Dave! His mouth opened up and he fell over backward and laid there like an ol' whale rollin' around!"

"That's enough of that, Zac," Alona said. "I don't want to hear any more about that fight."

"Fight!" Truman said with mock surprise. "Why, that wasn't no fight, sweetheart. If it had been a fight, he'd still be there on the ground. I just gave him a little love tap. And you seen me help him up."

"Yeah, and you heard what he said, Mom," Zac said,

his eyes shining. "I bet it'll be a long time before he sticks his big nose into somebody else's business."

"That's enough. Go with your dad now and behave yourself in Sunday school."

"Don't I always?" Zac said with a hurt look.

"No, you don't," Tim said. "You're always askin' fool questions."

"I don't either ask fool questions! If I ask a question about the Bible, it's important."

"Important! The last time Dad was teaching about Jonah and the whale you asked how much the whale weighed."

"Well, that's important!" Zac said stubbornly. "If he's big enough to swallow ol' Jonah, he'd have to weigh a heap."

"Come on, boys. We can fight about Jonah and the whale later." Truman grinned and winked at Alona. "I don't know if I ever teach these boys anything. They spend most of their time arguing."

"They learn a lot, Truman." Alona smiled. "Don't let them dominate the class—especially Zac."

Truman pulled Zac away as he tried to launch into an argument with his mother on that issue. Truman taught the elementary-age boys, and though Carl was younger than the other children in the class, he had convinced his dad that he was not about to be in any "baby" class when he could be with him.

Alona went at once to the nursery, where she found the pastor's wife already busy changing diapers. "Let me help you with that, Betty."

Betty Hodges, a slight brunette with two boys of her own, shook her head. "We're going to have to have help. We have every crib full this morning."

"Well, that's good. We'll put them two to a crib if we have to."

As the two women worked together efficiently, Betty

remarked, "I can't tell you, Alona, how much my husband and I appreciate you and your family."

Alona looked up with surprise. She had just finished pinning a diaper on a chubby baby, and she picked him up and held him over her shoulder after guarding it first with a diaper. "Why, it's been our blessing to be here, your husband such a fine preacher and all. I wish he was preaching at the revival next month."

"Charles thinks that since our congregation hears him all the time, it's good to have an evangelist in."

"He won't preach as good as Brother Charles, that's for sure."

Betty laughed. "I wish everybody was as supportive of my husband as you are."

"Well, they should be!"

Alona served her time in the nursery during the Sunday school hour, then was relieved by Elaine Simmons, who insisted, "You've missed every sermon the past three Sundays. Now, you go listen to it."

"Well, I probably need it, Elaine."

She left the nursery and made her way to her family in the church. The service had already started, but she spotted them midway down on the center aisle. She stepped in the pew next to her husband, picked up the hymnal, and began singing "The Old Rugged Cross." She had a beautiful voice and had been urged to sing in the choir, which she had done for a time, but now she divided her time between serving in the nursery and singing in the choir.

She loved the old hymns, and as they sang, she felt her heart lifted up with thanksgiving. Glancing at her boys and her husband, she breathed a prayer. "Lord, I thank you for giving me such a fine family."

After the offering and the choir anthem, Brother Charles got up and preached for half an hour. As good a preacher as he was, there were some folks who got nervous if the sermon went past noon, so the minister always did his best to finish on time. When he gave the invitation, no one came forward to give their lives to Christ. Brother Charles looked disappointed as always, and after he'd dismissed the congregation, he moved to the back to shake hands with people as they filed out the door.

"That was a pretty good sermon, Preacher," Truman said. "Why don't you give me next Sunday's sermon, and I'll polish it up for you and improve on it."

Brother Charles laughed, for Truman always said something like this. "I'm sure you could, Truman, but I guess I'll have to struggle along on my own."

As the Jennings family headed down the church steps, Truman said, "I came to a decision during that sermon."

"Was it something about the sermon?" Alona asked.

"Yes, I guess it was. He was talking about making decisions, so I decided we ought to go on a picnic today."

"Truman, you're crazy!" she said. "What a thing to say!"

"What's wrong with that? A man's supposed to take care of his family, so I've decided to take us all on a picnic. Let's stop at home and get some sandwich fixin's and our swimsuits, and then maybe we can swing by the grocery store and get a watermelon."

"Well, I don't think you heard a word of the sermon," Alona said, not able to restrain a smile. "But a picnic would be nice."

★   ★   ★

The boys splashed in the cool river, yelling like wild animals. They were wearing shorts, and Alona watched as Truman joined them wearing a two-piece swimming suit. Their collie, Buddy, sat close beside her. He had worn himself out chasing squirrels, and now she reached over and hugged him. "Buddy, won't you ever learn you can't catch a squirrel?"

The dog barked and licked her ear.

Alona watched with a smile on her face as Truman picked the boys up one at a time and threw them high into the air, letting them splash back into the river. After they grew tired of that game, Truman led them to a tree with a long vine that hung over the river, and they swung on it like monkeys. When Truman's turn came again, instead of swinging on the vine, he climbed into the tree and dove into the river. It was a familiar sight, but it still made Alona nervous. She knew Truman would dive from the top of the Washington Monument if he had a chance, but now the boys were copying him and climbing the tree to dive off from higher and higher branches. Zac, like his father, would probably have gone to the top, but Truman told the boy to stay a little lower. Tim was more cautious. He was not the daring type, and Truman had to urge him to climb a little higher.

Carl took just one dive and then trudged through the water to sit on the shore beside Alona. He threw his arm around the dog and gave him a squeeze.

"Don't you want to swim anymore, Carl?" Alona asked.

"Hootie doesn't want to swim."

"Well, why don't you leave Hootie with me, and you go swim with your brothers."

"He likes to be with me all the time."

Alona merely smiled at this. Carl's imaginary friend troubled Truman, but it did not bother Alona in the least. When she was Carl's age, she'd had an imaginary friend named Delores, but she'd grown out of it, as she knew Carl certainly would too.

Carl watched as his dad and brothers switched from

diving to seeing who could make the biggest splash with a cannonball. "Hootie, you stay here," Carl instructed. "I'm gonna go make a huge splash off that third limb."

"Be careful, Carl."

"I'm always careful, Mom. You look out for Hootie."

"Oh, I'll take good care of Hootie."

*   *   *

That night Alona fixed what she called a Depression supper. The main dish was a chicken potpie, and the dessert was something she called Depression pudding. She mixed up butter, sugar, jam, flour, and milk with a few other ingredients and then baked it. When it was done, she heated up a sauce of brown sugar, water, and cinnamon and served it over the pudding.

One good thing about having hungry boys and a hungry husband was no matter what you fed them, they devoured it as if it were the best food in the world. Alona enjoyed their time together at the supper table, where it was always lively. Her boys were so different from one another. Sometimes they seemed to have been born to different parents. Ten-year-old Tim was very sensitive and interested in artistic things; Zac was fearless, tough, and determined to be a great athlete like his father; and Carl was inquisitive and good at taking things apart, even at the age of six. The kitchen seemed to resound with their arguments and laughter, and afterward they all pitched in to wash the dishes and straighten up the kitchen.

"Let's go listen to the radio," Tim said after the last dish was put away.

"Yes, I want to listen to the *Hit Parade*," Alona said.

"Shoot, Mom. *Jack Armstrong* is gonna be on and after that *The Shadow*!" Tim exclaimed.

The radio was always a matter of argument. Carl liked *Little Orphan Annie,* which the older boys disdained. They preferred *The Shadow,* and they went around imitating the program. "'Who knows what evil lurks in the hearts of men?'" they would say slowly in their most sinister voices. "'The Shadow knows,'" they would answer and then imitate the ghostly laughter that emanated from the radio.

Everyone settled in to listen to the programs and then Truman turned the radio off. "Okay, we're gonna have our devotional time." The boys at once ran to get their Bibles. Truman and Alona had given each of the boys a Bible for their fifth birthday, complete with his name engraved on the front. It gave Alona a sense of pride as she saw her boys settle down around her husband on the rather dilapidated couch. Truman opened his Bible and said, "We're going to read one of the psalms tonight. This is about the time that David was running away from his son Absalom. It was about the worst time in his life. You fellows find the third psalm."

He waited through all the page turning, and finally he said, "You remember that Sunday school lesson a while back when we learned about how David's own son rose up against him? Well, this is that time when he was running from Absalom. Let's read it. 'Lord, how are they increased that trouble me! many are they that rise up against me. Many there be which say of my soul, There is no help for him in God. Selah.'"

"Dad, what does *Selah* mean?" Tim asked.

"I don't know. It must be important, though. It's in the Bible." Truman shrugged. "So, never mind that. The next verse says, 'But thou, O Lord, art a shield for me; my glory, and the lifter up of mine head. I cried unto the Lord with my voice, and he heard me out of his holy hill. Selah.'

"Now what do you reckon that poor David felt like?

He had been a king, but now his own son was trying to kill him, and he's on the run. What do you reckon he did?"

"I guess he ran some more, didn't he, after he said this prayer?" Carl offered.

"No, wrong guess. Look at the next verse. He says, 'I laid me down and slept; I awaked; for the Lord sustained me.'"

Truman looked up and shook his head with admiration. "There's a fellow that's facing death, and what did he do? Why, he prayed, and he asked the Lord to help him, and then he just laid down and went to sleep. Now, that's what I call faith. And that's the kind of faith I want you boys to have. Faith like your mama's got."

"What about the raincrow summer, Dad?" Carl asked. "Me and Hootie heard you talking about how bad stuff was coming when all the crows come."

"Ah, there's nothing to that! Ask your mom. She's like David—not afraid of anything."

"Well, I don't quite have David's faith," Alona said quickly.

"Don't pay any attention to her. Your mama's got more faith than any ten men I know of." Truman held out his hands and the boys put their hands in his. Alona pulled her chair closer to add her hands to the mix. "We're gonna pray that you boys will always believe in God no matter what happens."

The prayer that followed was simple, but Alona's eyes were wet with tears as she heard her husband praying words of praise for her. She hugged each one of the boys after the prayer, and they went off to bed. As soon as they were gone, Truman said, "Let's go sit on the porch awhile. I'm not sleepy."

"I'm not either."

"Good. I want to sit beside a good-lookin' woman for a while and look up at the stars."

They went outside and sat down in the swing, which creaked as they settled into it. "This old thing is gonna fall down and bust our rears one of these days," Truman said. "I'd better do some tightenin' up on it this week." He put his arm around her and drew her close. "Look at them stars. How about that? And the Bible says God knows every one of their names."

The two sat there for a long time looking at the stars and talking quietly. After a while he took her by the chin and kissed her. "I just want you to know how lucky I am to have a woman like you and boys like we've got. You know what I want now?"

"I can guess," she said, laughing at him.

"Well, that too, but the other thing I want is to have three girls."

"Three girls! What for?"

Truman was laughing. "So we'd have a matched set. We can put three on one side of the table, three on the other side, me at one end and you at the other end. That's reason enough."

"I hate to break it to you, but we're in the middle of a depression. It's hard enough to put food on the table for three boys."

"Three little girls won't add much to the bills. I want them all to be just like you."

Alona leaned over and put her head on Truman's shoulder. A shooting star lit up the sky, tracing a fiery trail across the darkness of the heavens.

"Did you make a wish?" Truman asked.

"Yes."

"What was it?"

"I wished for God to keep us safe."

"I wish that too." He held her tightly, and for a long time they sat there, letting the silence soak into their spirits and staring up at the stars that twinkled and flashed against the darkness of the night.

CHAPTER THREE

THE END OF SOMETHING WONDERFUL

★ ★ ★

The month of August brought a bit of relief with the slightly cooler temperatures. Often Alona watched the massive flocks of crows pass over the house and thought of what Truman had told her about the raincrow summer, never without a feeling that something ominous lay ahead.

America had been in a state of apprehension since the beginning of 1938. Eight million people in the country were jobless, and nobody knew what was going to happen next in Europe. Adolf Hitler, supreme commander of the German armed forces, had a sinister quality that made everybody nervous. Hitler had proven that he was to be feared when in March he had sent his armies into Austria, where he was cheered by crowds in the street. The hysterical salutes of his ardent supporters, many of them waving banners emblazoned with swastikas, were a frightening sight.

Americans tried to carry on business as usual and

were cheered by a new movie called *Bringing Up Baby*. Dizzy Dean was traded from the Cardinals to the Cubs, and heavyweight champion Joe Louis annihilated Max Schmeling in the first round after Louis's previous defeat by the German fighter. Father Divine paraded down the streets of New York with fifteen hundred followers who believed their leader would provide them heaven on earth, and Howard Hughes broke all records by flying around the world in just three days, nineteen hours, and fourteen minutes.

People died, babies were born, and all across the United States the Depression, which had been going on for almost a decade, numbed the nation.

★   ★   ★

Alona and her friends from the women's Bible study were sitting around Alona's living room, each intent on her own quilting project. Alona was starting on the first of the quilts she had decided to make for each of her three boys, and some of the ladies were working on individual squares of a Dutch girl pattern as they listened to *Stella Dallas*, the popular soap opera, on the radio.

"I just don't see how Stella is going to make it." Emma Hayes looked up from her square at the other eight members. "It seems like everything she does turns out wrong. I declare, I just find myself crying when I think about all her problems!"

Alona smiled. "I don't think we ought to shed tears over a woman who doesn't even exist."

"But it's so sad!"

"I know, but it's only make-believe. Those aren't real people on that program," Alona said.

"It's silly, but it just breaks my heart to think about all of Stella's problems."

Betty Hodges, the pastor's wife, smiled benevolently at Emma. "If you want something to cry about, I can tell you some stories about real people."

"I don't want to hear about that," Emma cried. "I just can't bear to hear bad stories."

Laughter went up around the room, and all the women fixed their eyes on Emma. "You love to cry," Maylene Strawler said. "That's your problem, Emma."

"What about you, Alona?" Emma challenged, looking across at Alona. "I've seen you cry in church a few times."

"Yes, I certainly have, but that's about something real, Emma."

The argument went on for some time with Emma determined to enjoy weeping over Stella Dallas and the others trying to convince her that such emotion was ridiculous.

A knock broke into the conversation, and Alona got up. "Excuse me. I don't know who that can be."

"It's probably Alice," Betty said. "She said she wanted to come but would be late."

Going to the front door, Alona could see a man she didn't recognize through the screen. "Yes?" she said.

"Mrs. Jennings?"

"Yes, I'm Mrs. Jennings."

"My name's Burt Sinclair. I wonder if I could talk to you."

"If you're selling something, Mr. Sinclair, we're not in the market."

"Oh no, ma'am, I'm not selling anything." The tall, gangly man pulled off his hat and twisted it around in his hands. "I work for the quarry."

An alarm went off in Alona's mind. "Would you like to come in?"

"It sounds like you've got company, ma'am."

"Just my Bible study group. We're making quilts."

Simmons twisted his hat nervously and chewed on his lower lip. "Mrs. Jennings, would you mind coming out on the porch?"

Her alarm increased as she stepped outside. The boys were down the street playing ball with their friends. She could faintly hear the sounds of the youngsters from the vacant lot two blocks away. She closed the screen door behind her. "What is it, Mr. Sinclair?"

"Well, it's . . . it's not good news, ma'am."

Alona knew at once it was Truman. "Is it about my husband?"

"Yes, ma'am. I'm afraid it is."

"An accident?"

He met her gaze for a moment, then dropped his eyes. "Yes, ma'am. A real bad one."

Alona froze. "How bad?" she whispered.

"Well . . . ma'am . . . I hate to have to tell you that . . . well . . . he's dead, Mrs. Jennings."

The earth seemed to stop for Alona. The words had no meaning. Truman so full of life and vigor, laughing, shouting. He couldn't be dead!

The man went on, "I hate to be the one to tell you, but they sent me down here. He was killed right off, ma'am. He didn't suffer or nothin' like that."

"What happened?" she asked, the words barely audible.

"Well, somebody set off a charge before they was supposed to. It took down a shelf of rock. It came right down on Truman, ma'am. It happened so quick there wasn't no time for nobody to help." He continued twisting his hat, a wretched expression on his face. "We . . . took him to the doctor, ma'am, but it wasn't no good. He was gone before we got him there."

Alona felt as if the wind had been knocked out of her, and she could barely get her breath. She tried to think clearly, but fear hovered over her like a giant, dark specter. If the sun had suddenly disappeared from the sky, she could not have been struck harder. She whispered, "Where is he now?"

"The doctor. He called the funeral home—Mae's Funeral Home, Mrs. Jennings. He's there."

"Thank you, Mr. Sinclair."

"We're all right sorry, ma'am. Everybody liked Truman."

Alona turned slowly. Her arms tingled as she fumbled for the handle on the screen door. Her movements were awkward, and she had to will herself to step inside. The door slammed behind her.

She moved woodenly down the hall and into the living room. Betty Hodges looked up. "Was it Alice?" And then she saw Alona's face. She jumped up, knocking over her sewing basket as she rushed around it. "What is it, Alona? What's happened?"

"It's . . . it's Truman. He's dead."

Cries went up and gasps from all the women as they rose and gathered around Alona. Betty Hodges put her arm around Alona's shoulders, tears running down her face. The others were crying too, and finally Emma asked, "What happened? Tell us."

Alona forced herself to give the report. Her mouth was as dry as cotton, and she stood there hearing the voices of the women but not understanding any words. They might as well have been speaking a foreign language.

"I'll go get Charles," Betty said. "The rest of you stay here."

"You don't all have to stay," Alona said. "I've got to tell the boys."

"Shall I go get them for you?" Mary Devrees offered.

"Yes, and when they come, let me be alone with them."

"What's wrong, Mom?" Tim asked.

"Yeah, we were winning. Why'd we have to come home?" Zachary asked.

Alona's three boys stood in a row before her. The other women had gathered their belongings and left her alone with them, and now she sat in a chair facing them. Lifting her eyes, she looked at the boys, and something in her face frightened all three of them. Carl began to tremble. "What is it? What's wrong, Mom?"

"It's . . . it's your dad, boys. He's . . . he's had an accident."

Tim's voice came out in a strained fashion. "Is he hurt bad?"

"You must be very brave. All of us must be brave." Taking a deep breath, Alona said, "Your father was killed this afternoon in an accident in the quarry."

Tim, the most sensitive of them, simply sat down on the floor and began to cry. He was the oldest, but in a way the other boys were stronger. Zac's eyes filled with tears, and his hands were unsteady. "What happened to him, Mom?" Carl climbed onto his mother's lap, his arms around her neck. She told them the few facts she knew, and finally she said, "Come here, Tim. Get up off the floor." She put her arms around him and gathered Zac to the group as well. "He's gone to be with Jesus, boys. We must remember that. It's sad for us, but he's with the Lord now."

Tim choked, and his voice was thick. "I don't want him to be dead. I want him to be here with us."

"What will we do, Mom?" Carl asked, his voice breaking. "How will we get along without Dad?"

"We'll have to trust Jesus. He'll take care of us."

Tears were running down Zac's face, but at the same time anger marred his features. "Why did God let my daddy get killed?" he demanded.

Alona had no answer. In fact, she had been asking the

same question. "I can't answer that, but I know that God always loves us and always wants the best for us. It's going to be hard, because we all loved your dad so much, but we still have each other, and we'll trust in the Lord to take care of us." She pulled the boys even closer, feeling nothing but a terrible emptiness. And in her grief, she knew that this feeling would only get worse.

★ ★ ★

The rain was falling out of gray, leaden skies as Pastor Charles Hodges pulled his car up in front of the Jennings' house. "You wait here, Alona. I've got an umbrella." He opened the door, grabbed the umbrella from under his feet, and walked around the car. Opening the passenger door for Alona, he said, "You boys wait here for a minute. I'll come back for you." He waited until Alona got out, shielding her from the downpour, and walked with her to the porch. When she was under the porch roof, he went back and opened the car door again. "Come on, boys. Get close."

Carl and Zac came in close enough, but Tim apparently hadn't heard.

"Come on, Tim," Hodges urged. "You're going to get soaked."

"I don't care!" Tim said woodenly, his face set in a deadened expression.

Hodges herded the boys under the umbrella until he got to the porch, and Alona said, "You boys go in and put on some dry clothes."

As the boys went in, Hodges thought of the graveside ceremony, which had been spoiled by an unexpected shower. The rain had poured down, soaking everyone except the immediate family and a few others who were able to crowd underneath the green tarpaulin tent that

Mae's Funeral Home had raised over the grave. Most of the people had stayed, simply choosing to get thoroughly soaked until the service had finished. They had filed by to shake hands with the boys and Alona, giving whatever words of comfort they could.

"I never saw so many people at a funeral in my life," Pastor Hodges said. Indeed it was true; the church had been packed. "Truman had so many friends. Why, all of the boys who've been in his Sunday school class for the last four years were there, as well as the ball players."

"I didn't know he had so many friends," Alona said stiffly. Her face was pale and set, and she found it difficult to speak, but she managed a semblance of a smile. "You've been just wonderful, Pastor. I don't know what we would have done without you."

"I don't think I've done much. There's not much to do, is there? It's at times like this," he said quietly, "I realize the weakness of human language. We want to express what's going on inside of us, but the words just aren't there."

"You seemed to find the right words for your sermon today. I'll never forget it as long as I live. It was just what I always thought about Truman, and you said it so well."

Hodges tried to smile. "I think the Lord was with us." He looked out at the rain for a moment. "Betty has offered to stay with you for a day or two. I'm going to go get her now if that's all right with you."

"No, don't do that. I'm all alone now." Then Alona caught herself. "I didn't mean to complain like that, but I meant—"

"I know what you meant, and in a way you're alone and in the most painful way. But you know the church is supposed to step in at times like this and do what it can. I was reading an article about how when a cut is made in the human body, the white corpuscles all rush to heal it. I think that's kind of what a church should be, Alona.

When one of us gets hurt, the others should come rushing to help. It doesn't always work like that, but—"

"Well, it has in this case. I've never seen such kindness from people in my life, Brother Charles."

"I wish you'd let me get Betty."

"Maybe later. But for a day or two I'd just like to try to pull myself together and be with the boys."

"We'll respect your wishes, but don't hesitate to call us. We'll be available."

Alona watched as he went out to the car. He waved as he closed the umbrella. She waved back and tried her best to smile, then watched him as he got into the car and drove away. She went into the house and was met by Buddy, who whined and reared up on her. The dog was sensitive to the moods of the people around him, and he had been disturbed by all of the people filling the house over the last couple of days. He had gone into every room looking for Truman, and now he whined as if trying to speak. "Get down, Buddy," Alona said. He dropped to all fours and went over to his favorite rug and flopped himself down, staring at the wall. Alona squatted beside him and scratched him behind his ears. "I didn't mean to hurt your feelings. I really didn't."

She went into her room to change her clothes, and when she came out, she went to the kitchen and looked around. The church ladies had brought more food than an army could have eaten. The table was full of dishes and bowls, the icebox was packed, and every countertop was full. "If this food would keep, we wouldn't have to cook anything for a month." She opened the cupboard to get a coffee cup and noticed Truman's favorite cup. The sight of it was like a dagger to the heart. She stood staring at it, engulfed in loneliness. She grabbed a different cup and poured herself some leftover coffee. She took a sip, barely registering that it wasn't hot.

Footsteps approached, and Tim came into the

kitchen. "You want something to eat, Tim?" she asked.

"No, ma'am." He stood there looking so forlorn and lonely, his lips trembling, that Alona went to him at once. When she put her arms around him, he said, "What will we do without Dad, Mom?"

"We'll go on, and you'll make him proud of you."

Tim looked at her. "Do you think he can see us?"

"Nobody knows really about that. Maybe so. The book of Hebrews says that we're surrounded with a cloud of witnesses. Maybe he's looking at us right now wondering how his boys are doing. In any case, we'll all see him someday. And, Tim, I'm depending on you to help. You're the oldest, and I'm going to need you to be strong."

He stood straighter and pulled away from his mother. "I'll help you all I can, Mom."

"Here's what we're going to do." Alona's throat felt thick, but she forced herself to continue. "We're going to talk about your daddy. We're not going to pretend we don't miss him. We're going to talk about the good times we had with him."

"Mom, I can't."

"Yes you can. Tonight we're going to make ice cream, and you'll have to turn the crank just like your daddy did. And after that we'll listen to the radio and maybe play games."

"I don't think I can do any of that, Mom."

"Tim," Alona said quietly. She pushed a lock of his tousled hair back from his forehead. "As long as you are alive and remember your daddy, why, he's alive too. He lives in you and in your brothers, and we have to hang on to that. Will you try and help me with that?"

He bit his lip; then he looked at his mother and nodded. "I'll try my best, Mom."

CHAPTER FOUR

NEW HOME

★ ★ ★

School started in September, and with the boys gone all day, Alona had more time than she knew what to do with. Since Truman's death, life with her boys had been difficult. The boys had all been stunned by the loss of their father, but it affected them in different ways. Tim had grown more quiet and had lost weight, and it seemed to Alona that he was hurting more than his brothers.

Zac showed his grief in a far different way. He had always been an outgoing lad, willing to tackle anything, but now there was an anger in him. He didn't speak of it often, but from time to time, Alona picked up on the bitterness that he felt toward God for the loss of his father. She had tried to reason with him, but she could still see the resentment in his eyes and in his body language. He had announced that he had no intention of going to his Sunday school class with the new teacher, Mr. Jones, who had taken Truman's place. It had taken all of Alona's tact to finally talk him into going.

Six-year-old Carl had an imaginative mind, and more

than once he had come to Alona asking innumerable questions: Where do people go when they die? How can Daddy be in heaven? I saw him in the casket and they buried it. Will he look the same when I see him in heaven? He dwelled on these technical aspects of death, but at times he looked so lonely—and he spoke more and more to Hootie, which troubled Alona greatly.

While Alona tried hard to help her boys work through their loss, she did not know how to overcome her own grief. At night she would reach out in her sleep for Truman and awake to the dreadful realization that never again would she be able to touch his warm flesh or hear his laugh. And then she was never able to get back to sleep. She had also lost weight, and the occasional glance in a mirror told her her features were drawn.

One evening while the boys were playing tag with the neighbors outside, she answered the door to a small man in a business suit. "Yes. What is it?"

"My name is Hawes. I'd like to speak with you, Mrs. Jennings."

"What about?"

"I'm a lawyer for your husband's former employer. I've come to discuss a settlement."

"Come in, Mr. Hawes." Stepping back, Alona allowed the man to enter. She had been expecting a representative from the company or a lawyer to come. He took off his hat and followed her into the living room, and she waved him to a seat. "Won't you sit down?"

"Thank you, ma'am." Hawes put his briefcase on his lap and laid both hands flat on it.

"I offer you my condolences on the loss of your husband, Mrs. Jennings." His voice was soft, yet there was a peculiar hardness about him.

"Thank you."

Hawes waited, but when Alona said no more, he

cleared his throat and opened his briefcase. Pulling out a single sheet of paper, he said, "The company has authorized me to offer you this settlement."

She took the sheet of paper, skimmed it, then looked up. Their eyes met, and Hawes could not hold her gaze. He focused on something past her shoulder and shifted nervously in the chair.

"A thousand dollars? That's the company's offer?"

"Yes, ma'am."

"That's pitiful! You know it is, Mr. Hawes."

"I'm unable to argue the point with you, Mrs. Jennings. You probably know that business times are hard. The quarry is hanging on by its fingernails. This is all that the board authorized me to offer. I'm sorry."

"I'll have to talk to a lawyer."

"Yes, ma'am, I understand, but I may as well put the matter plainly. I know you have a family and you need money. If you bring a lawsuit against the company, we are prepared to fight it in court. It could go on for two or three years or maybe even longer. These things are very slow."

"That sounds like a threat, Mr. Hawes."

"No, ma'am, not at all! It's just the way it is. I know this amount is not large, but in truth it's better than nothing."

"Your company is responsible for my husband's death."

"That would be very difficult to prove in court. It would be hard to get any of the other employees to testify."

"Because they might lose their jobs?"

"Oh, I didn't say that!"

"That's what you meant," Alona said as she stood up. "I will think about this. Good day, Mr. Hawes."

"Of course. And once again, my sympathy." His sympathy was as hard and lifeless as the briefcase he carried.

After he left, she sat down again and studied the paper more closely, but she found no encouragement there. Buddy came to her side and looked up at her with his big eyes.

"It's all right, Buddy." She stroked his head absently. "I'll have to talk to somebody about this. We're going to need money and fast."

★ ★ ★

Pastor Charles Hodges sat behind his desk listening to Alona. He had been concerned about the family. They still came to church regularly, but there was a lack of animation in their faces. The boys, especially, were unresponsive. He had tried to get them involved with the children's activities at the church, but none of them showed much interest. As Alona told him about the insurance settlement, he ran his hand across the scarred walnut finish of his desk.

"A thousand dollars?" he repeated when she stopped. "That's pathetic!"

"I said it was pitiful." Alona shook her head. "But what should I do, Pastor?"

"You should talk to a lawyer."

"I mentioned that to the man who brought this offer. He said if I took the company to court the case would go on for a long time, but of course, he would say something like that, wouldn't he?"

"Do you know Marvin Weatherby?"

"Yes. He sings in the choir."

"He's also an attorney, and I think you should talk to him. I'd be happy to call him for you and make an appointment."

"Pastor, I couldn't afford to pay a lawyer."

"I don't think Mr. Weatherby would charge you for

looking this over and giving his advice. Even if it went to court, he may be willing to take the case pro bono. I know he's done that in the past for people who can't afford to pay."

"I guess if you think it's best . . . I'm going to have to think about finding a job."

Hodges shifted uneasily. "That could be difficult. Jobs are hard to come by."

"I know, but there must be something. . . ."

"Before you do, talk to Mr. Weatherby about this."

"All right. Go ahead and make the appointment."

★ ★ ★

As soon as the boys hit the front steps, Alona called out, "Come into the kitchen, boys. I've made some cookies." They all filed in, and she set a plate of fresh-baked cookies on the table. "Here, this will hold you until supper."

Zac grabbed one and crammed most of it into his mouth, chewing fiercely. "These are good, Mom," he said with a full mouth.

"Don't swallow them whole! You won't taste a thing."

Buddy had followed the boys into the kitchen and was whining up at Alona. She broke a bite off of a cookie and gave it to him. "There you go, Buddy. Now, don't bother me for any more."

Buddy looked up hopefully, but when he saw that the well had run dry, he plopped down, leaning against the wall.

While the boys ate their cookies, Alona sat down at the table and asked them about school. They all shrugged and didn't have much to say. Tim especially seemed lackadaisical about the whole thing.

When there was a moment of silence, Alona said, "I've had to make a decision about our finances. A lawyer from the quarry came to see me a few days ago. He offered a settlement of a thousand dollars."

"A thousand dollars!" Zac exclaimed, his eyes opening wide. "That's a lot of money!"

"I know it sounds like a lot to you, but it wouldn't go very far when it comes to paying the bills. It'd only be about eighty dollars a month for a year."

"Gosh, that isn't much!" Tim murmured. "Is that all they'll pay?"

"That's their final offer."

"They're a bunch of crumbs! That's what they are," Zac said, picking up a cookie and biting it fiercely. "Why don't we sue 'em? I've heard about that."

"I talked to a lawyer about it, and he says the chances are we might get a little more if we fought it in court, but it would probably take a couple of years, and we need the money right now to pay the rent, so I'm going to have to take it."

Tim's face was twisted with anger. "So that's all they think Dad was worth!"

Only Carl seemed halfway satisfied. "Well, it will help, won't it, Mom? I mean, you can pay the rent, and we'll have enough to eat."

"We'll be okay for a while, but we're going to have to watch every penny."

"Mom, I want to quit school. I can get a job and help."

"That's sweet of you, Tim, but there's not much that a ten-year-old can do. Grown men can't find work now because of the way things are. No, you'll have to stay in school, but we'll have to be very careful about buying only the essentials."

The boys got into the spirit of the conversation, suggesting ways that they could cut down on their expenses. Carl even suggested giving up baths to save on the cost of soap.

Alona smile and mussed his hair. "We're not going to give up bathing, son. We'll just have to trust the Lord. He's never let us down before."

★ ★ ★

During the next year, the family cut their expenses to the bone and somehow managed to pay the rent each month. It had been a slow, hard year. Alona had gotten some work cleaning houses, which had helped somewhat, but by the time school started again in 1939, the money from the settlement was gone. There was no choice but to move to a cheaper place to cut expenses.

A truck was backed up to the front door of the house, and all three of the boys were helping carry boxes, along with two big men from the church and Pastor Hodges. Three women from the church were cleaning the rooms as each one emptied. When the last box was finally loaded, Pastor Hodges said, "Well, I guess that's all of it, isn't it, Alona?"

"That's all."

Hodge saw the sadness in Alona's eyes and said, "I still think we could have found some way for you to keep the house."

"It was kind of you to offer to help, Pastor, but we can't be beholden."

"I know you prefer to be independent, and I respect that. Well, come along boys. Let's go to your new home."

After Alona had thanked the women who had helped, the family loaded into the pastor's Ford. The two men got into the truck carrying the family's goods, and Hodges pulled out and made his way across town.

The section of town they were moving into was

pretty grim. Alona didn't say a word, but she felt her heart sink as they pulled up in front of one of the shotgun houses, the third from the end. Some of them had never been painted, while others looked just as bad with their peeling paint. The houses came right up to the sidewalk, which was strewn with litter. Although the weather was cold for September, many of the younger children were running around with bare feet.

Alona got out of the car while the men opened the back of the truck and started unloading the furniture. Alona and the boys each grabbed one of the lighter boxes and took them into the house.

The front door opened into a living area that was barely large enough to contain all her furniture. A door on the far side of the living room led directly into a bedroom, and the third room straight back at the rear of the house was a combination kitchen and dining area. Alona had looked at another house in the same row, and they were identical. This one was cleaner than the other one, and at least the roof didn't leak.

Hodges brought in a floor lamp and set it down. "I've already scheduled a work day for the men of the church, Alona. We'll put some new paper on the walls, lay some new linoleum. It'll look nice."

"Thank you, Pastor," she said quietly.

The boys had not seen the house before and were now making their way back into the living room after conducting a quick tour.

"Where's the rest of the house?" Tim asked, a pleading look on his face. "Where's the bathroom?"

"I'm afraid that's all there is," Alona told him, putting her hand on his shoulder. "The bathroom is out back."

"This is a crummy place!" Zac concluded after his tour.

"Shut your mouth, Zac!" Tim said. "This is our home. Don't be talkin' bad about it. It'll be fine, Mom."

"Thank you, Tim. The pastor said the men are going to come over and paper the walls and put down some new linoleum, so that'll help dress it up a little bit."

Alona had the men put her things in the bedroom, and the boys would sleep on cots—two in the living room and one in the kitchen—that they could fold down and put out of the way during the day. When everything was unloaded, Alona thanked the men who had helped and the pastor.

After the men drove away with the empty truck, Alona looked around at their sparse surroundings. It took all of her strength to say cheerfully, "Well, boys, we're going to make this place something to be proud of. You just wait and see."

★ ★ ★

Later that week the sun was low in the west, and Alona was cooking supper. The boys had gone over to the playground, since the house had no yard. When a knock sounded at the door, she opened the door to a scruffy-looking man wearing faded overalls and a pair of heavy brogans. "Yes, what is it?" she asked the man.

"My name's Alvin Scruggs. I'm yer neighbor three houses down. Just come by to welcome you an' see if you need any help."

"Thank you, Mr. Scruggs."

"Oh, Alvin's fine. What's your name?" He wore no shirt under his overalls, and his arms were wiry and covered with thick hair. He was as sorry a specimen of a man as Alona had ever seen.

"I'm Mrs. Jennings. You'll have to excuse me. I've got something on the stove. It's going to burn." She turned and went back to the stove and took the skillet off, and when she did, she heard the door slam. She went back into the living room to make sure he had gone and was dismayed to see that Scruggs had come inside and was grinning at her. "Like I say I just come by to offer my help. A widow woman like you needs a man."

Alona did not want to make any enemies, but she had an instant distaste for Scruggs. "Thank you, Mr. Scruggs. Now, if you don't mind, I need to get back to the kitchen."

Scruggs took a step closer and winked at her. He grinned, exposing twisted teeth stained by tobacco and snuff. "Reckon a good-lookin' lady like you needs a man. Too bad you lost yourn, but I'll be around."

"I think I'll be all right. Thanks for coming by."

"There's some pretty rough fellers around here, but I'll be careful that they don't bother you none."

Scruggs took a step closer, and she smelled the rank odor of his body and his breath. His eyes were burning, and Alona knew exactly what was on his mind. "It's all right. I don't need a man. I've got Buddy."

"Buddy? Who's that?"

"Buddy!" Alona called, and at once the big collie came bounding into the room. "Buddy—guard!" At once Buddy's hackles rose and he shot to the man, baring his teeth and growling a deep growl.

"Hey! Does that dog bite?"

"He'll take the throat right out of you if I tell him to, Scruggs."

"Well, that dog won't always be here," he said, balefully backing toward the door.

"No, but if he's not, I always keep this." Alona reached under a sofa cushion and pulled out her thirty-eight. "I keep this loaded. I'm not a real good shot, so my husband told me to just keep pulling the trigger until it's empty. He said I'd hit something that way." She lowered the gun and fired a shot ten inches from Scruggs's foot.

"Hey, you crazy woman! You wanna kill me?"

"I don't want to, Mr. Scruggs, but if I were you, I wouldn't come back here. I'm very nervous, and there's no telling what I'd do if you startled me." She lifted the gun again, and as she did, Scruggs yelled again and then backpedaled out. He hit the screen door, making it slam open, and fell down as he backed off the stoop. Alona followed him out onto the stoop, still holding the gun. "Good-bye, Scruggs. Don't come back."

He got up, cursing her and shaking his fist. Buddy started for the man, but Alona called him. "Buddy, come back!" She laughed and said, "Either Buddy will be waiting for you or this thirty-eight will."

"Say, that done my heart good, Alona."

Alona turned to see Judy Doakes, her next-door neighbor, coming. Judy was a heavyset woman, short and built like a barrel. She had a red face and merry black eyes, and the two had become fairly close in the last few days.

"I wish you'da shot him." Judy laughed. "He pulled the same thing on me and I guess every woman in the row." She had a loaf of bread in one hand and a jar in another. "Here. I baked some bread, and this here's some strawberry preserves. I want to officially welcome ya into the neighborhood."

"Why, thanks, Judy. I smelled the bread while it was baking. Come on in and we'll have a cup of coffee."

"Don't mind if I do."

Judy sat down and kept up a running conversation while Alona made the coffee. "Don't bother callin' the owner to fix anythin' that breaks. He takes the rent and that's all he does. My man Jim will help you if you have any problem."

"That's sweet of you, Judy, but I hope I'll be able to handle most things."

"Good for you, then. Good for you."

Alona set a cup of coffee on the table in front of Judy and sat down with her own.

"Well, this ain't the best place in the world to live. My kids are rough, but they're good-hearted. If they give you or your boys any trouble, you tell me and I'll wallop 'em good."

"I'll be sure to do that."

"I'd like to invite you to church tonight. We're Pentecostal folks. I always say we're Pennycost at any cost." She laughed at her own wit. "It's just a few blocks away. Take only five, ten minutes to walk there. Them meetings get plumb excitin' sometimes."

"I'd be glad to go with you tonight, and maybe you'd like to come to our church sometime. I'm Baptist."

"Maybe I'll do that, though I am pretty used to the way we do it at my church. My bunch gets kind of rambunctious." She got up to leave, saying, "Thanks for that mighty good coffee. I'll meet you out front at six forty-five tonight. Meanwhile, you keep that pistol handy, and I'm glad you got that big ol' dog. If Scruggs comes back, just shoot him. Nobody'll miss him."

Alona walked to the door with Judy and bid her good-bye, then went back to the kitchen. She picked up the gun, which she had left on the table, and swung the cylinder out. She pulled out the empty shell. "I guess five shots would be enough if I had to use it." She laid the gun down, then leaned forward and placed her elbows on the table. She put her head down into her hands and began to tremble. She had never had to threaten anyone in her entire life, and she was just now realizing how close she had come to shooting the awful man. "I hope I never have to do anything like that again," she whispered.

★   ★   ★

Alona heard the boys come in the front door. She was standing at the kitchen stove, and their voices were filled with excitement, especially Zac's. "Ma," he yelled, "we're rich!"

Alona laughed, for this was typical of Zac's overstatements. When the boys came rushing in, she saw their eyes were glowing. "I'm glad to hear we're rich. I hear it's better than being poor. How did we get so rich?"

Zac could barely keep still as he told his mother the news. "Ma, we found out that old man Jimmerson is buying bottles," he cried. "We went collectin' them, and we sold him a bunch of 'em. Look, we got two dollars and ninety cents."

"Jimmerson! Why, that old man is a bootlegger!"

"I don't care what he does with them bottles," Zac said loudly. "It ain't our business. We got the money and that's what counts."

"That's right, Ma. We need every penny," Tim said anxiously. "You're not mad, are you?"

"No, I'm not mad, but just don't do it again. You don't have to now."

"Why?" Carl asked. "We always need money."

"Well, I was going to wait until we sat down for supper, but I guess I'll tell you now. I got a job."

"A job! What kind of a job, Mom?" Tim asked with apprehension.

"It's a good job. I'll be cooking at the Elite Café. Things are gonna be a little bit different around here."

"How different?" Carl asked quickly.

"Well, when you boys get home from school, I won't be here. You'll have to take care of yourselves until I get home. Tim, you'll be in charge. Maybe I can bring leftover food home for your supper, but it will be late."

"Oh, Ma, I don't want you to do work. I'd rather you be here," Tim said.

"I know you would, Tim, but I have to do it. The

money from the quarry has run out. Before long, we'll have some extra money to buy you all some warm clothes for school," she said, looking at their well-worn pants that were riding a little too high on their ankles. "You boys will have to help me do some of the housework."

"I don't mind doin' that," Tim said.

"I don't either," Carl agreed.

Alona went over and ruffled Carl's hair. "Your daddy would be so proud of you."

"When do you start, Mom?" Tim asked.

"I start tomorrow. Why don't you go ahead and wash up now, because after dinner, I'm going to the Pentecostal church down the street with our neighbor Mrs. Doakes."

CHAPTER FIVE

CHANGE OF PLANS

★ ★ ★

The calendar on the high counter that separated the pharmacist from his customers had a page-a-day format. Alona read the day's date: August 2, 1940. Staring at the calendar, she thought back over the past two years since Truman had died. She had assumed that her memories of him would fade as time passed, but that had not been the case. The truth was that as she lay in bed at night, or even while busy at work or at home, she had vivid memories of her life with Truman. She remembered another August second, three years earlier, when she had been at a ball game and had watched Truman throw his blazing fast balls, striking out thirteen batters. The drugstore faded and she could almost hear Truman's voice as he came rushing toward her after the game, crying, *"I guess we showed 'em that time, didn't we, sweetie!"* The memory was painful, as all such memories were, but she had learned to live with them.

"I'm sorry to keep you waiting, Mrs. Jennings. I've got your prescription here." Mr. Poch put a bottle of pills on the counter and cleared his throat. "Pretty expensive medicine. I'm only charging you my cost. Won't make a dime out of it. Never mind the tax."

Alona allowed none of the dismay she felt to show. The amount looked as large as Mount Olympus at the moment, but she reached into her purse and snapped open her change purse. She handed the pharmacist the correct amount. "I appreciate your helping me out all you can, Mr. Poch. I know you've done it before. I wish I could pay the full price."

"Don't you worry about that. I just hope you won't need to have it refilled."

"This should take care of it. Dr. Grayson said Carl will be feeling better in no time."

"That's good to hear. That little guy's one of my favorites, you know."

"I know. I appreciate the way you've treated me and my boys."

"You take care, now."

"Thanks, and you too." She left the drugstore and walked slowly toward the church, the hot sun beating down on her. She glanced over to see a group of sparrows fighting over a crust of bread on the edge of the street. It was quite a contest, and she shook her head. "Even birds can't agree," she murmured. Her thoughts were filled with doubts, and she hated that. Lately she had been struggling against doubt, and it seemed to be a continual effort to remain positive. She repeatedly went over the Scripture verse she had recently memorized: *But my God shall supply all your need according to his riches in glory by Christ Jesus.* Philippians 4:19. *All your need.* That was a good one to repeat to herself.

She turned the corner and went halfway down the next block and into the church. She glanced into the window of the sanctuary and found the pastor standing at the podium.

She opened the door and asked, "Are you practicing, Brother Charles?"

Pastor Hodges looked startled at first and then he grinned. "Well, hello, Alona. There are some folks in the congregation that say I need more practice. Maybe they're right." He stepped down and came toward her. "It's good to see you. How's Carl? Is he feeling any better?"

"Not really. But I just picked up some pills for him. Dr. Grayson says his ear infection should clear up in no time."

"That's good. It's still difficult to be patient, isn't it?"

"Yes, it certainly is. Brother Charles, do you have a few minutes?"

"For you, always. Let's go to my office."

The two made their way to the offices. Maylene Strawler, the pastor's secretary, smiled brightly. "Hello, Alona. How are you today?"

"Just fine, Maylene."

"Hold all my calls, will you, Maylene?" Hodges asked as he led Alona into his office. "Have a seat."

She sat down, then smiled wanly. "I feel like I ought to be paying rent on this seat. I've been here so many times the past couple years."

"Don't be foolish. That's what friends are for."

Alona had often wondered how a man could listen to other people's problems day after day. "You probably hear every hard luck story in town, Brother Charles."

"Yes, I suppose I hear my share. Not like a psychologist, though, or a Catholic priest. It makes me shudder to think what those fellows have to go through."

"I'm sure you hear enough. I really shouldn't complain. The Lord's been good to the boys and me. Except for Carl's ear infections, we've all been well."

"How's it going on the job?"

"That's why I stopped by. Harry is selling the Elite

Café, and the new owner's wife is going to do the cooking. That means I'm out of a job."

Hodges straightened up in his chair. "I heard about Harry selling the place, but I thought maybe you could stay on."

"No, that's going to be impossible, so I've got to find something else. I just wondered if you had any ideas. You know I'll take any kind of work I can do."

"As a matter of fact, I do know of something that might interest you, Alona. My friend Reverend Byron Sandifer is pastor of the First Baptist Church in Jonesboro. He's a very fine man. He was telling me about a job that was available, and I think you'd qualify for it."

"What sort of job is it?"

"It's a job assembling parts at a small factory that makes radios. It pays twenty dollars a week. It isn't much, but—"

"It's more than I've been making."

"And Brother Byron said that if there was someone who really needed help, he knew of a house that could be had rent free. It belongs to one of his church members—an elderly lady who doesn't want to rent it out but prefers to help somebody in need."

"In need! Well, I guess that's me. But I don't know anything about radios."

"Brother Sandifer said it's fairly simple. They would train you, of course. The worst thing about it is it's over in Jonesboro."

"I hate to move. I love the church so much, and we know people here. We wouldn't know anyone there."

"I hate it too, Alona. Why don't you let me look around town, see if I hear of anything else."

She shook her head sadly. "I doubt if you'd find anything. I need a job in a hurry, Pastor. Would you call and find out when I could go over to apply? And I hate to ask this, but I don't have any way to get there."

"Yes you do." He smiled. "You've got a broken-down Baptist preacher with a broken-down Ford, but I think we can make it. Let me call Brother Byron right now." He picked up the phone, and when the connection was made, he said, "Byron, has that job we were talking about been filled yet? . . . Good. I've got just the lady for it. Would you see if you could set up an appointment, and I'll bring her over for an interview? . . . Thanks, Byron. This means a lot to me, and if she gets the job, you'll be getting a fine family too. You won't find any better people in the world than Alona Jennings and her three boys. . . . Right. Call me when you set it up."

He put the phone down and nodded. "He said he'd try to set it up for tomorrow morning if that'll suit you."

"That'll be fine, Pastor."

"Let's pray before you leave that this will work out." They bowed their heads, and Hodges prayed a simple prayer. When it was over, he said, "I'm going to miss you, Alona, and those boys too."

"I'll miss you too, Pastor, but it's something I have to do."

★ ★ ★

Raymond Atwood was a big man in his late forties. He had a bulging stomach, was balding, and had a gruff manner. Pastor Hodges had given Alona a ride to Jonesboro and was catching up with some reading in the library at his friend's church until Alona was done with the interview. Reverend Sandifer had then driven Alona to the factory and told her he would wait in the car until the interview was over.

"So you lost your husband and you've got three boys?" the man asked from the other side of the desk.

"That's right, Mr. Atwood. I need a job. But the truth

is I don't know anything about the inside of a radio."

Atwood waved his hand, and she noticed his hands were dirty and his fingernails were bitten down to the quick. "Aw, that don't matter. If you got any ability at all, you can be trained. I guess the pastor told you the pay. It's twenty a week to begin. Of course, you'll get a raise if you work out."

"That's fine, Mr. Atwood. I'd like to start at once if possible."

"The preacher tells me you're gonna live in old lady Cunningham's house."

"I haven't seen it yet, but Pastor Sandifer said there is a fine lady who was making it available."

"Not a bad old house. How you gonna get moved?"

"My pastor will get some of the men from the church. One of them has a truck."

"All right, then. I guess you've got the job, and you can start after you get moved and settled in." He leaned forward across his desk and gave her a grin that didn't quite seem sincere. "You're gonna like it around here, Mrs. Jennings."

She thought she saw him wink but quickly dismissed it as a tick. "I hope so, Mr. Atwood. I thank you for giving me a chance." He walked her to the door. "Come in as soon as you get settled."

"Thank you, sir."

Alona left the factory and found Reverend Sandifer waiting for her. He was a tall, broad-shouldered man with a manner that Alona had liked at once. "Did it go all right?" he asked as she got into the car.

"He said I could start as soon as I get moved."

"That's great. Charlie Hodges says he's going to get the men of the church to move you when you're ready."

"Yes. They all pitched in the last time I moved too."

"That's what church folk are for. We'll be glad to have you here. We've got a good church, and you'll like my wife, Hazel. And I've got two boys. Mike's ten and Roger's twelve. The same ages as your older boys. I hope they'll be good friends."

"My boys will need some friends. They've lived in one town all their life and gone to one church."

As the pastor pulled out of the parking lot, Alona asked, "Is Mr. Atwood a member of your church?"

"No. Actually, I don't think he's a member of any church."

"Is he married?"

"Yes. I believe his wife goes to the Methodist church on occasions."

Alona wanted to ask more about her new employer but wasn't quite sure what to say. The man had made her feel uncomfortable, but there was not much she could do about that now.

"What do you say we go by my house and get Hazel?" Reverend Sandifer asked. "You can meet her, and then we'll show you Mrs. Cunningham's house. I told her yesterday that we might have a new tenant for her today."

"I'll be taking up a lot of your time, Reverend."

"Hey, you know I've never felt comfortable being called *reverend*. I know it's a title a lot of preachers use. My dad was a preacher. Everybody just called him Brother Sandifer, or real close folks by his first name, Ed. Most of the folks in our church call me Brother Byron."

"All right. And I'd really like to see the house."

"Why, this is a fine old place!" Alona exclaimed, walking through the frame house that sat back about fifty feet from the street. It was dwarfed by towering walnut trees and had been well cared for. "And it's got three bedrooms!" She opened the door to yet another room. "An indoor bathroom. We were almost getting used to having one outside."

"Oh, my dear, this will be heaven, won't it!" Hazel Sandifer said. "Byron, you make sure that the hot water heater is working."

"Mrs. Cunningham told me everything's working, but I'll check it to be sure." He grinned. "Do you need any furniture?"

"We'll make out, Brother Byron."

"You let me know if you need a bed or something. People always have extra stuff. We've got a garage full ourselves."

"The ladies and I will come in and give the house a good cleaning before you move in," Hazel said. "Then, when you get here, all you'll need to do is unload and set up housekeeping."

"That would be so wonderful, Mrs. Sandifer."

"Oh, please call me Hazel." The pastor's wife was an attractive woman with a good figure, blond hair, and blue eyes. She and her husband made a striking couple.

"Brother Charles told me you and your family are real special people so we'd better treat you right," Byron said with a grin and a wink. "So I guess I'll have to do that."

"He's been so patient to wait back at the church for me all this time," Alona said. "We'd better head back so he can get home."

"I'm ready if you are," Byron said. "Don't worry about the house, and don't worry about anything else. We'll look forward to seeing you at church as soon as you're moved."

"Thank you, Brother Byron, Hazel. You've both been more than kind."

★ ★ ★

Alona was pleasantly surprised at how easily the boys adjusted to a new town, a new church, and a new school. They had moved less than a week after her interview, and the boys did the standard complaining at first, but by mid-September, when they had been in school for two weeks, they appeared perfectly satisfied.

As for Alona, it was a huge relief to live in a house that was decent and easy to clean. The indoor plumbing was enough to make her feel rich. After his third bath in the indoor bathroom, Carl had complained, "We're gonna wash all our skin off if you keep makin' us take so many baths!"

Alona laughed. "I guess we did without a tub for so long I'm trying to catch up."

The house was a delight to her, but the job was more difficult than she had expected. She had a fair amount of manual dexterity, but it had been difficult learning how to assemble the radio parts. An older lady named Bess Johnson had trained her. She was an impatient woman, but Alona had gotten to know her and had discovered that her impatience came from many years of enduring a bad marriage.

Raymond Atwood had come by her station to speak to her almost every day. He had a way of putting his hand on her shoulder from time to time that made her feel uneasy. He made it seem innocent enough, but Alona always wanted to pull away. She had to keep the job, however, and she hoped she was making more of the gesture than was there.

The First Baptist Church of Jonesboro had received her and her boys with warmth and enthusiasm. The church was a short walk from the house—less than ten minutes. The boys had immediately taken to the pastor's sons and were spending a fair amount of time together. When Paul Root, the music director, had discovered that Alona had a strong, clear soprano voice and was an excellent sight reader, he had drafted her into the choir. She had protested, but he had teased, "I've got to have you, Mrs. Jennings. If you'll come quietly, we won't have any trouble."

Alona had laughed at his imitation of a policeman and had become an enthusiastic member of the choir. Mr. Root was already pestering her about singing a solo.

On their fourth Sunday as members of the church, during the morning service, rolling thunder was followed by the drumming of rain upon the roof. After the service was over, those who had umbrellas took refuge under them; others ran holding purses over their heads, men pulling their hats down firmly.

Brother Byron was standing at the door watching the rain coming down in torrents, and when he turned and saw Alona and the boys coming, he exclaimed, "You can't go home in this! You'll get drenched."

"We'll just wait until it clears off, Brother Byron."

"Well, according to my calculations, that will be a long wait. Stay here a minute. I'll find you a ride."

"Please don't bother!"

"Yes, I think I'd better." He went back into the church, leaving Alona and the boys waiting in the foyer. He came back in a few minutes with a rather short but powerfully built man with steel gray hair. "Mrs. Jennings, I'd like you to meet Oscar Moran. This is Mrs. Jennings and her boys."

Moran smiled. "Yes, I know. I was there when she joined the church. I don't believe you've missed a service, have you, Mrs. Jennings?"

"No, I haven't. I've enjoyed the good preaching."

"Yes, I'd have to agree. The pastor says you need a ride home."

"I hate to be a bother. It's not very far."

"No bother at all. The hardest part will be getting into the car without getting drowned. You wait here and

I'll bring the car right out in front."

"I've got some umbrellas here. I'll get them out, Mr. Moran."

She got the umbrellas out of her bag and the boys immediately started using them as swords. "What does Mr. Moran do?" Alona asked as the man went to get the car.

"He owns the foundry. He's a widower. His wife died about four years ago. She had two daughters by a previous marriage when he married her. They're both grown now."

"He never remarried, then?"

"No, but he's had enough chances. Look, there he comes. Plenty of room for you in that big Oldsmobile he drives. See you later, boys—get under those umbrellas or you'll drown."

Alona and the boys ran to the car, and when the doors were slammed shut, Moran said, "All aboard. Tell me which way to go."

"Go down here and turn left on Oak Street, and I'll direct you from there."

"This is a big car," Zac said. "It's an Oldsmobile."

Oscar Moran turned around and grinned at the boy, who was leaning over the front seat staring at the dashboard. "That's right. You know your cars, young man."

"I bet it's got a big engine in it. How big is it?"

"Zac, don't bother Mr. Moran."

"Let the boy ask questions, Mrs. Jennings. How's he going to learn?"

"That's right, Ma. I'm gonna get me a big car like this one day."

"What's your name, son?"

"Zachary. But everybody calls me Zac."

"Do you think you could drive this car, Zac?"

"Sure I could! My legs aren't quite long enough yet, but I could do it."

"And you fellows. What are your names?" Moran got their names and repeated them. "Well, you'll all be driving cars like this one of these days."

"I could drive this one," Zac spoke up.

"Well, maybe you'll get the chance some day. If you're good boys, that is."

"I'm *always* good," Carl said.

"You are!" Moran was amused. "I don't believe I ever met a boy that was always good."

"Well, I am! Isn't that right, Mom?"

"Almost always, Carl." She smiled. "He is a good boy. But not perfect, as he sometimes thinks."

"You've got three fine boys." Moran turned around for a quick glance at the boys. "When I was a younger man, I thought I'd have five or six just like these."

"Don't you have any boys, Mr. Moran?"

"No, but I've got two stepdaughters."

"What's a stepdaughter?" Carl asked.

He explained what a stepchild was. "When I met my wife, she was a widow with two teenage girls. My wife died a few years ago, and I never did have any children of my own."

"Maybe you'll have one someday," Zac said.

"That's not likely, son."

Alona had been directing Moran as he drove, and finally she said, "It's that house."

"Oh, that's Mrs. Cunningham's place. A nice house."

"She's letting us have it rent free. So kind of her."

"She's a generous woman. Look, the rain's almost stopped."

He stopped the car and then turned and named the boys off. "Let's see. Tim, Zac, and Carl. Is that right? You boys take care of your mother." He fished into his vest and pulled out a card. "Here, Mrs. Jennings."

"What's this?" she asked, taking the card. It said Moran Foundry, Oscar Moran, owner and president, along with a telephone number. "Any time you need any transportation just call me."

"That's very generous of you, but I hope I won't have to do that."

"It won't be any trouble at all. I'm glad to have met you, Mrs. Jennings, and we're delighted that you've come to be a member of our church."

The boys got out, and Zac got the last word. "Don't forget. Someday I'm going to get to drive your car."

Moran laughed. "That's right, son. You will."

As Zac watched the car drive off, he said, "Gee, we can get a free ride anytime we want to, Mom."

"No we can't."

"Why not?"

"We can't impose on Mr. Moran."

"But he said he doesn't mind. He doesn't have any kids or any wife to sit in that big old car. We might as well ride in it," the boy announced.

Alona told him that they wouldn't be needing any more rides, but Zac was still arguing when they entered the house.

CHAPTER SIX

A Heart for Boys

★ ★ ★

The Saturday afternoon practice for the Christmas pageant was going as well as could be expected, which meant that half of the children knew their lines and the other half didn't. Alona sat halfway back in the sanctuary and watched as the pastor's wife attempted to bring order out of chaos. She had watched the practices so many times that she knew all of the lines by heart, and now, except for those times when one of her three were speaking a line, she allowed her mind to drift.

The year had been difficult for the world. Alona thought often of the day that Truman had explained the meaning of a raincrow summer, how it would be followed by dangerous and hard times. She thought of how in August 1939, Germany and Russia had shocked diplomats everywhere by signing a nonaggression pact, which meant, as far as Alona understood it, that the German army, which was now the largest in the world, would be able to concentrate on the western front of Europe without worrying about fighting Russia on another front. They had already begun in September

1939 by invading Poland. This invasion broke twenty-one years of rather shaky peace in Europe, and the Germans had, with their blitzkrieg or lightning war, defeated Poland easily. Britain and France had declared war on Germany at once, but America stayed neutral.

With the world teetering on the brink of a war, the likes of which had never been seen, Alona read the papers each day and listened to the broadcasts with a sinking heart. She wondered how her boys might be affected if the war ever moved beyond Europe. She hoped it would never come to that.

Alona's life had gotten somewhat easier since moving to Jonesboro. She was surprised to find that she was becoming quite good at assembling radio parts, and the steady income, with no rent payments, was easing the financial strain. She loved the house that she lived in and had paid a visit to Mrs. Cunningham to thank her personally and deliver some homemade bread. Mrs. Cunningham was in her late eighties but was in possession of all her faculties, and it had been a joy for Alona to visit with her and thank her for letting them have the house rent free. Mrs. Cunningham had told Alona that she had been widowed herself thirty years ago and understood the loneliness that came after being married to a good man.

The sound of Tim's voice broke into her thoughts, and she quickly looked up as he delivered his lines. "We need a room, innkeeper." She was proud of Tim. He was not outgoing enough to make a good actor, but he did his best. The thought occurred to her that Zac might have made a better Joseph. He would have banged energetically on the innkeeper's door and boldly asked for a room. But he was too young for such a role and was thoroughly enjoying playing a shepherd boy.

When the rehearsal was over, she and the other few parents who had been watching applauded. She stood up and waited while the boys gathered around her, grinning broadly.

"You are doing so well. All of you."

"Aw, it's duck soup, Mom," Carl boasted. Which it was, since he had only one line to speak.

The four of them started out of the church and were intercepted by Oscar Moran. "Hello. How are you fellows tonight?"

"Great, Mr. Moran," Zac said, speaking for the others. "How are you?"

"I'm fine, Zac." Moran turned and said, "How are you, Mrs. Jennings?"

"Very well. I've been watching the rehearsal."

"I caught a little of that before the deacons' meeting. You fellows did fine. It's going to be a great pageant."

"If they don't forget their lines," Alona said with a smile.

"Aw, Mom, we never forget our lines. That's those other dumb kids," Zac announced.

"Don't call kids dumb," Alona reprimanded him.

"That's right," Mr. Moran said. "You must always be polite." He turned to Alona. "It's cold outside. Let me give you and the boys a ride home."

Before Alona could speak, Zac popped up. "Mr. Moran, maybe we should stop and get some ice cream cones at Stanley's Drugstore."

"Zac, where are your manners?" Alona admonished. "Besides, we have the chocolate cake at home that I made last night."

"Why, I think ice cream is a fine suggestion," Oscar said. "Or maybe we should get something even bigger. Like a chocolate sundae or a strawberry milk shake. You know," he said, sounding serious, "I've often wondered how much ice cream a boy could eat. Never have found out. Maybe I could experiment on you."

"Sure," Zac said instantly. "I'd be glad to be an experiment!"

"Me too!" Carl said. "Let's experiment with a vanilla shake and see how many I can eat."

"Boys, you stop that!" Alona scolded. "You sound like beggars."

"Not at all," Moran protested, shaking his head. "Perhaps we might find out how much ice cream the mother of three boys can hold as well."

"I appreciate your offer, Mr. Moran, and your generosity, but I think I'll hold out for chocolate cake myself. Would you like to join me for some after we stop at the drugstore?"

"That would be absolutely delightful, Mrs. Jennings."

"Please just call me Alona."

"I will, and you must call me Oscar," he said as they made their way to the coatrack. "By the way, that's an unusual name—Alona. Where did your parents get it?"

"My mother read that in Hebrew it's the word for an oak tree. She wanted me to be a strong woman, so they tagged me with it. I've spent most of my life spelling it for people and trying to explain it."

"I think it's a lovely name, and I am looking forward to sampling your chocolate cake."

The trip to the drugstore settled very little about the capacity of boys. All three of them were able to consume both the sundae and the milk shake that the soda jerk had set before each of them. After the shake, Alona insisted that was enough and they all piled in the car again to go back to the house.

Alona found Moran's attachment to her boys rather touching. She knew he felt affection for boys in general, and he had been more than generous with her boys in particular. More than once he had taken them home, insisting on stopping to get something good to eat each time.

As the group entered the house, Oscar walked in but stopped immediately as Buddy came bounding forward. He took a step back, explaining, "I'm afraid I'm allergic to some kinds of animals. All cats and some dogs. My eyes tear up and I sneeze like crazy if I get too much animal hair on me."

"Buddy, you'll have to go outside," Alona said as she took Oscar's coat and hat. Buddy gave her a hurt look and his head drooped as Tim let him out.

"Why, he actually looks crushed!" Oscar said with astonishment. "He looks like we've hurt his feelings."

"He's very sensitive," Alona explained. "He'll go outside and pout for a while, but he'll be all right."

"When he stays in the house and gets his feelings hurt," Zac added, "he goes over and faces the wall and won't come away until somebody sweet talks him out of it." He grinned. "He always gets over it, though."

"Come into the kitchen." Alona smiled. "It's warmer there, and cleaner too. I haven't had time to do much housecleaning."

"Don't worry about that. A good chocolate cake makes up for all kinds of housecleaning."

Alona led the way into the kitchen and indicated where Oscar should sit. The boys sat down as well, following Alona's every move as she got out the cake and served it onto two plates.

"Mom," Zac asked, "how come you only got out two plates?"

"You can't *possibly* want cake after all that ice cream!"

"Sure we do," Tim insisted. "I've got one little corner left that's not full."

"Me too!" Carl said. "And give me the biggest piece."

"You're a hog! That's what you are!" Zac snapped. "Give *me* the biggest piece!"

"Stop arguing, boys. You sound like hungry wolves dying for a meal. I'll give you each a half a piece. I don't want you groaning about stomachaches later on." She got out three more plates. "Do you have time for me to make coffee, Oscar?"

"No coffee for me. I've cut way back. I'm trying to watch my diet too, or at least I'm supposed to."

"How about milk, then?"

"That sounds good."

"Why do you have to watch your diet?" Zac blurted. "To keep from getting fat?"

Oscar laughed. "That too, but I have a little heart problem that the doctors fuss at me about."

"What's wrong with it?" Carl asked curiously. "Doesn't it work right?"

"I had a spell with it about a year ago, but you know doctors. They get all upset. I'm fine really."

Alona put a piece of cake in front of everybody and poured milk for the boys and for Oscar. Finally she sat down herself.

"What was it like when you were a boy, Mr. Moran?" Zac wanted to know.

"Well, these are hard times we live in, Zac, but I think it was even harder back then. My family was happy when I was a boy, but we had to work hard to make ends meet. Things got even harder for me when I got older, though. My mother died when I was twenty, and my father remarried a younger woman two years later. They had a son—my half brother Jason, but Jason's mother died in childbirth. Then our father died when Jason was only ten, and I wound up raising him myself."

"Do you have any other brothers or sisters?" Alona asked.

"I have one sister. She's married to a colonel in the army. They move around constantly. He's about ready to retire."

"What about your half brother? Where is he now?"

Oscar seemed somewhat at a loss at the question. He

took a bite of cake before he answered. "Actually, he lives with me right here in Jonesboro. He works for me too."

"I don't believe I've met him. Doesn't he ever come to church?"

"No. Jason's not much of a churchgoer."

"That's too bad, when you're such a good example for him."

Oscar suddenly grinned. "I'm not a saint by any means, Alona."

"How old is he?"

"Let's see. He's twenty-eight." The boys wanted to know more about Jason, but Alona noted that Oscar was having a hard time talking about him.

"Some young men have a hard time finding themselves," Oscar explained, "and Jason's one of those. He's tried a lot of jobs. He was even a pilot for the navy for a while."

"A pilot! Gosh, that's what I want to be!" Zac said.

"You want to be a fireman. That's what you told me yesterday!" Carl snapped.

"I'll be a fireman first and then a pilot later. Would he take us up in his airplane, do you think, Mr. Moran?"

A sober expression crossed his face. "No, Jason doesn't have an airplane now. It was like some of his other efforts. He had a bad crash, and it shook him up so badly he hasn't been able to fly again. He's afraid of it now. I don't understand that." He shrugged his thick shoulders. "When a man makes a mistake or has hard luck, he just has to get up and try again. That's what I always had to do."

"I suppose it's harder for some than for others. You obviously have a lot of determination."

"Well, thank you. I do have that. Some call it bull-headed stubbornness." He laughed and shook his head. "I guess that's about right. I've had to be stubborn to keep this business going. It all but went down during the first year of the Depression, but it's doing well enough now."

Moran stayed for half an hour and heaped praises upon Alona's cake. When she walked him to the door, the boys scattered to their bedrooms. "You know, Alona," Oscar said as he put on his overcoat and hat, "I envy you those fine boys."

"They're not perfect, but they are good boys. And I want to thank you for paying attention to them. They miss their dad a lot. It means something to them to have a man show them some attention."

"No thanks necessary, because it's a joy to me. If you ever have to take them to the doctor, or have some difficulty with them, give me a call. You have my card."

"I do have it, Oscar, and I'll use it if I have to."

"Don't hesitate. Thanks again for the cake. It was delicious."

Alona closed the door and was thoughtful as she went back to the kitchen to wash the dishes. She thought about how odd it was that Oscar seemed so unwilling to talk about his half brother Jason. *He doesn't have any other relatives except for a sister. I would think the two of them would be closer, especially since Oscar pretty well raised Jason after their parents died.*

Later that night, as she settled in between the cold sheets, she thought about how large the bed seemed for one person. She deliberately refused to think about Truman and instead thought about the Christmas pageant and her job. The job worried her, because Mr. Atwood was becoming more and more familiar, and she was at a loss as to how to discourage him without losing her job. She pulled the covers up under her chin and asked God to give her wisdom and to help her with the difficult situation.

* * *

Alona had come to watch the next to the last dress rehearsal for the Christmas pageant. The performance was almost over when Oscar came down the aisle and slipped into the pew beside her. "Hello, Oscar," she whispered.

"Hi, Alona. Is the practice going well?"

"Yes. Everybody seems to know their lines."

"It must take a lot of patience to take children and train them to go through something as complicated as this. I admire the pastor's wife."

"She's such a talented woman, and so very patient."

"She is, and her husband's a good preacher too. A fine couple. We're lucky to have them here."

When the rehearsal was over the two applauded with the other spectators. The children went offstage to change, and Oscar turned suddenly and said, "I don't want to offend you, Alona, but there's something I'd like to ask you."

"Why . . . how could you possibly offend me?"

"I don't know. I don't have the most tact of any man in the world." He chuckled. "Most people would say I don't have *any*. But there's something I'd like to ask you to let me do."

Alona had been approached by many men since her husband had died—some had been crude and others more sophisticated. Until now, she had thought Oscar was just a friend, and she felt sad somehow, for Oscar Moran had never appeared to be the kind of man who would chase after women.

"Just tell me what it is, Oscar."

"I've told you I have two grown stepdaughters, but they both live in Louisiana. We write two or three times a year, but Christmas is pretty lonely in my big house.

I've always wanted children of my own, especially boys, but it just didn't work out that way."

"You would have been a good father. It's too bad you didn't have children."

"Thank you. That's kind of you. What I'd like to do— and please don't be offended by this or take this the wrong way—I'd like to see to it that your boys have a very good Christmas."

"But we will have a good Christmas, Oscar. We have a tree, and I've been baking cookies and breads. On Christmas we'll have a nice dinner and sing songs— we've kept up with all the traditions Truman and I started."

"Of course you have, and I think that's wonderful. But, well, to put it bluntly, I know you don't have much money, and toys and other gifts are expensive, especially as boys get older. So I would like to help with that part of your Christmas."

"Oh no, Oscar, I couldn't possibly let you do that!"

He was quiet for a moment, then said, "I know it's hard to accept money from somebody who's not a member of the family, and I know your pride may be a bit hurt. But, Alona, I'd like to ask you to put your pride aside so that I can help the boys get some nice gifts. No obligation at all, of course."

Now it was her turn to be silent, and she thought for a long time. *Maybe he's right,* she thought. *Maybe I do need to let him do this for the boys. Zac is dying for a twenty-two rifle, and I can't afford it. Tim would love to have some art supplies, and Carl wants toys that I can't possibly afford.* She took a deep breath. "Maybe you're right, Oscar. It does trouble my pride that I'm not able to buy things for the boys that other kids might have."

"I'd be surprised if you felt any other way. But it would make them so happy. You wouldn't even have to tell them where the gifts came from."

"Oh no, I couldn't do that!" she said at once. "You'd have to own up to buying them the things."

"Whichever way you want to do it as long as you let me help. Will you do that?"

She nodded and smiled. "I think it's a wonderful thing for you to do, and I appreciate it so much."

"Good! When you go home, why don't you make a list of what those boys want. I'm sure they've managed to get that across to their mother."

"They certainly have!"

"We can go shopping together, and then we'll wrap the things, and you can hide them at the house."

"That would be fun. I've never gone shopping with someone else buying the presents."

"It'll be fun for me too. I haven't had anybody to buy for since my stepdaughters were living at home, and that's been a long time."

"Tomorrow night is the last practice," she said. "Do you want to go shopping right after work tomorrow? I can leave Tim in charge of the other boys until suppertime. Then we can wrap the gifts while they're here at the church."

"That sounds great. I'll pick you up in front of the factory when you're done at work." Oscar grinned. "You know Christmas has been difficult for me, but this makes it much better. Here they come," he said abruptly. "You'll have to be careful not to say anything that might make them suspicious about our plan. They're smart boys."

"I'll be careful."

"Good. I'll see you tomorrow, then."

★　★　★

The next day Alona could hardly keep her mind on her work. Mr. Atwood came by once and frowned.

"I believe you're so caught up with Christmas, you're not paying attention to what you're doing, Alona."

"I guess you're right," she said, somewhat flustered. "I'm sorry."

"But overall, you're doing a good job," he said. He started caressing her shoulders and the back of her neck. She immediately jerked and looked up at him, but he winked and said, "I'd like to have a Christmas gift from you."

"From me?"

"Nothing expensive. How about a kiss."

"I know you're teasing, Mr. Atwood," she said hopefully. She looked around to see if any of the other workers had heard his comment. They all seemed to be concentrating on their work.

"No, I'm not teasing." His smile disappeared. "You don't need to be so standoffish, Alona. I know you're alone, and a woman needs a man."

"I'm afraid you'll have to go somewhere else for that sort of thing." She saw something change in her boss's eyes.

He removed his hands abruptly and glared at her. "You'd better think that over. Jobs are hard to find." He swiveled and strode away, and the joy was gone from Alona's heart. She tried to put the incident out of her mind and concentrate on her work for the last hour of the day. She watched the clock and left the minute her shift was over. She was relieved to see that Oscar was already waiting for her at the curb.

"What's wrong?" he asked. "Don't you feel well?"

"No, I feel fine. It's just something that happened at work."

"Is it Atwood? Has he been chasing you?"

Startled, Alona lifted her head, her eyes wide with astonishment. "How'd you know that?"

"He gets after practically every woman who works

for him. Have you decided what you'll do about it?"

"I don't know. I can't afford to lose this job."

"Well, do me a favor," Oscar said. "Put it out of your mind until after Christmas. You don't want to let that man spoil the season."

"You're right," Alona said firmly. "Now I'm going to spend so much of your money that you'll have to go put a mortgage on that big house of yours."

Oscar laughed. "I'd like to see you try."

Alona and Oscar had a wonderful time shopping for the boys, and before long, the back of the car was pretty well filled up with presents. Oscar dropped Alona off in front of her house and said, "I'll be back to drop off the gifts as soon as the boys are at practice."

Alona heated up some leftovers for a quick dinner and then walked the boys to the church. "I'll be back when you're done, boys. Have fun."

"Bye, Mom," they called in unison.

Alona walked quickly home and found Oscar waiting outside when she arrived. "Hi, Oscar. I can't believe you're doing all this for us."

"I'm having more fun than the boys will when they open all of this." The two each grabbed all they could carry and with two trips each managed to get everything inside. "I'll help you wrap them, although I'm not much good at that."

"Let's get started. We don't have much time."

Just over an hour later they were hiding the presents in the attic, and Alona was finding herself getting more and more excited. "The boys are going to go crazy," she said as they went downstairs. "They've never had this many nice things." She handed Oscar his coat and hat. "Thank you, Oscar. It's a wonderful thing you're doing. Would you like to come over when we open presents Christmas morning?"

"No, that's just for you and the boys," he said kindly.

"Well, I am going to put your name on all the gifts," she said as she put her coat on.

"I wish you wouldn't, but you know best." They walked out to the car. "Let's get back to church before the boys suspect we're up to something."

As they drove back to the church, he said, "You've made me very happy allowing me to do this little thing."

"It's not a little thing, Oscar. Giving is never a little thing when it's done with a good heart. And you have such a heart."

"Do you think so? Most people that work for me wouldn't agree. They say I'm a hard man, but, Alona, I've had to be hard to keep the business afloat. My employees would be out of work if I didn't run a tight ship."

"I'm sure you would never harm anybody intentionally. Times have been very hard on everyone lately."

Oscar pulled into a parking spot and the two went inside to find the rehearsal was just ending. "I'll take you and the boys home," he said, "and then I'll see you at the performance tomorrow."

"All right, Oscar, and thank you so much."

His whole face glowed as he smiled. "It was more fun than anything I've done in years."

★ ★ ★

On Christmas Eve, the church drew a good crowd for the pageant the children had worked so hard on. Oscar and Alona found a place about midway back in the sanctuary, leaving the front pews for parents who hadn't seen any of the rehearsals. No one forgot their lines, and except for a few angel halos and wings being a bit off center, the children did a magnificent job, bringing the people to their feet with their applause. The boys joined them after they had taken off their costumes. Oscar took them all home and wished the boys a very merry Christmas as they piled out of the car and ran inside, excited by the success of the pageant and the anticipation of Christmas morning.

"I wish you would come by tomorrow and join us, Oscar," Alona said as she got out of the car.

"No, it's your time to be with your boys. I wouldn't want to interfere. Merry Christmas, Alona." He smiled at her as he pulled away from the curb.

She wondered at his generosity as she made her way inside. Her boys had never received elaborate gifts for Christmas, even when their father was alive. So she knew they did not have big expectations this year. Alona had not breathed a word to suggest anything different, and after she got them all tucked into bed, she waited anxiously until they were sound asleep before tiptoeing to the attic. It took her several trips to get the presents downstairs. She had affixed Oscar's name to the ones he had bought, which was the bulk of them.

She slept fitfully until she finally heard the boys stirring. She put on her slippers and housecoat, went downstairs, and built a fire in the stove in the kitchen. When it was going well, she sat down on the living room couch, enjoying a few moments of silence by the Christmas tree before the commotion started. The tree was bright with tinsel and decorations, and the presents were mounded underneath.

She had only been sitting for a minute or two when all three of the boys burst in, then stopped dead still.

"Mom, where'd you get all those presents?" Zac cried.

"It was Santa Claus," Carl said, but he knew better.

"No it wasn't," Tim said. "It was you, Mom."

"All the gifts are marked who they're for and who

they're from. Why don't we take them out one at a time."

The boys were already going through the presents like a whirlwind. "Look, this one's from Mr. Moran!" Tim cried.

"This one is too—and this one!" Carl said.

Zac was picking up presents and reading name tags furiously. "Mom, so many of these are from Mr. Moran."

"Yes, it was something he wanted to do for you. Since he doesn't have any kids of his own, he wanted to give you all a good Christmas."

"Let's get started!" Zac said. "Can I do this one first?"

"I suppose so."

Zac ripped the paper off, threw it up, and yelled, "It's a twenty-two rifle!"

"You'll have to be very careful with that. I don't want you to hurt anybody with that thing."

"I know how to use it," Zac said. "I ain't gonna shoot nobody that don't need shootin'," he said, imitating a voice he'd heard on the radio.

It took much longer than usual to open all of the gifts. Tim was shocked when he found a sketchpad, colored pencils, and watercolors. "How did Mr. Moran know I like art, Mom?"

"Hmm . . . I guess some little bird told him."

Tim laughed.

Carl had received a set of Lincoln Logs, among other things, and was already constructing a fort out of them in the middle of the paper and presents. "You can build anything with these," he said.

When the boys had unwrapped all their gifts, Alona made a big deal over the presents they had bought for her: a bottle of perfume, some handkerchiefs, and a book she had mentioned wanting. "It was so sweet of you boys to get me exactly what I wanted."

"Gosh, Mr. Moran didn't buy you anything!"

"No, he just wanted to make Christmas extra special for you boys."

"He must be rich!" Carl exclaimed. "This stuff costs a lot of money."

"You'll have to tell him how much you appreciate it."

"We will," Tim said. "Do you think we don't have any manners?"

Alona laughed. "I know you have very good manners. I was just reminding you. Now, let's clean up this mess and then you can look at your new things. Zac, you can go out and shoot tin cans. I've been saving some for you."

The boys were thrilled at this, and after they cleaned up all the paper, Alona watched them enjoying their presents, thinking of Oscar Moran with a warm feeling. And then she thought about another man who was quite different from Oscar—Raymond Atwood. She had put all fears of him out of her mind for the last couple of days, but now she knew that the holiday was over and it was back to work, and a dread came over her as she realized that Atwood was not going to change.

PART TWO

January–April 1941

★ ★ ★

CHAPTER SEVEN

JASON LENDS A HAND

★ ★ ★

The woodbox beside the cookstove was practically empty, holding only two rather small chunks of white oak firewood. Carl and Zac were sick with some sort of virus that was going around town, and Tim was going to stay home to look after his brothers. Alona had managed to cook breakfast but knew someone would need to chop wood later on. The first week of 1941 had been bitterly cold. Six inches of snow covered the ground, and every morning for the first six days of the year frost had coated the windows.

The boys were all in the living room, with Zac and Carl each covered with a blanket and curled up in a ball on opposite ends of the sofa. "Get plenty of rest, boys. I've left sandwiches for lunch." She left the house and shivered as she walked to work wearing a coat that was too thin for the unseasonably cold temperature.

She made her way toward the factory, which was a walk of a little over a mile. On her way, she noticed how beautiful the icicles were that hung down from the eaves of the houses—like crystal daggers reflecting the reddish rays of the morning sun. She passed by the birdfeeders that a neighbor kept well supplied with scraps and seed and noticed that the few birds that had gathered were puffy and moved slowly in the cold. Most of the colorful birds had already flown farther south, but the male cardinal made a brilliant red splash against the white background as he pecked at the sunflower seeds. Alona stopped and watched for a moment to see if he would perform the ritual she so delighted in. He picked up a sunflower seed, cracked it, and then hopped across to the female cardinal dressed in brown with none of the male's showy crimson. She opened her mouth, and he shoved the seed in. The act never ceased to delight Alona. "That's a good husband," she whispered. "Go at it, boy." She watched for a moment as he fed the female before hurrying on toward the factory.

She had made it a habit of going to work early, in order to have a few moments of quiet to pray, and the place was virtually empty when she arrived. She welcomed the warmer air inside and went into the cloakroom, where she hung her coat and hat and took off her galoshes. As she turned to leave the cloakroom, the doorway was filled with the ominous presence of Raymond Atwood.

"Good morning, Mr. Atwood."

He took a step forward. The cloakroom was small, and the large man towered over her. "I've told you a hundred times you can call me Ray."

"All right. I'll try to remember that." She started to move forward, but before she could, Atwood reached out and grabbed her, catching her off guard, and planted a kiss on her lips. He was a strong man, and she struggled futilely, turning her head aside to avoid his lips. "Please let me go!"

"Oh, come on. You're a good-looking woman in the prime of life. You've been married, and you know what it's like. What do you want to be so standoffish for?"

"This isn't right, Mr. Atwood. Please don't ask me to do anything that's wrong."

"I got a wife that pays no attention to me and won't have anything to do with me in bed. I figure that gives me the right to find affection somewhere else. Look, you've been struggling with those boys of yours. Why don't you let me help you? I can double your salary. You can do the same work. You and me can go away for weekends sometimes."

"I couldn't do anything like that. Please let me go!"

Atwood's grip only tightened. Alona managed to get one arm free and slapped his face. The blow made a meaty sound, and she saw the imprint of her hand on his cheek.

He cursed but let her go. "You're so holy, ain't ya?" he sneered. "Well, you may be too holy to work around here. You think about what I'm telling ya. I'll give you the rest of the week to think about it. If you don't like my terms, you can go find a job somewhere else." He turned and left the room.

Alona stood for a moment, still shocked by the encounter. Fear came over her at the thought of losing her job, for the Depression was still bitter hard. There were still soup lines in the big cities and hobos roaming the countryside asking for food and work.

She took a deep breath and bowed her head. *Lord, you know I want to be what you want me to be, and this man wants me to do an evil thing. I don't have any other help but you, Lord, so I'm asking you to give me the courage to do the right thing.* She stood there for a moment battling the thoughts of how she would provide for her family if she lost this job, but even as she prayed, she knew she had no choice.

She put her coat back on, along with her hat and galoshes, and went to the large room where the radio parts were assembled, stopped at her worktable, and picked up the few things she had there. Resolutely she walked to Atwood's office, which was at the far end of the assembly area. Without knocking she stepped inside. Atwood was sitting at his desk and looked up with surprise. He got up at once with a grin on his face.

"I reckon you've decided to be smart."

"I've decided to quit. Pay me what you owe me, Mr. Atwood."

For a moment Atwood stared at her in disbelief and then his lips drew together in a pale line. "All right," he said. "But don't come crawling back when you can't get work." He went across the room, opened a small safe, and took out the cash box. "There. I'm paying you for the rest of the week. It shows I've got the right kind of spirit."

Alona took the money without counting it and put it into her purse. "I appreciate the work you gave me. Good-bye." She turned and closed the door and walked steadily toward the entrance. As she approached the door, her friend Mary Alworth was coming in.

"Hello, Alona. You just get here?"

"I just quit, Mary. It's been good to work with you."

Mary, a tall woman with worn features, stared at her. "You're doing the right thing, Alona. This is no place for a woman like you, not with a man like that around." She reached out her hands and Alona took them. "I'll be thinking about you."

"Thanks. I appreciate that. Good-bye, Mary," Alona said briefly and then left the building. As she walked home, she felt empty and drained. Fear was knocking at the door, and she knew that if she allowed herself to dwell on it, it would only get worse. She held her head up and began humming one of the hymns the choir was rehearsing for the coming Sunday.

Arriving at the house, she went in, and the boys all

stared at her. "What's wrong, Mom?" Tim asked. "Are you sick?"

"No. I quit." She told them nothing about Atwood, but went on, "I need another job, so we'll pray for that."

"That's good, Mom," Carl said. "Now you can stay home and bake cookies more often."

She ruffled his hair. "You're always thinking about food, aren't you?"

He grinned but then started coughing.

"Tim, since I'll be home today, you can go ahead and go to school. If you walk quickly, you'll only be a few minutes late."

After he left, she put on her older work clothes and then went out and managed to split enough wood to get the fire going. It was hard work for her, but it gave her an opportunity to diffuse some of her anger and spend some time praying. "Lord, you probably get tired of hearing me ask you for help, but I've got nobody else to ask. Please provide for me and for my boys, Lord. That's what I would ask of you today."

★ ★ ★

Jason Moran stood in front of his half brother silently. Oscar's face was red, and his voice was raised in anger. "Can't you do *anything* right?" Oscar almost shouted. "I depended on you to take care of getting that work done for the Adams account and it's not done! You're like a child! I can't trust you to do anything."

Jason had learned long ago not to interrupt Oscar when he was in one of his fits of anger. They came rarely, but when he was crossed or when one of his workers disappointed him, the rage flared up in him. Jason met Oscar's eyes, and suddenly he saw something change in his brother's face.

"What's the matter, Oscar?"

His brother had stopped speaking, and his face began changing. Pain etched its way across the set of his lips, and his color faded so abruptly that Jason was alarmed. "What's the matter?" he asked, quickly stepping forward. "Are you in pain?"

Oscar reached across with his right arm to rub his left forearm. He looked down at his left hand and flexed the fingers, still saying nothing, but his face was becoming pasty pale.

"Here, sit down, Oscar." Jason guided his brother to a chair and sat him down, bending over him anxiously. "I'd better go get Dr. Roberts."

"No," Oscar wheezed, struggling for breath. His right hand went to his chest and he kneaded the flesh. "I'll be all right. These things pass away."

"Don't be foolish! Something's wrong. It's your heart again."

"All I need . . . is to be quiet. I'll talk to Dr. Roberts later."

Jason stood there uncertainly. Oscar was a difficult man, but he himself was difficult. The two of them had always been different in appearance as well as in behavior. Oscar took after their father, inheriting his short stature and bulky muscles, along with his fiery temper. Jason's mother, Karen, had been a tall, willowy woman with auburn hair and light blue eyes, which Jason had inherited. No one ever took them for brothers, for physically they had nothing in common.

As Jason stood beside his half brother, waiting for the spell to pass, watching him carefully and ready to run for the doctor, he thought about how different they were on the inside. Jason was accustomed to thinking of his older half brother more as a father, for Oscar had raised him after Jason's mother died. It had been a hard struggle, and Jason would always be grateful, for he

would have been in an orphanage if it had not been for
Oscar. But he himself was so different temperamentally.
He naturally had a light spirit, whereas Oscar was a
sober man, even gloomy at times. Jason had early shown
a love for having fun, which Oscar had tried to suppress.
This particular trait had caused Jason to get into many
difficulties as a teenager, but Oscar had always been
there, ready to take him back, although not without ser-
monizing.

"I still think I'd better go get Dr. Roberts, or let me
take you to his office if you won't let me bring him here."

Oscar was breathing more easily now. "Just leave me
alone for fifteen minutes." He took a bottle of pills out of
his desk and put one under his tongue. "I'll be all right.
These pills help a lot."

"You really should go home and get some rest."

"And who would take over here if I did? You certainly couldn't do it."

"Fred's a good man. He knows everything about the
business."

But Oscar's stubborn spirit showed in the set of his
chin. He sat in his chair, taking deep breaths and still
rubbing his chest. "It's going away now. I'll be all right."
He took a slow, deep breath. "You're not any good
around here, Jason, so I've got another task for you."

★ ★ ★

"Don't try to talk. I can't take your temperature if you
won't be quiet."

Zac Jennings had great difficulty staying quiet even
long enough to get his temperature taken. And his occasional coughing spells didn't help the situation either.
He was propped up on the couch, wrapped up in a blanket, as was Carl on the other end of the couch.

Zac waited impatiently until his mother took the thermometer out of his mouth and then piped up at once. "Mom, Carl was makin' faces at me while you were taking my temperature."

"Don't look at him, then."

"I have to!" Zac responded.

"No you don't." Alona looked at the thermometer and shook her head. "You've still got a fever. How do you feel?"

"I feel rotten." He started coughing.

"Well, you'll feel better tomorrow."

"You said that yesterday!" Zac snapped with irritation after he finally stopped coughing.

Alona almost bit her tongue to keep from snapping back. "I'm going to go out and get some more wood. You boys can listen to the radio."

"I get to pick what we listen to!" Zac said at once. "I'm the sickest."

"No you ain't! I'm the sickest!" Carl said.

"You'll have to take turns. It's ten o'clock. You can pick the station for an hour, Zac."

"I want to be first," Carl said.

"You can be second. Every hour you can switch turns, but you've got to be still and get plenty of rest."

"But it's so it's cold in here. I'm freezing!" Zac protested.

"I know. That's why I'm going to go out and get some more wood. I'll be—" Interrupted by a knock at the door, Alona turned and left the room. She opened the door to a tall man she didn't know.

"Mrs. Jennings," he said. "I'm Jason Moran."

"Oh, you're Oscar's brother!"

"That's right."

"Please come in, Mr. Moran."

"Everybody just calls me Jason."

As he stepped inside, Alona asked, "Did Oscar send

you?" She had to look up to Jason—he was at least two inches over six feet and very fit. He looked nothing at all like his half brother. He had rich auburn hair, a wedge-shaped face, and the bluest eyes she had ever seen. They were as blue as the cornflowers that dotted the hills in the beginning of spring.

"Oscar sent me to take the boys to the doctor. The pastor told him they've been sick."

"Oh, I couldn't permit that."

"But he told me to do it, and I have to do what he says."

Alona smiled. "Are you going to kidnap them? Because that's what you'll have to do."

Jason had heard a great deal about her indirectly but was surprised at how attractive the woman was. Oscar hadn't shown much interest in women after his wife died, but Jason had figured out that he was interested in this one. He took in her glowing orange hair, large gray-green eyes, and tall strongly built figure and found himself admiring her. "Mrs. Jennings, I don't want to sound pushy or anything, but this is something that Oscar wants me to do, and he usually gets his own way."

"I'm afraid he's not going to get his own way this time, Mr. Moran."

"Jason."

"Jason, then. The boys will be all right. Just tell Oscar that I appreciate it but I can't permit him to do this."

Jason laughed. "He'll probably shoot me. Sometimes I think he's going to."

"You work for him, I understand?"

"That's right. I work at the foundry, but he's upset with me today, so he sent me over here." He hesitated, then said, "Are you sure you won't let me take the boys to the doctor?"

"I'm very sure. Thank you very much, Jason."

He turned and left the house without another word.

As the door closed, Alona thought, *He's so different from Oscar. I would never take them to be even distant relatives.*

Putting the incident out of her mind, she bundled up and went outside to split a few more pieces of wood. She had bought a load of wood from a man who had stopped by with a load in the back of his pickup. It was sawed into two-foot lengths but not split. The ax was dull, and the wood was tough and spongy. She awkwardly handled the ax but managed to get enough to keep the house warm for the next day or two. She carried the wood in and put some in the woodbox in the kitchen and some in the living room. As she deposited the load in the living room, she heard a car pull up. "Who can that be?" She went to the door and saw Dr. Roberts getting out along with Jason Moran.

She waited until the two men approached. "I'm surprised to see you, Dr. Roberts." She was fond of the man, who was a member of their church.

He grinned. "I had to come, Mrs. Jennings. Jason here threatened to start rumors about me if I didn't."

"You're a stubborn man," Alona told Jason.

"No I'm not. Other people are stubborn. I'm just . . . firm, you might call it." He smiled, exposing very white teeth. "I was more afraid of not doing what Oscar said than of offending you."

"That's enough of this foolishness, Alona. Let me see those boys."

"All right, Doctor. Come in." She opened the door, and the two men entered.

"I'll just wait here in the hall," Jason said.

"Go on into the kitchen. There's coffee on the stove."

Dr. Roberts, a short, rotund man of sixty with silver hair, went at once into the living room and gave Zac and Carl a good examination. "Well," he said, putting his stethoscope back in his bag, "they've got what everybody else has. In a couple days they'll feel much better.

Meanwhile, give them a teaspoon of this cough syrup—" he took a bottle out of his bag—"every few hours and especially before bedtime."

"How much is it, Dr. Roberts?"

"It's a free sample."

"Now, Doctor, I don't believe that."

He smiled. "I don't care whether you believe it or not. You give the boys what I tell you and don't argue."

Alona shook her head but she couldn't help but grin as she accepted the medicine he held out. "I'm going to get a spoon and give them the first dose right now." She went into the kitchen and quickly came back with a spoon.

"Say, I've just recruited a sinner for the choir," he told her as she gave each boy some cough syrup. "Oscar's been telling me that Jason's got the best voice he's ever heard. Clear as a bell and powerful he says. I told Jason I'd come visit your boys if he'd agree to sing in the choir. He's scared to death of his brother, so he agreed. Don't know what the pastor and the music director will think, though."

"Why would you say that?"

"Jason's not a Christian. He made a profession of faith when he was very young, about fourteen, I think, and did well for a time. But he got away from the Lord somehow or other. Have you heard about that trouble he had in the navy?"

"Oscar told me he crashed his plane."

"Yes, he did. It's a miracle he got out of it. But it did something to him. You should have known him before that. Full of life, ready to try anything. Now he drinks too much, although I guess any drinking at all is too much for a Baptist. The way I figure it, he's better off in church even if he's not living a Christian life. He'll get to hear some good preaching and be around good people.

It may be just what he needs to help him get back into a relationship with the Lord."

"I think that's a wonderful idea, Dr. Roberts."

"There's a good man inside Jason somewhere. It just got lost somewhere along the line." He snapped his bag shut and went over to the couch to pat each of the boys on the shoulder. "These boys will be all right."

"Thank you so much for coming. That was so kind of you."

"Don't you give it another thought."

The two went into the kitchen to get Jason and found him sitting on a chair, stroking Buddy's head, with Buddy's paws propped up on his lap. "Just push him away, Jason," Alona told him.

"I think this dog is love starved." Jason grinned at her. He leaned over and let the dog lick him on the face. "You see? He'll even kiss a stranger. You've been ignoring this animal."

Alona laughed. "Ignoring that dog! Not likely. He's spoiled to death."

"Are you ready to go, Jason?" Dr. Roberts asked.

"You go on ahead, Doctor. I know you have other house calls to make. I'm going to walk back to the foundry."

"Are you sure I can't give you a lift?"

"Nah. I like to walk. Thanks anyway."

Alona showed the doctor to the door, thanking him again for coming. She went back into the kitchen to find Jason talking to Buddy.

"He's a beautiful animal. I've always liked collies." He held Buddy's head between his hands and moved it gently back and forth. "They're smart, nervy, and loyal to a fault. I had one when I was growing up. When he died, I thought I was going to die too."

Alona offered her sympathy and sat down at the table with him, talking about dogs.

"I'd better get going now," he said after a few minutes.

"I really appreciate your bringing the doctor. I . . . I was starting to worry about the boys."

"It's pretty hard to take charity, isn't it?" Jason grinned wryly. "I've taken a lot of it the last few years. Haven't ever learned to like it, though."

"Do you enjoy your work at the foundry?"

"I hate every second of it, but Oscar's been good to me. Anybody else would have kicked me out on my ear a long time ago."

"I understand he raised you from the age of ten."

"Yes, that's true." Jason shrugged. "I never had a mother, you know. She died when I was born. And when our father died when I was ten, Oscar just took over. I'll always be grateful to him for that. No telling where I'd be today if it weren't for him."

"Dr. Roberts tells me you're going to be singing in the choir."

Jason sobered. "That's his fool idea. I'll do it, though, because I promised."

"It's a wonderful choir. I enjoy it so much."

"I guess you need one sinner there to balance all the saints."

"You shouldn't talk like that! You're a Christian, aren't you?"

"I think I've lost my birth certificate. I guess I used to be saved, but I haven't acted like it for the last few years."

"What happened?" She was hoping she could get him to talk about it.

"I'm like that sheep. The one out of a hundred that wandered away."

"That happens sometimes. But you'll be in church now, so if you let Him, the Lord will bring you back."

She saw that he was disturbed by the remark, and his

face was stiff. Even as she watched him struggle for a reply, she thought what a handsome man he was. Oscar had told her he was twenty-eight, which made him just a couple of years younger than she was. "It will be good. You'll see," she said.

"Maybe so. Can't hurt, I guess." He got up and left the house without saying another word.

Alona was surprised by his abrupt departure, but she started making preparations for the noon meal. She had just taken the pans out of the drain pan in the sink when she heard a loud smack coming from the back yard. She looked out the window and saw Jason lift the ax and strike a blow at one of the round sections of log. It fell apart easily. He picked one of the split logs up and struck it again. He was strong and had evidently split a lot of wood before, for every strike split the wood as cleanly as if it was cloven rock.

"I shouldn't let him do that, but he's got a stubborn streak. I expect he'd do it no matter what I said." Jason was still splitting wood by the time lunch was ready. She went to the back step and called, "Jason, come in and have some lunch."

"That sounds good." He swung the ax into the chopping block and then came inside, his face flushed from the exercise.

"You can wash up in the bathroom." She showed him where it was and went into the living room to call the boys to lunch.

When Jason came back, Zac said, "You don't look like your brother."

"No, I sure don't. Which one of us do you think's the most handsome?"

"You are," Carl said at once.

"Well, that's nice of you to say so, but he's a far more reliable man than I am."

"He gave us lots of presents for Christmas," Carl said.

"Yes, I heard about that. He loves kids. He raised me for much of my life. He's been more like a dad to me than a brother."

They all sat down at the table to eat their soup and sandwiches, with Zac firing questions at their visitor. When he found out that Jason had been a pilot in the navy, he grew very excited. "Tell us about it," he said. "What's it like to fly?"

Jason told them a little about the exhilaration of flying and explained how the planes landed on aircraft carriers. But then he dropped his head for a moment. "At one time it was the biggest part of my life, but I don't fly anymore."

"Why not?" Carl demanded. "If I could fly an airplane, I'd want to fly all the time."

Alona saw something change in the tall man's face. She wasn't sure, but part of it may have been sadness. He said quietly, "I had a pretty bad accident, so I don't fly anymore."

"That's enough questions. You boys are through eating. Why don't you go back and get all warm and cozy on the couch and listen to the radio."

When they were gone, she said, "You'll have to excuse the boys. They're full of questions. My oldest son, Tim—he's at school—is fairly quiet, but those two younger ones never stop."

"It's all right." He turned the coffee cup around in his hands, and she noticed how strong they looked, with long fingers. "That's sad about your accident . . . with the plane, I mean."

"It was pretty well the end of the world for me."

Alona did not pursue the subject. "You never married?" she asked. Then she laughed. "I'm as bad as the boys. We're a bunch of busybodies around here."

"That's all right. No, I never married. Wouldn't saddle a woman with a fellow like me. I'd be the world's worst husband."

Alona didn't know how to respond.

"What about your son Tim?" Jason went on. "What's he like?"

"Like I said, he's very different from my other two boys. Very artistic."

"Is that right! In what way?"

"He likes to draw and paint. He says he'd like to be an artist."

"Well, he and I will have something in common, then."

"Oh? Are you a painter?"

"I thought I might be at one time. I still fiddle with it and I enjoy it, but I'm not too talented."

When he looked up, she noticed again how bright his blue eyes were. They were very penetrating, and there was a strength in his face that she rarely saw in a man. *He's so handsome,* she thought. *It's a wonder some woman hasn't married him, no matter what he says.*

"I've got an idea. I've got a lot of painting supplies. I don't use them much anymore. I wonder if Tim would like some of them."

"He would love them, but what he needs even more is somebody to talk to. A man, that is."

"I'm a good talker. And I suppose a fair listener too. I'm just not much of a doer, as my brother will tell you."

"Your brother has been very kind to us."

"He's grown fond of your boys and of you too." He took a sip of his coffee. "It's been a long time since I've seen him show any interest in a woman. At first I thought he just liked being around the boys, but now that I've seen you and gotten to know you a little bit, I don't think it's only that."

"Oh, there's nothing to that!" Alona said, her face

burning with embarrassment. "He just likes the boys."

"So you say. But about Tim. I'll drop by later and bring him some paints and easels and things."

"That would be wonderful. He got a few supplies from Oscar for Christmas, but I'm sure he would make good use of anything that you don't think you'll be using."

"That's settled, then. Thanks for the lunch. I'll fill your woodboxes, and then I'll be going."

He left the house, and Alona sat at the table thinking about how different the brothers were. Jason made one trip in to fill the woodbox in the living room and another trip for the kitchen.

"That'll do you for a while. I'll see you later."

"Thanks so much. I really appreciate all you've done—especially bringing the doctor."

"You'll have to thank Oscar for that. It was his idea. But I did enjoy chopping the wood. At least I'm good at that. When Tim gets home from school, tell him I'll come by later with the paints and stuff."

She watched him go, walking away with a quick stride. "Tim will like it so much," she whispered aloud.

CHAPTER EIGHT

A New Voice in Choir

★ ★ ★

"Oscar, I wanted to thank you for what you did for my boys—sending Dr. Roberts over."

Oscar Moran had been about to enter the Sunday school room for his class. He smiled at Alona. "I hated to think about them being sick and not getting any medicine."

"I'm afraid I wasn't very nice to Jason at first. I practically ran him off. That's my foolish pride, of course."

"I wish you wouldn't take it that way, Alona. I've got plenty of money. You know that, and I spend more on all kinds of foolishness than a doctor's visit costs."

She laughed. "I can't imagine you doing anything foolish."

"Well, I spend way too much money on cigars, for one thing, which the doctor doesn't even want me to smoke. I sneak around at times, though, and have one."

Alona laughed and put her hand on Oscar's arm. "I can't imagine you *sneaking* around to do anything. You're the most straightforward man I've ever known in my life."

He grinned. "I guess I've been called worse things than straightforward."

"I've got to get to the nursery now."

"Jason told me about how he had to promise Dr. Roberts he'd join the choir in exchange for his making the visit."

"I think that was a good idea the doctor had."

"I suppose so. He hasn't been in church since he left the navy. I've tried to persuade him to join me, but he can be a pretty stubborn fellow at times. And, of course, you can't make a person go to church."

"He does have a fine voice, the doctor says."

"Oh yes, he's always been a great singer! He took after his mother in that respect. She had a beautiful voice. As a matter of fact, he's a great deal like her in appearance, as well as in personality. I'm more like our father."

"Well, we can always use some good, strong male voices in the choir. I have to go now. I think we might have a full nursery this morning. Thank you again, Oscar. It was very generous of you."

"It was nothing at all," he said and waved.

Alona turned and went directly to the nursery, where she found the pastor's wife manning the fort. Since Hazel always came to church early with her husband, she was always there when the first babies arrived. Alona and Hazel would leave the nursery to another pair of ladies when they went to sing in the choir during the worship service.

Alona went over and looked in one of the cribs, where a baby girl with a ribbon clipped into her hair stared owlishly up at her. "Hello, you sweet little thing." Alona leaned over the crib and let the baby grasp her finger. "I wish I had three just like you."

"What in the world would you wish that for, Alona?" Hazel asked.

"That's what my husband always said. He wanted three girls to go with the three boys. He always said we needed a matched set."

Hazel knew how much Alona still missed her husband. "How are the boys?" she asked.

"They're absolutely fine now. They're completely over that bug. Did you hear what Oscar did?"

"No. What was that?"

Alona told her how Oscar had sent Jason to take her boys to the doctor, and how she had refused and then Jason had simply brought the doctor to her. "I think he's got some of Oscar's stubbornness in him. He simply wouldn't take no for an answer."

"I'm glad Jason's going to sing in the choir. Paul told me that he'll be coming. We'll have to pray for him."

Alona picked up a chubby baby boy who was fussing and sat down and began rocking him. "Oscar's been so helpful to me, but I guess he is to everyone."

"No, not really."

Alona looked up with surprise. "Why would you say that?"

"I'm sure he's generous with his donations to the church, but he's rather tight with his workers. I suppose with this depression he has to be. Everyone says that he saved his business when others went down by being tight and hard."

"I never see that in him, but of course I don't work at the foundry." She rocked the baby for a few moments. "I wonder why he never married again."

"Plenty of women have wanted to marry him but none of them have succeeded. Do you know about his heart trouble?"

"No, what's the problem?"

"He had a heart attack about a year ago. He seems to have gotten over it, though. Dr. Roberts pulled him through. Put him on a strict diet, made him quit smoking, and tried to get him to exercise."

"I didn't know that. He looks healthy enough."

"He still weighs too much. Dr. Roberts keeps trying to get him to lose more weight." Hazel looked at Alona with one eyebrow raised. "Everyone's talking about how much Oscar seems to care for you. I've heard rumors of wedding bells."

"Really! That's foolishness! It's nothing like that."

"Are you sure?"

"Of course I am. He's just interested in my kids."

"Has he ever asked you out?"

"No. Not in the way you mean." To change the subject, she said, "Jason is very different, isn't he?"

"Yes, he is. You'd never know he and Oscar are related. After Jason's plane crash, he started drinking. He nearly drank himself to death. Oscar went searching and finally found him living in a run-down shack some forty miles away. Practically pulled him out of the gutter and convinced him to come here. Gave him a roof over his head and put him to work at the foundry."

"From what I understand, he led a good Christian life until the crash," Alone said. "I guess that took all the strength out of him."

"I don't think a thing like a crash would have fazed Oscar."

"No, it wouldn't. Oscar would have stood up and gotten into another plane that same day. Some people are strong and some aren't. I guess Jason just doesn't have that kind of strength."

★ ★ ★

"Alona, I'd like to take the boys to my hunting camp for a few days. I'm getting a group of guys together."

Alona invited Oscar in and led him into the living

room. "Your hunting camp?" she asked. "What's that?"

"I own some land out north of town. I built a pretty nice cabin on it. I used to go to it more than I do now, but it's not much fun going alone."

"And you want to take the boys?"

"Yes. And I've also invited the pastor and his boys, Mike and Roger. James Glover is going to be there with his son Leon. They're all about the same age as your boys."

"It sounds wonderful! What would they do?"

"We'll try to get a deer or two and do some fishing."

"You go fishing in January? That doesn't sound like fun to me."

"I don't go often, but you can usually catch something if you can stand the cold."

"It sounds like a wonderful adventure for the boys. How long would you be gone?"

"We'd leave Friday afternoon after school and come back Sunday night. It's a nice cabin, tight and warm. I've taken the pastor and his boys before. We always have a good time." He suddenly looked down at the floor and was silent for a moment. He continued with a wistful note in his voice. "I've let the men of the church take their boys to the camp many times, but this time it'll be almost like having three boys of my own along."

"I'll let you tell them, Oscar. They're playing in Zac's bedroom. It seems like I spend my life thanking you."

"No need to thank me. It's something that I've wanted to do, and I consider it a privilege that you'll let me spend time with your boys."

★ ★ ★

"Are you ready to go, fellas?" Oscar Moran asked. "We're going to meet up with the other men in just over an hour, but I want to stop at a store and get you some warmer clothes first."

"These are the warmest we have, Mr. Moran," Tim told him.

"It'll be cold out there sitting on a deer stand. You fellows need to be fixed up."

Oscar drove downtown with the boys packed in the car along with all their supplies. "Boys, I want you to have fun on this trip."

"We will, Mr. Moran," Zac said eagerly. "You bet we will!"

"That's the idea, but I have to tell you now there are rules. It can be dangerous in the woods. You'll be handling guns, and there'll be other people out hunting. You have to do everything I say, and I mean *everything*. Your mother would never forgive me if anything happened to you, and I'd certainly never forgive myself. Whatever I tell you, you must do it instantly as a matter of safety. Understood?"

"We'll listen to you, Mr. Moran," Tim said quickly. "We've never gotten to do anything like this before, so we'll do what you say."

"That's good. Carl and Zac, do I have your word too?"

They all agreed that they understood the rules.

Moran drove to the sporting goods store and fully equipped the boys with warm boots, heavy socks, pants, and bright orange wool mackinaws and hunting caps. They all strutted around in the store in their new getups.

"Can we wear these and put our old clothes in a bag?" Zac asked.

"I don't see why not." Oscar grinned. "You're certainly colorful enough. Nobody would mistake you for a deer. That's why you have bright clothes like that."

"Gosh, Mr. Moran," Tim said. "Thanks so much for these clothes. They feel great and they're so warm." The other boys chimed in, and Oscar waved his hand and cut them off.

"I'm glad to do it, boys. It makes me feel young myself to be around you fellows. Let's be on our way."

★   ★   ★

Paul Root, the music director of First Baptist Church of Jonesboro, had big ideas for the music program. Usually his ideas were bigger than the talent he had available, but he never grew discouraged. He loved his work, no matter the skill level of the people. He had invited Alona to meet him at the church on Saturday afternoon before choir rehearsal while the boys were on their hunting trip. Normally the choir practised on Wednesday night, but he had called a special rehearsal in order to read through the new music.

After the two exchanged greetings, Alona told him about the trip and how excited all three of the boys had been before they left.

"It's good for Oscar too," Paul said. "He told me all about it. I think he was at least as excited as the boys."

After a little more talk, he said, "I was hoping you would help me with the Easter cantata. It's going to be quite an undertaking, Alona. It's more difficult than most of the music we do. I was wondering if you would mind working with the sopranos and altos for part of each rehearsal. I'd like to have sectionals to help each group feel more comfortable with the music."

Alona was pleased that he had asked her. Now that she wasn't working, she had plenty of time on her hands, and she was confident that she would do a good job. It would also give her an opportunity to use her piano skills, which were getting a bit rusty. "I would enjoy that, Paul. Thanks for asking."

He showed her a few of the pages that he thought would be most difficult for the women while she marked the spots with bookmarks.

"What do you think about Jason joining the choir?" Alona asked curiously

"I think it's great. Have you heard him sing?"

"No, I haven't."

"You'll be surprised. I think he could have been a professional singer if he'd wanted to."

"Have you heard people talking about the way he lives? I've heard that drinking is a real problem for him."

"Yes, I've heard that too," Paul said reluctantly. "I guess he gets to thinking about what he could have been and it gets him down. But I think it's a good thing for him to be in church."

"That's exactly what I think."

"You encourage him all you can, Alona, and I'll do the same. And we've got to recruit some more people for the cantata."

"Maybe we can get some of the Methodists to come, or the Pentecostals."

"I'd even take an Episcopalian," Paul said, then laughed. "I'll take anybody who can sing."

As the choir members started arriving, Paul greeted them each enthusiastically.

Alona was keeping an eye out for Jason, and when he arrived, she went up to him at once. He was already being greeted by two of the other tenors. "I'm glad to see you, Jason."

"Gosh, I feel like I've been ambushed." He looked around nervously. "I'm as out of place here as a bullfrog on a highway with his hopper busted."

"You shouldn't feel like that."

"Yes I should. I'm not living for the Lord, and I know it, and everybody else knows it too."

Alona felt sorry for the man. She did not know him

very well, but she knew his talent and even his life were being wasted. "We all have our problems. Some people's are just easier to see than others'."

Paul Root called out that he was ready to start and asked everyone to take a seat. He asked them to pause for a moment of prayer and then he passed out the new music. "We're going to have the best Easter cantata we've ever had!" he exclaimed, excitement glowing in his eyes. "I'm going to count on all of you to come faithfully to practice and recruit anybody who has any talent at all, whether they come to this church or not. We'll sing together and we'll pray together, and we'll show this town what Easter should be like—at least in music."

They started sight-reading the new cantata, and Alona was surprised to hear the clear, powerful tenor of Jason Moran's voice. *Why, he's great!*

After the rehearsal, as they were putting their music folders on the shelves, Alona said, "You have a beautiful voice, Jason."

"Thank you, Alona. I like the cantata we're working on." They went to the coatrack and Jason held her coat for her. "Have you eaten any supper yet?" he asked.

"No, I haven't."

"Why don't we stop off and get something at the café? And then I'll give you a ride home. Oscar gave me strict orders to take you home after practice."

"That sounds good. I'm starved."

The two got into his car and went to the Royal Café. Jason ordered a steak and she ordered a sandwich. While they were waiting, they talked about the musical program.

"I still think this is some kind of a mistake for me to be singing in the church choir." He gazed off into the distance, sorrow and regret in his eyes. "I drink sometimes, you know."

"Do you?"

"You probably already knew it but you're too nice to say so. Well, I do drink. Sometimes when I get down, I just can't seem to help it."

"Oscar told me you crashed your plane when you were flying for the navy."

"That's right. Before that, it was the happiest time of my life. I love to fly." He told her about what it was like to fly far above the ground, looking down at cars that looked like toys and clouds that looked like cotton. After their food arrived, he said, "When my plane went down that day, it didn't hurt me physically, but it did something inside me. I got in another plane the next day, but I froze. Couldn't even start down the runway. I guess I just lost my nerve. I was so lucky to walk away from that plane. I'm still not sure how I survived it."

After the two had finished their meals, they sat there drinking coffee for a time, and finally they got up and left. He was silent as he drove her home, and when he stopped in front of her house, she waited until he got out and opened the door.

"Thanks for the meal," she said.

"You're welcome. It's good to be doing something different for a change. I'm pretty lonesome, but I'll bet those boys of yours aren't. I'll bet they're having the time of their lives."

"It was wonderful for Oscar to take them for the weekend like he did," Alona said as he walked her to the house.

"He's a generous man."

"I'm looking forward to the cantata." She opened the front door.

"I think it will be a good one. You have a beautiful voice."

"Well, thank you. I don't sing as well as you do."

"Maybe we can do a duet sometime."

"Maybe so. Good night, Jason."

"Good night, Alona."

★　★　★

When the boys came piling into the house the next evening, they were all trying to talk above the others. "I shot a deer, Mom," Zac yelled, "and we dressed it out, and I brought some of the meat home."

"And I caught a six-pound bass," Carl said, "but we ate him!"

"It was great, Mom," Tim said. "We had so much fun with Roger and Mike—and Leon too."

"Where did you get these new clothes?"

"Mr. Moran said we needed warmer clothes. He bought them for us before we left. Ain't they keen?" Zac said, strutting around.

Oscar came in, arms loaded with packages of venison. "You won't have to worry about meat for a few days. Have you ever cooked deer?"

"Yes, I have. I always soak it overnight in saltwater. It makes it tender." She motioned for him to put the packages on the counter. "Can you stay for a cup of coffee?"

"Absolutely."

The boys could not speak fast enough as they all sat at the kitchen table and told Alona about the weekend. Oscar sat back, saying little but smiling. After he finished his coffee, he said, "Well, I've got to go."

"I'll go to the door with you."

"Mr. Moran, it was the best time we ever had, all of us," Tim said. "Thanks a lot." He put his hand out, and Oscar shook it.

"Tim, it was the best time I ever had too." He shook hands with the other two boys as well. "We'll have to do something like this again. You save some time for me, all right?"

The boys assured him they were ready for anything, and they stayed in the kitchen while Alona walked Oscar to the front door.

"They had such a wonderful time," she said.

"So did I." He buttoned his coat. "There's a concert over in Dayton next Saturday. I don't know how good it'll be, but I know you love music. Would you like to go with me?"

"That would be nice, Oscar."

"Good. I'll pick you up about five o'clock. We'll go get something to eat before the concert. Can you get someone to stay with the boys?"

"Oh, I'll leave Tim in charge. He's very responsible."

"They're fine boys." Oscar shook his head. "I know you must be very proud of them."

"I am."

"I'll see you Saturday, then."

Alona closed the door, and as she walked back to the kitchen, she suddenly realized, *He is interested in me*. The thought troubled her. She had never thought of remarriage, but now she began to wonder if Oscar Moran could be a man she might learn to love. She knew she could never marry again unless she felt the Lord's blessing on it. When she went into the kitchen, the boys were still talking about their adventure.

"Did Mr. Moran take good care of you?" she asked.

"Oh, Mom, he spent all the time with us! He's very careful with guns, and he taught us all how to shoot. Even Carl got to shoot the big deer rifle."

"He bought us all these nice clothes, Mom," Zac said. "And he told us he has a pool table. He said we can come over sometime and play pool."

"That would be fun."

"Would you go too, Mom," Tim wanted to know, "if he asked you?"

"I expect I would, Tim. I've never played pool, but it might be fun."

He started to ask another question, but then he suddenly broke it off. She thought she knew what the question would be, but Tim would have to ask it himself.

CHAPTER NINE

AN ELEGANT HOUSE

★ ★ ★

"Tim, you've done a great job on this painting."

Tim stared at the painting on the easel rather doubtfully. "You really think so, Jason?"

"Sure do. See how you've blended the various grays in the sky to make it look overcast? And here you've got this little bit of vermilion to show that the good weather's about to come."

"I don't think I did very well with the trees."

"It's a lot better than the last time. You're doing well, son—you're really making progress." Tim seemed to enjoy having the time with a father figure as much as he did painting. Jason stood beside Tim, his hand resting on the boy's shoulder. He understood a little about how the boy felt, for when he had shown an interest in painting when he was young, not much older than Tim, Oscar had shown no understanding at all. Jason had worked hard to save his own money for paints and canvas and books, but he had never been able to persuade Oscar to let him take lessons. Later, after joining the navy, all of his free time went to studying the technical aspects of flying.

Tim turned suddenly. "I'm using up all the canvases, and they cost a lot of money."

"You have to use canvas to learn how to paint. Sometimes I painted over old paintings and then I wished I hadn't."

"Why, Jason?"

"Because I wish I'd kept all my paintings. Kind of a record of my life at that time. You want to keep all these, Tim. One of these days you'll look back and you'll remember how you struggled with these. It'll be easy for you then."

"I don't see how you paint your leaves so easily," Tim said, leaning forward.

"I'll show you. Here. Let's work on this tree together. Watch me do a little, and then you try to do what I've done."

The two worked for over an hour, Tim's face alight with eagerness, and Jason smiling from time to time thinking how much the boy was like him when he was that age.

Jason put his brush down. "Well, I've got to be headed to work. It's going to be—" The door opened, and Alona stood there smiling.

"Can I come in or is this for artists only?"

"Come in, Mom. Look at how I've done this tree. Isn't it neat? Jason showed me how to do it real easy."

Alona was pleased at the happy, excited expression on Tim's face. Zac took this same sort of excitement and interest in sports, and Carl in making mechanical projects. But painting was the only thing that brought such joy to Tim. "That is really wonderful!" she said as she came closer. "You've even got the old windmill in there. I'd know this place anywhere."

"He's doing real great, Alona," Jason said. "He'll

never be as good as I am, of course." He winked at Tim.

"You are so egotistical, Jason Moran!"

"Like Dizzy Dean says, it ain't bragging if you can do it."

"I guess there's some logic to that."

"I've got to get to work—back to the salt mine," Jason said.

"Thanks for showing me how to do the leaves, Jason."

"I did my best, but at some point you'll need a real teacher."

"Gosh, I wish I could have a class in painting instead of English or some of the other stuff I have at school!"

"You'll need that too," Jason said. "Do your best at everything. I'll teach you what little I know, which isn't a lot, and someday you'll be a full-fledged painter."

"That's what I want to do more than anything!"

"You stick with it, then." Jason turned to Alona and said, "I'll see you tonight at practice."

"It's going well, isn't it?" Alona said as she walked with Jason out of Tim's bedroom and toward the door.

"Yes, it is." Jason put on his overcoat and donned his hat. "You know, I've really enjoyed singing in the choir, and Brother Byron is a great preacher."

"I think so too, and the cantata is going to be wonderful. Everyone in the choir is aware of how much you add to it."

"I'm lucky they haven't kicked me out." He grinned. "I'll see you later, Alona."

★   ★   ★

Oscar pulled his Oldsmobile up in front of Alona's house, turned the engine off, and leaned back in the seat. "Did you like the concert?"

"Very much, and the dinner was wonderful. I hope I didn't embarrass you by eating so much."

"I think we were both equally guilty about that. Doc Roberts keeps on me to lose weight, but I can't seem to stop eating. When I was younger it was easier."

"You really ought to pay attention to what the doctor says."

"Now, don't you start in. Jason stays on my back every day about eating too much."

"You should listen to him."

"I know I should, but there are very few pleasures in life that I really enjoy. Eating's one of them." He shrugged his shoulders and smiled. "But I enjoyed tonight very much. I hope we can do it again sometime."

"Of course we can."

"You know, Alona, I get very lonely at times." He stared out at the street for a moment and then said quietly, "I'm sure you do too."

"Yes, of course I do, but I have my boys to keep me busy."

"Would you and the boys like to go to one of the Civil War battlefields sometime? There's one not too far away. I think they'd enjoy it and it would be educational."

"Yes. Why, I think that would be very nice."

"Let's plan on that some weekend, then." He reached out his hands and took both of hers. "It was a wonderful evening. Thank you so much for going."

★ ★ ★

In mid-March they finally found a Saturday when they could all be free to make the trip to the Civil War battlefield. Oscar had invited Alona and the boys to have dinner at his house after they got home. "We could go to a restaurant," he said, "but I'd like for you to see my house. My brother will be there, and the housekeeper will take care of everything."

Alona agreed, for she had been curious to see his house.

The battlefield was great fun for the boys and interesting for Alona. The boys were full of questions, and Alona found that Oscar knew an awful lot about the Civil War and could answer most of their questions.

When they returned to Jonesboro, they stopped at the foundry and Oscar gave them a quick tour, again answering the boys' many questions. Zac was fascinated by the place, but Tim didn't like it much. It was noisy and dirty, and Oscar said as they left, "It's not the place for a lady, Alona, but I'm proud of it."

"I know you must be, Oscar. Everyone says it was nothing less than your determination and strength that kept it going when other businesses were failing. You have a right to be proud of it."

"Do you think so? Well, I must admit I am." He tried to see the building through her eyes. "It's not lovely, but it's provided work for a lot of people who needed it, and of course, it's done some good things for me too. Now, let's go to the house. I'm starved."

Oscar's home was on the edge of town, in a very nice neighborhood where all of the houses had huge lots. Oscar's two-story colonial-style house had huge pillars out front, with gables on all four sides of the structure. Although the grass was dormant, she could tell the lawn had been carefully tended. There were flower beds everywhere with splotches of color from winter jasmine, pansies, violas, and other winter flowers.

"I'll show you about the grounds some other time, but it's getting dark now. Come on, boys. I'll bet you're hungry."

Oscar opened the front door, and a tall, gaunt woman

dressed in a severe gray dress stood in the spacious foyer watching them. "This is Mrs. Darrow, my house-keeper," he told the Jennings family. "Mrs. Darrow, this is Mrs. Jennings, and these are her boys. This is Timothy, Zachary, and Carl."

"You are very welcome. Dinner is ready whenever you'd like, Mr. Moran."

"We'll be ready as soon as we get washed up. Is Jason here?"

"No, sir."

Oscar frowned. "I told him I was bringing company for dinner, but he's generally late. Well, come along, boys. I'll show you where you can get washed up. Mrs. Darrow, you can show Mrs. Jennings where she can refresh herself."

"Certainly, sir. If you'll come this way, Mrs. Jennings."

Alona followed the tall woman into a spacious bedroom on the main floor. "This is one of the guest rooms," Mrs. Darrow said, "and there's an adjoining bath. Will you require anything else?"

"No, thank you. This is a lovely house."

"Yes, Mr. Moran is very proud of it. He spared no expense. Of course Mrs. Moran did most of the decorating."

"Were you with them when she was alive?"

"Yes. I've been here for sixteen years." Mrs. Darrow's face was rigid, and there was a hardness about her. "The dining room is down the hall," the woman said and left.

Not a very pleasant woman, Alona thought, *but she's been with the family a long time. I suppose Oscar feels he has to keep her.*

Alona was overwhelmed with the elegant dining room, and it was obvious that the boys were also. The flowered light green wallpaper on the walls contrasted with the heavy green floor-length velvet draperies covering the windows. Two crystal chandeliers hung over the dark mahogany table with ten chairs surrounding it, and a large mahogany cabinet containing crystal, china, and silver stood to one side. Paintings of horses and landscapes hung on the walls in ornately carved frames opposite a beautiful white marble fireplace on which stood a gold mantel clock, a crystal vase with fresh flowers, and old tin-type photographs of the family.

None of them had ever seen such an ornate dining room or been served such a meal. They started off with a beef-based barley soup served with crackers, and then a green salad with vinegar-and-oil dressing with herbs. The main course was roast beef with carrots, onions, and potatoes; freshly baked bread and butter; milk for the boys; and coffee for the adults.

Mrs. Darrow served the meal efficiently, doing what was necessary but exuding no warmth. Alona felt the woman's eyes on her and wondered why she had incurred her enmity.

If Oscar noticed that his housekeeper was less than warm toward the visitors, he didn't show it. He and the boys carried on a lively conversation about the battlefield as they ate. "Someday you boys need to go to Gettysburg," he remarked. "It's the best preserved of all the battlefields of the Civil War."

"Would you take us there someday, Mr. Moran?" Carl asked.

"Well, we'll have to see. It's in Pennsylvania. A long trip from here, but worth it."

The meal was half over when Jason finally got home. His face was flushed, and it was obvious that he had been drinking. Alona glanced at Oscar and noted the stern disapproval on his face.

"You're late, Jason" was Oscar's only greeting.

"I know. I'm sorry." Jason sat down, nodded to

Alona, and said hello to the boys. He ate his dinner silently, adding nothing to the conversation, and the tension was almost palpable.

After their dessert, a rich, creamy custard that seemed to melt in their mouths, Oscar invited the family into the parlor so he could show them some slides he had taken on a trip to Europe. The room was just as beautiful as the rest of the rooms Alona had already seen. It had white walls accented with gold lilies. Alona wondered if Jason had painted the lilies. Four floor-length windows were on two of the walls, hung with gold and red draperies. There were two large sofas covered in red damask, and two armchairs with gold-colored fabric flanked the massive black marble fireplace. A piano stood against one of the interior walls, and the floors were covered with beautiful carpets of black and red, outlined with gold.

Oscar had already set up the slide projector and turned off the lights. Jason had joined the group in the parlor, but he remained silent as Oscar described what they were seeing on the screen.

"I don't know if I'll ever be able to get back to Europe again," Oscar commented sadly. "This European war is out of hand."

"I heard the president speak on the radio last week," Alona said. "He said we're going to starting sending arms to France and England."

"Yes. It's called the Lend-Lease Act. It allows President Roosevelt to lend all kinds of war supplies to the Allies without the U.S. actually becoming involved in the war."

Jason finally spoke up. "Eventually we'll be involved in this war."

"Don't talk like that, Jason," Oscar said. "We've got to stay out of it."

"I don't see how we can do that. Hitler's determined to rule the world."

"It's a European war," Oscar retorted. "We'll supply the Allies with arms and let them do the fighting."

Jason said no more, but Alona stored his words away and resolved to ask him later why he felt that way.

"Jason, why don't you take the boys into the pool room," Oscar said.

"Good idea," Jason said as he stood up. Alona thought he looked relieved.

"Jason can show you boys how to play while I show your mother the rest of the house."

"This way, guys. You can learn from the master."

As soon as they were gone, Oscar shook his head. "Jason's been drinking."

"Yes. I could tell."

"I wish he wouldn't do that, especially when you and your family are here. It sets a bad example for the boys."

"Does he do this often?"

"No. I will admit it's rare. He gets to thinking about that crash and just can't handle it." Oscar stood up. "I guess all I can do is pray for him. Come along. Let me show you the rest of the house."

They walked down the hall into the library. The walls were lined with shelves of books, hundreds of them, with colorful leather bindings. An overstuffed couch was in front of the fireplace, two easy chairs with ottomans were between large windows, and a massive oak desk anchored the far wall.

From there they proceeded to the pool room, where Jason was showing Carl how to make a bridge out of his hand and get ready to make a shot. Carl missed the ball he was aiming at but struck three others, which made him just as happy.

Alona followed Oscar upstairs, where there were five bedrooms, all beautifully decorated with thick carpets on the floors, ornately carved beds with matching armoires, and a small sitting area. Each room also had its own fireplace. Oscar showed Alona the kitchen, and she was relieved that Mrs. Dawson was not there. A butcher block island stood in the middle of the massive space, and gleaming pots and pans hung above the stove. The cabinets were full of china, crystal, silver, and other items befitting the wealthy.

Oscar told Alona that Jason had a suite of his own in the basement and then he led Alona out the back door, down the path, and to the greenhouse. He snapped on the light and told her about the special heating system he'd had installed, and Alona admired the many varieties of beautiful flowers.

"My wife was fond of flowers," he told Alona. "I know very little about them. I hire a gardener to come in now and keep it up."

"They're gorgeous."

"And so are you, Alona." He put his arms around her and pressed his lips to hers. She did not resist, although it did not feel comfortable to her.

He stepped back awkwardly and his face was flushed. "I'm sorry. I haven't had much practice."

"Neither have I, Oscar."

"I hope I didn't offend you."

"Of course not."

He smiled. "I'm glad. I wouldn't want to offend you in any way."

"Well, it is getting late."

"Yes. If you want to go gather up the boys, I'll drive the car around and give you a ride home."

"All right. I'll see if I can pull the boys away from the game. But you know how boys are when they're having a good time."

"No hurry. I'll have the car out front whenever you're ready."

"Mom, I'm the best at pool," Zac said when she stuck her head in the room. "I beat Carl and Tim both."

"You didn't beat me!" Carl argued.

"Yes I did!"

"I'm not sure that pool's such a good idea for you boys." She looked over at Jason for support.

He understood what she wanted. "You want to stay away from pool halls," he told the boys. "As a matter of fact, I started going wrong in a pool hall. Took my first drink there. I wish I'd never gone inside one of them."

The boys were silent for a moment and then they went back to their bragging and arguing.

"I'm no model, Alona," Jason said quietly.

"You could be, Jason."

"I made a mess of my life."

She reached over and touched his arm. "I think you know from listening to our pastor that Jesus specializes in messes."

He laughed. "That's a funny way to put it, but you're right. Don't give up on me."

"I never will."

He seemed to be struggling with something and said, "You like Oscar pretty well, don't you?"

"He's been very kind to me and the boys."

"I guess I'd be dead if it weren't for him. He's kind of a man's man, you know. Never had much need for women."

"But he was married."

"Yes, but it was sort of a marriage of convenience."

"A marriage of convenience! What do you mean?"

"Well, his business was struggling and Helen Grimshaw had money."

"He married her for money?"

"And for her children. As you know, she had two girls. Oscar thought they'd have other children. He's always wanted boys."

"That's why he's interested in me—for my boys."

"Any man would be interested in you, Alona."

"I've got to get the boys out to the car. Oscar's waiting. I'll see you at church tomorrow morning, Jason."

He stood quietly, a tall figure, physically strong but with a weakness he could not control. "I think I'm a token sinner they keep around to remind themselves what can happen if they're not careful." He sighed. "Good night, Alona."

CHAPTER TEN

ALONA GETS AN OFFER

★　★　★

Jason did not show up at church the next morning, which bothered Alona, especially after his remark the previous evening about being the "token sinner." She had thought a great deal about both Jason and Oscar, and her mind was not at rest about either of them. Jason's troubles were deep and spiritual in nature, and perhaps emotional as well. The plane crash had snapped something in his character, making him an emotional cripple. He had given up on life after that, and now he seemed merely to exist. The fact that he was absent for the first time from choir concerned Alona, for she knew he was prone to deep bouts of depression and would inevitably turn to the bottle to blot out whatever demons were gnawing at him.

After the service, she met her boys in their usual gathering place in the hallway, and they asked her if they could go home with the Sandifer family. Hazel had invited the boys to have lunch with them and then spend the afternoon playing with Mike and Roger. Alona agreed to let them go and then headed out the door, her raincoat pulled tight around her neck.

Rain was coming down in a steady drizzle, but as soon as she stepped outside, she saw Oscar's big Oldsmobile parked out front. He got out and came right over with an umbrella. "Come on. You don't need to walk home in this terrible weather."

"Well, that's thoughtful of you, Oscar." She stayed under the protection of his umbrella, waited until he opened the car door, and then slipped in.

When he got in he shivered. "This kind of weather is horrible. I'd rather it be snowing and below freezing. For some reason this rain makes me cold right to my bones."

"Me too. I'm sure it'll clear up in the next day or so."

As Oscar started the car and pulled away, Alona cast a quick glance at his profile. He had strong features, rather blunt and forceful. His hat was pulled low on his forehead, and as he always did, he was giving his whole attention to the road ahead of him.

"That was a good sermon this morning, wasn't it?" Oscar asked.

"It really was. The pastor is so good at helping me see the Bible from a different perspective. I especially liked the things he had to say about James one, verse nineteen."

"About being quick to listen and slow to speak and slow to get angry? That's probably the one thing I need to work on most. I'm not good at controlling my temper."

"It's hard sometimes."

After a brief silence, Oscar asked, "How is practice going for the cantata?"

"It's going as well as can be expected, I guess. The piece was really written for a much larger choir with more voices than we've got."

"I've heard Paul Root has drafted everybody who doesn't actually croak like a frog."

Alona laughed. "Yes, he has. But he's a good choir director, and he's going to get a good performance out of us."

"How's Jason doing in choir?" Oscar asked.

Alona hesitated. "He's been doing very well, but I was concerned when he didn't come to church this morning."

"He's been acting a bit strangely at work. It's happened a few times before. He starts getting quieter and quieter, and then the first thing you know he drops off the edge somehow." There was sadness in his voice, and he shook his head. "I think sometimes I've not helped Jason very much. Maybe I should have left him where he was."

"You couldn't do that, Oscar. He was in terrible shape, wasn't he?"

"Yes, he was, but I don't know whether that changed much. Oh, he doesn't drink as much now. Only when these spells come on him, but inside he's still the same."

"What was he like growing up?"

"Always laughing. Pretty much the opposite of me. I was always struggling, working as hard as I could. Jason worked too, but he made a game out of it. He used to sing all the time. His friends all called him Songbird, but he didn't seem to care."

"He told me the happiest part of his life was when he was in the navy before the crash."

"Yes, it was. I tried to talk him out of going into the service. I thought it was something only fellows that couldn't do anything else might do. But he fooled me. I talked to the officer in charge of his squadron once. He told me Jason was the best soldier he had ever trained, and he said Jason could have a great career in the navy. When he'd come home on leave, I never saw anybody so happy. Then he crashed that plane. He was lucky to survive. He just walked right out of the wreck. But that was the end of the good times for Jason."

"It's such a shame. He has such potential."

"Potential everywhere you look."

Oscar stopped the car in front of Alona's house. The rain had started coming down harder, and he said, "Wait a minute until it lets up."

The two sat there quietly, Alona thinking about Jason.

"I want to tell you, Alona, how much I admire you."

"Why . . . thank you, Oscar. That's very nice. I admire you too."

"To tell the truth, what I feel for you goes deeper than admiration. You're a beautiful woman, but that's not too important. Oh, I suppose it is, but what I really admire about you is your determination. I haven't known you long, but I know you've sacrificed your own happiness to raise those boys. You've probably done without a number of things you might have wanted. You've kept them together. They've got good spirits. That came from you. Not many women could have done that."

"Oh, I'm sure many women have done it."

Oscar was silent for a moment and then he sat up straighter and cleared his throat. "Have you ever thought of me as a man you might marry, Alona?"

While the question wasn't entirely unexpected, she had not settled on an answer. At times she had thought about how easy her life would be and how much better off the boys would be if she married a man who was able to support them, but since Oscar was so much older and had never remarried after years of being a widower, she had not really thought the idea through.

"I was never very romantic, Alona." He shook his head and laughed. "Jason, he's the romantic one. But not me. To tell the truth, my first marriage was pretty much a mistake, although I can't complain. You may have heard about it."

"You told me that your wife had two girls when you married her."

"Yes. She had been married before. She wasn't an especially attractive woman and had no real suitors. Her father wanted her to have a home. We had worked together, and he knew I was honest and a hard worker. They had money, and I needed help with the foundry. Her father came and talked to me about her."

"You mean he offered his daughter to you?"

"He wasn't quite that blunt. But he did tell me that Helen was lonely and he went on to say how much he liked me. He said he was afraid some fortune hunter would sweep her off her feet but not provide a good home. So he told me that if I ever felt anything for Helen, I shouldn't hesitate. That he and his wife would support me."

"What did Helen think about it?"

Oscar seemed embarrassed. He reached up and rubbed his hand across his brow. "I don't know," he said lamely.

"You don't know! How could you not know, Oscar? She must have been happy, sad, angry—something!"

"I'm being honest with you, Alona. I really don't know. I didn't do anything for six months after her father and I had that discussion, but I thought about it. The business was in terrible shape. It was about to go under, and I knew I couldn't make it unless I had some financial support. But that wasn't really why I finally approached her. I asked her to marry me, but not just because her father was willing to finance the business."

"What was your other reason?"

"I thought we could have children. She was still a young woman. I didn't love her, Alona, and she didn't love me. But she was a decent person, and I respected her. So I decided I'd be very honest with her."

"What did you say?"

"I told her that I didn't really love her the way a man should, that I wasn't romantic, just as I've told you, but that I would like her to marry me. I told her that I'd spoken with her father and that he was agreeable and that I thought we would have a comfortable marriage. I even told her that her father had offered to support me financially if I became his business partner."

"You told her that? What did she say?"

"She said she would marry me. I always suspected her father told her all about this before I asked her."

Alona could not think of a single intelligent remark to make, and finally he went on.

"I know that sounds a little cold to you, but I really wanted children—a family."

"So you're asking me to do what your first wife did, to make a business arrangement out of marriage."

Oscar groaned and smacked his forehead. "I've made a big mess out of it, Alona. Let me start all over again."

"I don't think there's any need, Oscar."

"Yes there is. Listen to me, please. You're not the same kind of woman my first wife was. She was rather cold and distant. Respectable, as I say, and she was a good housekeeper and a good hostess, but there was no warmth to her at all. Of course, there wasn't a lot in me either, to be honest."

"I still don't see the difference."

"The difference is you, Alona." He reached for her hand and held it. "You're different. You're warm and alive, and you've got an inner joy in you, and people brighten up when they see you coming. I do myself. It's true," he insisted. "I feel great every time I see you. So that's one difference. I know I'm older than you are—maybe you feel I'm too old."

He seemed to have more to say so she let him keep going.

"The doctor says I'm unable to have children, and I'm

really too old to start out with infants anyway. I want some children, Alona. I think your boys like me, and I love them. So that's why I'm asking you to consider me as a husband and as a father to your children. Will you think on it? I won't press you for an answer now, of course."

Alona was in a difficult position. She could not help but think of her sorry financial state. After she had lost her job, the little money she had managed to save had drained steadily away. She had tried to find another job but hadn't found anything yet. Oscar was still holding her hand, and there was an eagerness in his face. But inside, a voice kept saying, *It won't be like your marriage to Truman.* But then she thought, *But no marriage would be like that one. He was my first love, and that will always be special, no matter whom I marry.*

"I don't know what to say, Oscar. I respect you. Everybody does. You've been there for your brother, helping him in every way you could. You're very faithful at church, and you've been wonderful with my boys. And, of course, we both know I'm having financial difficulty since I lost my job. It's been . . . well, it's been hard, and I don't know which way to turn. Naturally I'm tempted. It would be so easy to say yes. You have a beautiful home, and I know you'd be good to the boys. And you'd be good to me."

"I would. Indeed I would, Alona!"

"I know you would," she said and squeezed his hand.

"I don't want to press you, but just let me tell you this. I know you can't love me as you did your first husband. You talk about him enough that I understand that, and I don't expect it. But I could do so much for your boys. They'll be going through some difficult ages. It's a hard time for young men, and I've never cared as much about money as people think I do, but this is one time I'm glad I do have money. I can give your boys whatever they need. And when it's time for them to go to college, they could go and get a fine education. I think Zac might even like to come back and work in the foundry. He's so good with his hands. Tim and Carl will probably have other ideas. But we could do it together. They could become wonderful men—men you will be so proud of."

He stopped abruptly. "I'm sorry. This sounds like a business proposition, but it isn't. I won't say anything else, and I won't speak of this again. But if you can think of me as a husband, you just say the word, and I'll be the happiest man in the world."

He got out of the car and came around to her side. Holding the umbrella over her head, he walked her up to the house. "Good-bye, Alona" was all he said before he turned and walked back to the car.

Alona watched the big car as it pulled away. Her heart was beating fast, and she felt weak in the knees. Slowly she turned and went inside the house. After hanging up her raincoat, she knelt down beside the sofa. "Lord, I don't have any idea what to do," she prayed. "I envy those people who always seem to know what you have for them, but I'm weak. Please show me what to do. If you'd have me marry Oscar, then I'll do it, but if you wouldn't have me marry him, I won't. I promise you that."

CHAPTER ELEVEN

THE VALLEY OF DECISION

★ ★ ★

Jason tried to concentrate, but his head seemed to be splitting open. It felt as if someone were driving a railroad spike from one temple to another.

"You're not fit to do your work here, Jason!" Oscar's voice sounded rough and disgusted. "When are you gonna sober up?" Jason turned to leave when Oscar started again. "No, you're not gonna go back to that dive and drink anymore. Get a truck from Roy, load up those white oak logs that have been sawed into lengths, and take them to Mrs. Jennings. Then stay there and split them all up. Maybe that'll sober you up."

"All right, Oscar."

Jason's voice was hoarse, and he had a terrible taste in his mouth. He went to find Roy Hanson, the foreman, and said, "Oscar wants me to fetch the wood he bought for Mrs. Jennings."

Roy grinned at him. "Are you sure you can handle it? You don't see two trucks, do you?"

"I can do it, Roy." Jason tried to smile. "The Bible

says, 'Be sure your sin will find you out.' I guess that's the way it is."

Taking the keys, Jason went to the truck and glanced at the load of logs that had been sawed into eighteen-inch lengths. He got into the truck and drove to the Jennings' house. He drove to the back of the house and backed up by the chopping block. He began to shove the logs off and by the time he had them all unloaded, he was sweating under the late March sun. Jumping off the truck, he picked up the ax, saw that it was dull, and spent some time searching for a file. While he filed the ax, he thought back with disgust to the previous night. He had bought a quart of whiskey and drank most of it before passing out. He had gone to work this morning with a terrible hangover, knowing that if he encountered Oscar, he would never hear the end of it.

A bluebird had alighted on the clothesline and cocked its head, seeming to examine him. "On your way, bluebird. You look too happy for me," Jason muttered. He gripped the ax and swung it, but his aim was bad. Viciously he jerked the ax back and blinked, focusing his eyes. The next time he just nicked the edge of the log. He took a deep breath and tried again. This time the wood split. Methodically he bent over to pick up the two pieces, and his head seemed to come off with the pain. He straightened up, closed his eyes for a moment, took a deep breath, and began to work again.

As a rule, splitting wood was something Jason Moran liked to do. There was a pleasure in striking cleanly and watching the wood split. But his aim was off, and his legs and arms felt weak, so there was no pleasure in the work. He had been working steadily for an hour when he heard the back door open. He looked up and saw Alona bringing him a cup of coffee.

"You don't have to chop all that wood. With what

you've done already, I've got plenty to last a good long time. Here, take this coffee."

"Thanks," he said, but he kept his eyes averted. He knew they were bloodshot, and it didn't take a genius to know that he had a hangover.

"Have you had breakfast?"

"Yeah. I had some."

"Would you like me to fix you some eggs?"

"No. The coffee's fine."

"Sit down for a while and rest. I've been watching you. You're working too hard."

"Oscar wouldn't think so."

"Did you two have a quarrel?"

"I got drunk last night and came to work with a hangover. He ran me out. Told me to bring this wood and chop it. He said it was all I was fit for." He took a sip of his coffee. "And he's right."

"No, he's not right. You're fit for lots of things."

"Chopping wood is about my limit, Alona."

"You've done a wonderful job with Tim. He's so excited about the painting techniques you're teaching him."

"Well, I'm glad of that. He's a great kid. Got lots of talent."

They watched a pair of squirrels chase each other around a tree and finally disappear into the leaves.

"Have you ever thought of flying again?" Alona asked.

"No, not if I can help it."

"You told me once you loved it."

"I did, but I can't do it anymore."

"Why not?"

"The first time I tried to go up after that crash, my hands froze on the throttle. I couldn't make a move. And then I started to shake all over. I got out of the plane and never went in one again."

"It seems such a shame. You like it so much, and Oscar said your officer said you had great ability."

"I guess my ability leaked out of me when I hit the ground in that crash."

Alona squeezed her hands together and said tentatively, "Did you know that Oscar's asked me to marry him?"

Instantly Jason lifted his head. His blue eyes, bloodshot though they were, were very direct. "Are you going to?"

"I don't know. Marrying again is not . . . it's not something I've really thought about."

Jason turned the cup around in his hand for a time, then lifted it and drained the rest of the coffee. "Oscar has always wanted boys. He'd do anything for them."

"Yes, I know that, but marriage is different. It's not a business matter."

"It might be with—" Jason broke off and shook his head. "I can't say anything against Oscar."

"What do you think I should do, Jason?"

His eyes flew open with astonishment. "Have you lost your mind, Alona?"

"What do you mean?"

"I made a wreck out of my own life, and you're asking me to help you with a decision like that? I can't tell you what to do." He handed her the coffee cup, then went back and picked up the ax. He raised it and it came down cleanly, splitting a thick log in two. "Alona, you don't want to share a bed for the rest of your life with a man you don't love." He went back to work. She stared at him for a moment, then walked quickly back into the house, ashamed for some reason she could not pinpoint.

★ ★ ★

The boys had gone to school, and Alona could not concentrate on the housework. She put on a light coat, went out the front door, and walked to the church. She went to the office and greeted the secretary, who told the pastor she was there.

"Come in, Alona," he called through the open doorway.

"Is this a bad time, Pastor?"

"No, not at all. Sit down." He rose and waited until she had seated herself, then sat down across from her. "I hear the Easter program is going first rate. Paul is so excited about it. I've never seen him so pleased, and he says nothing but good things about your role in it."

They talked for a few minutes about the cantata and then she said, "I need some advice, Pastor."

"Well," Brother Byron said with a slight grin, "I don't often give people straightforward advice."

"You don't? Why not?"

"I prefer to listen to people and then I say things like 'yes' and 'I see.' Sometimes I just say, 'hmm,' but very rarely do I say, 'Do this.' It's good for people to talk things out. What's on your mind?"

"I . . . I don't know what to do. Oscar has asked me to marry him."

"I'm not too surprised. I don't think anyone else will be either."

"Has it been that obvious?"

"Pretty obvious. You see, Oscar's never showed any interest in any other woman, and there have been some attractive women who have tried to get his attention. Why is this a problem for you?"

"Don't you see it?"

"I guess not. We men are pretty thickheaded. Tell me about it."

Alona talked about the situation for the next ten minutes, sometimes rambling, bringing up her marriage and how happy she had been, speaking about her worries about the boys and her financial problems, talking about the age difference between herself and Oscar Moran. She finally got to the heart of the matter. "I just don't feel for Oscar what I . . ."

When she hesitated, Brother Byron said, "You mean you don't have the same feelings for him that you had for your husband?"

"That's right. I don't."

"But you really didn't expect to feel that way about any other man, did you, Alona?"

She thought for a moment and then shook her head. "No. I guess I knew I could never feel that way again."

"And I guess you know that I'm not going to say 'Don't marry Oscar Moran,' or 'You should marry Oscar Moran.' I couldn't say that to you. I know you well enough to know you've prayed about it."

"I have, Pastor, but I don't have any answer."

"It's tough to discern God's will, isn't it? How many times have I been there. It's like you're going down a road and you see a fork in the road coming, and you've got to take one or the other, but you don't know which one. And you start screaming out, 'God, which one—right or left?' and God doesn't say anything."

"It's exactly like that," Alona said with surprise. "What do you do?"

"You take the one you want to."

"But that doesn't sound right."

"What's the other choice? If you don't take either one, you'll crash right into the fork. There're probably trees back there or a house. When this church called me about taking this position, I had no idea whether God wanted me to come here or not. I agonized and I prayed and I fasted, and the longer it went on, the less sure I was about what to do. It was like God locked up heaven and closed it down. Put a sign up that said *No trespassing*. But

I had to make a decision. I had to say yes or no."

"And what did you do?"

"I had to use human wisdom. Since God didn't tell me directly, I took what seemed to me to be the best road. Even with my frail human wisdom I could make some kind of choice. I had felt for some time that my work was done at the church where I had been pastor for six years. I'd been praying for a new opportunity for a door to open, and suddenly a door was open. So when I didn't hear a direct message, as Paul did on the road to Damascus, I just said, 'Lord, you can always stop me, but I'm going to this church unless you intervene.' So I called the church and told them I'd come, and I watched in case I got a red light. But I didn't get one."

He leaned forward and smiled. "And it was the right decision. My advice to you is to do what your heart tells you, and if God gives you a yellow light, be careful. And if He gives you a red light, just say, 'No. I made a mistake. I won't do it.'"

Alona smiled. "You have the nicest way of refusing to give me any direct advice, Pastor."

"I've had a lot of practice at it. Let's pray now that whatever happens, God will get glory out of it." Alona bowed her head and folded her hands together. Byron Sandifer prayed an earnest prayer, and when he said amen, he got up and walked around his desk. "Why don't you talk to my wife about this. It may help to get another woman's perspective."

"I will. She's such a sweet woman and has such great insight."

"She's home now. I'll call her and tell her you're coming, but I won't tell her why. It's good for women to talk."

Alona did have a long talk with Hazel Sandifer. She was a good listener, and in the end she gave no more direct advice than her husband had. But she and Alona prayed together, and Hazel put her arms around her. "You and I will keep on praying, but I think my husband gave you the best advice that anybody could give a woman facing a decision like yours."

For the next couple of days Alona prayed almost constantly. She was completely out of money—even for groceries. The cupboard was almost bare, and the boys were starting to complain about the simple meals they were having. Alona got down on her knees once again and prayed aloud, "Lord, I have no guidance. I'm going to call Oscar and tell him to come by, and I'm going to agree to marry him. If you don't want me to do this, make something happen. Please don't let me make a mistake."

She went next door to use the telephone. The Carruthers family was always willing to let her use their phone. After chatting very briefly with Pearl, she called the foundry. When she got through to Oscar, she said, "Hello, Oscar. It's Alona."

"Alona, is anything wrong?"

"No, but I'd like to talk to you."

"Would you like me to come out to the house?"

"Yes, I would."

"I'll come right now. I'll be there in a few minutes. I'll see you then."

Alona put the phone down, thanked her neighbor, and returned home. She sat down in a rocker in the living room and began to rock back and forth. Her mind had been filled with confusion, but now somehow the decision seemed simple. "I've done all I know how to do," she murmured. "Now I'm going to see that my boys have a chance."

She got to her feet when she heard the car pull up and opened the door.

"Well, here I am," Oscar said as he took off his hat.

"What is it? Are the boys all right?"

"Yes, they're all right. Come into the living room." They went into the living room and stood face to face. "Oscar, you asked me to marry you, and I've kept you waiting for my answer. Now I'd like to tell you that if you still want me to be your wife, I will."

"Of course I still do."

"Wait a minute," she said, putting out her hand as he stepped forward. "I haven't told my boys yet. I'll have to talk to them and see how they feel about this. Their opinion is very important to me, you understand."

"I know that. Of course you must talk to them. I would expect nothing less."

"All right. I have to say something else . . . and I'm afraid it may sound harsh or uncertain." Alona was speaking rapidly now and forced herself to be calm. "I want to be as honest with you as you've been with me."

"I appreciate that. Please go on."

"You know I had a good marriage and that I was very much in love with my husband."

"Yes. I'm glad about that."

"I . . . I don't feel for you what I felt for him. I don't think I'll ever feel it for any other man."

"It's not reasonable that you would. I don't know much about things like that, but you married when both of you were young. He was your first love. It was different, special. And you can never repeat things like that. I'm glad you told me this, and I want you to talk to the boys. Talk to them tonight, or this afternoon."

"I'll talk to them as soon as they get home from school."

"Will you call me as soon as you have your answer?"

"Yes. I will."

He took her hand and lifted it and kissed it. Then he laughed. "I've never done that in my life—kissed a woman's hand."

Alona smiled. "It was nice. You did it very well."

He laughed again. "I feel like I'm on top of the world. I know the boys like me. That's in my favor, but I won't say any more. Call me when you have an answer for me. Either way, even if you decide not to marry me, I'll think no less of you."

"That's kind of you, Oscar. I'll call as soon as I've talked to the boys."

She waited until he had left and then sat down again in the rocker. She thought for a long time about their brief conversation and tried to predict what the boys would say. She waited, wondering if she would feel that she had done something wrong. Perhaps that would be the way God would stop her. She continued rocking in the quiet house, but she felt nothing—neither joy nor apprehension.

"Boys, you can go outside and play in a minute, but there's something I need to talk to you about first."

"I'm always afraid when you say that, Mom," Tim said nervously. "It usually means bad news."

"I'll bet it's about money. We're broke, aren't we?" Zac spoke up.

"Well, we are broke, but that's not exactly news. Here, sit down on the couch, all of you." She pulled a chair over in front of them. "You look like three baby birds, all waiting with your mouths open for me to poke some food down your throat."

"Come on, Mom," Carl said. "What is it? Have we done something wrong?"

"No, of course you haven't." Alona hesitated as she studied their faces. Zac's especially, who was a living memorial of Truman, looking more like him than the other two. Carl also resembled him, but Tim had only a faint resemblance. He had taken her characteristics, and now she saw that he was the most afraid of what she was going to say.

"This is nothing to be afraid of, boys. It's a decision I have to make, but I need your opinions."

"Are we going to have to move again, Mom?" Tim asked.

"Well, that's possible, but that's not what I wanted to ask you." She hesitated, then gave a half laugh. "I'm a little embarrassed. I don't know how to say this, so I'll just say it right out." She took a deep breath. "Mr. Moran has asked me to marry him."

Astonishment washed across Carl's face. "Did he really!"

"Yes. He really did."

"Which Mr. Moran?" Tim asked.

"Oscar."

"It'll be great, Mom!" Zac said. "We'll move into his house, and we can play pool anytime we want to, can't we?"

"There's more to it than playing pool, Zac. It would be different. Yes, we'd move into his house, but I need to know if you're ready to accept him as your stepfather. What about you, Tim? You're the oldest."

He swallowed hard. "It means you wouldn't have to work, doesn't it, Mom?"

"Yes, but I don't mind working."

"I hate it when you have to work. I hate it when you have to worry about money all the time. You wouldn't have to if you married Mr. Moran, would you?"

"No. That's true enough."

"He's been real good to us, Mom," Carl said. "Remember he took us hunting and bought us clothes? I think you oughta do it."

"He'd be your dad. You understand that. Not your real dad. You'll never forget Truman."

"Would my name be Carl Jennings or Carl Moran?"

"It would be Jennings. You'd still have your father's name unless Mr. Moran decided to adopt you legally."

"Why would he do that?" Tim asked quickly.

"Well, purely for legal reasons. For instance, if he wanted to leave you something in his will, it would be easier if you were his legal sons." She hurried on to say, "He's not taking the place of your father. Nobody can ever do that."

"What about you, Mom?" Tim said. "Do you want to marry him?"

Alona turned to this tall son of hers who was so much like her. He alone of the three understood the heart of the matter and cared for her feelings. "I think he's a very fine man, and I think he would do wonderful things for you boys, and I think we would get along very well."

For the next ten minutes Alona sat there answering all their questions. It was easy enough to see how the boys stood. Carl and Zac could see only the advantages, but Tim was worried, as she had known he would be. She tried her best to be as honest as she could. When it seemed they had finally asked all of their questions, she said, "I'm going to leave it up to you boys, because we're a family. I don't mind working. It's hard, but we'll make it somehow. It would be easier, and you boys could do many things if we had more financial security, but we're not going to make the decision based on that. Would we be a better family, do you think, if I married Oscar and we went to live at his house?"

Of course Carl and Zac at once agreed that they would. But Alona was watching Tim's face. She saw he was trying to control his emotions and could not imagine what they were. "What do you say, Tim? This is not a majority decision. If any one of you says no, I'll say no too, so it's up to you, Tim."

"Mom, I can't decide for you."

"Do you think you could be happy?"

He cleared his throat and searched for words. "I want you to be happy, Mom, and I want you to have an easier life. I don't care about anything else."

"There's my good boy!" Alona cried. She rose up, hugged him, and then hugged the other two. "All right. I've prayed about this, and I've asked you all about it, and I've sought guidance from the pastor and his wife. I'm going to take this as a yes."

"When will you marry him, Mom?" Tim asked.

"I imagine it will be quite soon. Will that be all right?"

He managed a smile. "Sure. It'll be fine, Mom. It'll be good. I'm all for it."

Alona wasn't certain if this was the exact truth, but she took him at his word. "All right. End of conference. You can go ahead and play now."

Later that night, she waited until the boys were in bed, and then she went next door to use the phone again. Pearl and her husband were still up, and they left her alone to make the call.

She dialed Oscar's number at home, and when he answered, she said, "I talked to the boys, Oscar."

"How did they take it?"

"They gave me their permission."

"I'm so glad they did. Were they happy?"

"Yes, they were." She did not go into detail but said, "If you'd like to come over tomorrow morning, we can talk more."

"All right. But let me ask you now. Do you want a big church wedding and a fancy dress and all that?"

"No, not really."

"Neither do I. What do you say we just get married in the pastor's office. Then we can go away for a few days to get used to each other."

"But what about the boys?"

"They can stay here with Jason. I think he enjoys their

company almost as much as I do."

"All right, Oscar. I'll look for you in the morning."

"I'm very happy, and we'll be happy together, Alona. I'll see you tomorrow."

She hung up the phone and thanked Pearl and Ed and then went back home and crawled into bed. As she lay there thinking about the day's events, tears suddenly began rolling down her face. She could not control them, and her shoulders began shaking. She buried her face in the pillows so the children wouldn't hear her sobs. She did not know why she was weeping. She was not a crying woman. Finally she ceased to weep and rolled over on her back. She wiped her tears away with her palms and then said, "I'm being silly. The boys will have everything they need—even college. It will be a good thing." Moonlight was shining through the window, laying its silver beams upon the floor, and from far off came the mournful sound of an owl, always the saddest of sounds to her. She saw a feathered shape pass the window. The cry was repeated, and she turned over and buried her face in the pillow again.

CHAPTER TWELVE

"It's for My Boys"

★　★　★

Jason listened as Oscar gave him the final instructions about taking care of things while he and Alona were gone on their honeymoon. He glanced up at the calendar and noted that it was April 5, 1941, Alona and Oscar's wedding day—something Jason never thought he would see. He had to pull his attention back to Oscar's instructions.

"For the time being, you can store all the furniture from Alona's house in our empty shed. It's sound and tight. She'll want to keep some of the furniture, I'm sure, and the pictures and things. Just store everything so she can sort through it later. She's got all their clothes and personal items in boxes, and she said they're all in her living room. You and the boys can bring the stuff over here and get it all to the right room."

"We'll take care of it, Oscar."

"I've already showed the boys which room they will each get, and Mrs. Darrow has cleaned them and made the beds."

"I think you've covered every detail. Don't worry

about a thing, Oscar. I'm not much good at business, but I can manage those boys."

"Good. That takes a load off my mind and off of Alona's, I'm sure."

"Good-bye then. Have a nice time."

"There is one more thing. . . . I don't want to have to say this, but be sure you stay sober, Jason. It's very important. Alona would be crushed if she knew you were drinking around her boys."

"You have my word on it."

Oscar looked up at his brother and said, "I hated to mention it."

"I understand. Like I said, you've got my word."

For some reason Oscar seemed dissatisfied. "Jason, you haven't said anything at all about Alona and me getting married."

"I'm sorry I didn't congratulate you before. I do wish you well, Oscar. You're getting a wonderful woman."

"I have the idea you think it's the wrong thing."

"Don't talk like that, Oscar. I want to see Alona happy and her boys taken care of. You can do that. It'll be good for all of you."

Oscar's face relaxed, and he smiled and slapped Jason on the shoulder. "Well, I had to pull it out of you, but thanks anyway."

★ ★ ★

"I'm only going to be gone for five days, Tim."

"I know, but five days sounds like a long time." Alona and the boys were standing on the front porch waiting for the Moran brothers. Oscar and Alona had decided that there was no reason to wait to get married, so they had allowed just enough time for Alona and the boys to get all of their belongings packed up. It was important to Alona that they be back from their honeymoon in time for the last rehearsal for the cantata the day before Easter. She had put so much time and effort into the concert that she didn't want to miss it.

The couple had gotten married in the pastor's study that morning and had spent the rest of the morning making final preparations for their honeymoon trip.

"We'll miss you, Mom," Carl said.

"And I'll miss you too. But Jason will be with you all the time. He's taking time off from work until we get back. I think he has big plans for things for all of you to do together."

"Look, there they come!" Zac said, pointing. They all looked to where the two cars had rounded the corner, the Oldsmobile in front and the Ford that Jason drove in the back. They stopped and the two men got out.

Oscar strode up to the boys and shook hands with Tim. "Tim, I hope you'll take good care of your brothers while we're gone."

"Yes, sir, I will."

Oscar kept his hand. "When we get back, we'll have time to talk about things we're going to do. All right?"

"Yes, sir. That'll be fine."

"And you, Zac," he said, shaking Zac's hand. "I've got an idea you'd like to do a little work at the foundry."

"I sure would, Mr. Moran!"

"Well, you're going to have to call me something besides Mr. Moran. All of you boys will."

"What should I call you?"

"Anything but that. We'll talk about it later. Maybe we'll get to be good enough friends we can call each other by our first names."

He reached down and shook Carl's hand. "You keep these two brothers of yours straight while I'm gone, all right, son?"

"Sure. I'll watch out for them. Can we play pool while you're gone?"

"That's up to Jason." He looked at his half brother and laughed. "It's like I'm leaving four boys. You be careful with these fellows, Jason."

Jason managed a smile. "I sure will, Oscar." He turned to Alona and said, "I hope you know that I wish you well."

Her voice was tight, but she managed a smile. "Thank you, Jason. That's good of you."

"Well, let's go," Oscar said. "We'll see you fellows in about five days."

The four watched as the newlywed couple got into the car and the big Oldsmobile pulled away.

Jason saw that the boys were troubled, despite their appropriate words, and he said enthusiastically, "Well, this is great! I've got the whole week off to be with you fellows, so you know what I'm going to make you do today?"

"Make us do!" Tim said with astonishment. "That sounds bad."

"It is bad. I'm going to make you fellows decide on something you want to do today. You name it and we'll do it—as long as it's not against the law."

"Can we go to a movie?" Zac asked instantly.

"We can go to three movies if we can find them. Anything else?"

"Will you let me drive the Ford?" Tim asked.

"Sure. We'll get out into an open field where you can't run into as many people. Let's see what's playing downtown, and then later we'll give you that driving lesson."

★ ★ ★

The trip to Atlanta felt strained to Alona, although Oscar was excited. He did most of the talking, and when his side of the conversation seemed to flag, she quickly asked him something about the business, which he was always glad to talk about.

Alona had an empty feeling and tried to ignore it. By the time they reached Atlanta, she was wound up as tightly as she had ever been. She was exhausted just from trying to think about what she was doing.

Oscar signed their names in the hotel's registration book and then said, "Look at this, Alona." He had written in big, bold handwriting: Mr. and Mrs. Oscar Moran.

"You'll have to get used to that," he said. "I imagine that'll be a bit difficult."

"Not too hard." Alona smiled back at him.

After the bellboy left their baggage in the room, Oscar asked, "Are you tired?"

"I guess I am. It's been a busy day, even though it's only midafternoon."

"Why don't you have a nice relaxing bath and then take a nap. I'm a little tired myself."

Alona knew this was his not so subtle way of getting her into the large bed that dominated the suite. "All right, Oscar," she said.

"I'll go downstairs for a while, then I'll come up and shower. Can I bring you something to eat?"

"No, I couldn't eat a thing."

"All right. I'll be back in about half an hour."

After he left the room, Alona opened her suitcase and took out the nightgown she had bought for her wedding night. She closed the heavy drapes on the window and then went into the bathroom and ran a hot bath. After she soaked in the tub for a while, trying to relax, she washed up and got out, slipping into the gown. She turned the lights off except for the one by the bed and then lay down and waited.

Ten minutes later she heard the door open, but she closed her eyes to give Oscar privacy. He came in, gathered up a few items, and then went into the bathroom. She could hear the water running for a short time. After a moment, Oscar returned to the bedroom. She felt rather than heard his footsteps on the floor, and then the light went out and the bed sagged. He reached for her at once and pulled her over toward him. She turned to meet him, not at all sure what to expect.

★   ★   ★

Jason came out of the theater a few days later with the boys, saying, "I think we've seen every movie in the county this week. What's next?"

"Hamburgers!" they all three cried and Jason laughed. "You boys ought to have hamburgers coming out of your ears."

"Well, I'm hungry!" Zac said. "You can't starve us to death, Jason."

"That's right," Carl agreed with a grin. "You promised Mom you'd take good care of us."

"You guys are a bunch of bandits. Okay. Hamburgers it is."

They went at once to the café, where the boys consumed hamburgers and French fries, washing them down with root beer, which all of them loved. After they were finished eating, Jason took them home, and even though it was ten o'clock, Zac said, "I want to play pool."

"It's too late," Jason groaned. "I'm tired!"

"Oh, come on! We can sleep late in the morning."

Jason laughed. "Oh boy, are you getting by with murder! You'd better enjoy it. Your parents will be home tomorrow, and then it's back to the real world."

"Come on. I can beat you, Jason," Zac said. He never had beaten Jason at pool, but he wouldn't give up thinking he could.

Pool was a noisy game with the Jennings boys. There was a great deal of shouting and teasing and carrying on. They were right in the middle of a game when the door opened and Mrs. Darrow stood there, wearing her robe with her hair up in curlers. They all turned to look at her, and she said frostily, "Do you know what time it is?"

Jason pulled out his watch and said, "I believe it is eleven thirty-two, Mrs. Darrow." He did not like the woman and was always very polite, as if to offset his distaste. "If you need to know the time, I'll always be available. Good night, Mrs. Darrow."

The woman glared at him angrily. "Things will be different when Mr. Oscar gets home." She turned and slammed the door on her way out. "Don't wait up for us!" Jason called cheerfully. Then he winked at the boys. "Go on and make that shot, Zac."

"She was really mad," Tim said.

"I'll bet she tells Mr. Moran," Carl said.

"We're supposed to call him something else. What can we call him?" Tim asked.

"You've got plenty of choices—Father, Dad, Pops, Oscar," Jason suggested. "But none of them sound really right, do they?"

"I don't really want to call him Dad," Tim said. "That was what we called our real dad."

"If you all put your heads together maybe you can agree on some name that you all like."

"I can't think of anything, Jason," Tim insisted. "Don't you have any more ideas?"

Jason thought for a moment and then shook his head. "Like I said, nothing sounds right. I think you ought to talk to him, Tim, and tell him the truth. That the word

Dad is reserved for your real dad, and *Father* sounds too formal. Maybe you could call him Mr. Oscar, like Mrs. Darrow does. I think he might like that."

"That's a good idea," Zac said. "I'm glad I thought of it."

Carl laughed. "You didn't think of nothin'! Jason thought of it."

"It's still a good idea," Zac said. "You do the talking, Tim. Tell him we all like that idea. Mr. Oscar. That sounds real friendly like."

"Okay," Tim said weakly. "I'll do it, but I sure hope he likes it."

"Try your best to get along with my brother. He's a good man in many ways. You'll find out he's kind of strict about discipline, but that never hurt anybody. Now, you guys go to bed."

"Are you going to take us fishing in the morning like you promised?"

"I don't remember promising that."

"Well, you almost did."

"Well then, we'll almost go fishing," Jason teased. "Now, get to bed."

★ ★ ★

As they approached the big house that would be Alona's home, Oscar was talking excitedly about his plans for the boys. Alona was forcing herself to pay attention, but she had been so quiet, he had asked more than once if she was all right.

Actually she was not all right. Truman had been a gentle lover, but Oscar was rough and demanding. That first night when he rolled back from her, she felt used, and that had not changed. She had not been expecting as much sweet talk and gentleness from him as she had gotten from Truman, but Oscar evidently had never heard that a woman needed to be spoken to and assured and touched in a gentle way. But she could not talk to him about it, and neither did he say anything.

Alona had tried to put this part of their life out of her mind, but she knew that would be impossible. *It's for my boys,* she had said to herself many times during the honeymoon. This had given her some comfort.

Oscar pulled up in front of the garage, and the boys came swarming out of the house. Jason stood back, Alona saw, watching them as they greeted and hugged their mother and shook hands with their new stepfather.

"How did things go, Jason?" Oscar asked.

"They went fine for me. I just let 'em do what they wanted to and kept 'em from killing each other or me. They're all hale and healthy."

When he greeted Alona, he seemed more reserved than he had been before. "Good to have you back, Alona. The boys have missed you."

"And I missed them."

That was all the conversation they exchanged, but Mrs. Darrow had quite a few remarks to make after the group went inside the house. She got Oscar off to one side and told him about everything that had been going on, including the late-night hours and the noise in the pool room. "It's disgraceful, Mr. Oscar!"

"Well, it was just for a short time. Jason did the best he could, I'm sure. But we'll be on an even keel now that I'm back."

★   ★   ★

The matter of the noise in the pool room came up the next day, when the boys were playing and shouting as they usually did over a game of pool. Oscar walked into the room and raised his voice to get their attention. "Boys!" When they were quiet, he said, "Mrs. Darrow is very disturbed about the way you act in this pool room. If you can't behave like gentlemen, I'm going to have to have the pool table taken out."

"Please don't do that!" Tim said. "We'll be quiet."

"Will you?"

Zac, who loved pool most of all, said, "We'll be real quiet, sir."

"Yes we will, Mr. Moran," Carl agreed.

Oscar frowned slightly. "Okay, then. Make sure of that. We don't want Mrs. Darrow to be upset. And I also wanted to talk to you fellows about what you should call me. *Mr. Moran* is a bit too formal, don't you think?"

"We talked about that, sir," Tim told him. "We kind of would like to call you Mr. Oscar, if that would be all right."

He considered it, frowning slightly, as if he had wished for more. "I guess that will be all right, at least for the time being. Now, you finish your game, but you'll have to be quiet about it. Mrs. Darrow's nerves are on edge."

"Yes, Mr. Oscar, we'll be quiet," Zac assured him.

As soon as Oscar left the room, Zac said, "It's not going to be as much fun now that he's here."

"Well, there's no getting around that," Tim said grimly. "So we either have to play quietly or we'll have to wait until he's gone."

"That wouldn't do any good," Carl said. "Old lady Darrow would tell on us."

"What fun is shootin' pool if you can't whoop and holler!" Zac said with exasperation.

★ ★ ★

Later that day, Alona was unpacking her things in the master bedroom. She looked out the window and saw Jason coming in the front door. It was almost dark, and she quickly went downstairs and opened the door. "Hello, Jason."

"Hello, Alona." He stepped inside and pulled off his hat. "You all settled in?"

"I'm getting there."

"I stored all your things like Oscar asked me to. I was real careful with them. Oscar says any of the furniture you want, he'll have me bring it and put it where you want it."

"I don't think I'll need much. Oscar has everything I could imagine. Jason," she said, "thank you so much for taking care of the boys. They told me about how you did everything they wanted. Tim said he'd never had such a good time in all of his life."

Jason smiled. "I guess I haven't either. I wish I had a steady job doing nothing but having fun with them."

"They'd like that."

Jason turned and faced her squarely, a serious expression on his face. "How are you, Alona?"

"Fine," she said quickly. "I'm just fine."

She dropped her eyes. She knew that he had seen something in her, and she turned quickly and walked away. She went back to the bedroom and closed the door, then she sat down on the bed and clasped her hands together tightly. For a long time she did not move. Then she whispered as she had done many times in the last week, "It's for my boys!"

★ ★ ★

Alona was thrilled to get back to choir on Saturday morning. The singers were gathering for their final rehearsal, as were the members of the five-piece string ensemble that would be accompanying them.

"Welcome back, *Mrs. Moran*," Paul said as he came into the sanctuary with a music stand in each hand. "Congratulations on your marriage."

"Thank you, Paul." She quickly changed the subject. "It looks like everybody's going to make it for this rehearsal." There was a buzz of activity in the room as people greeted each other and made their way to their seats.

"Do you think we're ready for this?" he asked.

"I certainly do. You've done a wonderful job with the rehearsals, and the extra people who have joined the choir have given us a nice balance."

He set the music stands down in front of the chairs for the violinists. "I couldn't have done it without your help at the sectionals. Thank you for pitching in like you did."

"You're certainly welcome. I loved every minute of it."

He checked his watch. "Ten o'clock. Time to get started."

As the rehearsal progressed, everything went even more smoothly than Alona could have imagined. And the string instruments added such richness to the piano and organ accompaniment. When they stopped for a break at eleven o'clock, the woman sitting next to Alona leaned over and said, "What a blessing this will be. I know the Spirit of God is going to be moving in this place tomorrow!"

PART THREE

May–December 1941

★ ★ ★

CHAPTER THIRTEEN

A DIFFERENT KIND OF MARRIAGE

★ ★ ★

Alona stared at the price tags on the knickers she was holding up. *Five dollars! I can't pay that much for a pair of boy's knickers! That's ridiculous!* Quickly she put the knickers back on the rack, then began searching for something a bit less expensive. But then she remembered Oscar's words when she had told him she was going shopping for the boys: "Get some nice clothes for them, Alona. These boys of ours deserve the very best."

She picked up the knickers again and checked the size to be sure they would fit Carl, then placed them on top of the other garments she had chosen. Although the nearly two months of her marriage had changed her in many ways, still the old habits of frugal economy died hard. Oscar Moran had the reputation of being tight with money where his business was concerned, but he was more than liberal toward his new family. He had, in fact, grown impatient with Alona on one occasion. She had mentioned that she couldn't afford to buy the best brand of shoes for Tim because they were too expensive. Oscar had frowned and shook his head. "You've got to change your mindset about things like this. We need to be careful with money, of course, but not that careful. When I was a boy, I had to wear hand-me-down shoes that were too small for me. They just about ruined my feet. We don't have to skimp on buying things for our boys. I wish you would understand that."

"Could I help you with anything, Mrs. Moran?"

Alona turned to see the saleswoman standing there, a bright smile on her face. Alona remembered a time when she had come in trying to find a bargain in socks for the boys. The same woman had not been smiling that day. As a matter of fact, she had given her a cold reception and turned her back on Alona. Evidently being married to the wealthiest man in town made quite a difference.

"I think I've got everything I need."

"Shall I ring it up then?"

"Yes. That would be fine."

She waited until the purchases were totaled up, and it came to thirty-one dollars. As she removed a wallet from her purse and pulled out a fifty, she thought how that would have been half of her monthly income at one time. She took the change, nodded to the woman, and then turned to go. She had just reached the door when she nearly bumped into her pastor, Byron Sandifer.

"Why, hello, Alona. Doing a little Saturday morning shopping?"

"Yes. Buying some summer clothes for the boys. Are you doing some shopping too?" she asked, although she couldn't imagine he was.

"Actually, I've been wandering all over town trying to think of a good gift I can give to Hazel."

"Is it her birthday?"

"No, it's our sixteenth anniversary."

"Have you come up with any ideas yet?"

He shook his head and grinned ruefully. "The only thing I can think of is a new vacuum cleaner. The old one hasn't been working well for a while." He lifted his eyebrows as though a thought had struck him. "Say, I bet you could help me. You know Hazel real well. Do you think I should go ahead and get her a vacuum cleaner?"

"Oh, Brother Byron, that is the worst idea I've ever heard!"

"What's wrong with it? She would use it all the time."

"It's a great idea to get her a new vacuum cleaner, but not for your anniversary—and not for a birthday either! You need to make this a very special day. She's a wonderful wife, and I know she makes such a good home for you and your boys."

"You're right about that. None better than the woman I married."

Alona thought quickly. She had grown very close indeed to Hazel Sandifer and knew more about her, in some ways, than her husband did. Hazel loved her husband dearly but had often complained, *"He's so practical, Alona! He loves me, but he forgets to say so. And he doesn't do those little things that a woman would appreciate.*

An idea leaped into Alona's mind, and she said firmly, "I know exactly what you should give her. But it might be a bit expensive."

"I don't care about that. I'll take out a loan at the bank if I have to. What is it?"

"You should take her on a trip—maybe to Atlanta. Go to a first-class hotel and get a really nice room. Surprise her with some flowers or maybe just a single flower. Take her out to a nice restaurant, and tell her that she's prettier than she was when you married her. And write her a poem, telling her how much you love her."

"I couldn't write a poem if my life depended on it!"

"Sure you could. Just use the words *moon*, *June*, and

spoon, and say you love her. Borrow a couple lines from Shakespeare. Write it on some beautiful paper using your neatest handwriting, and she'll love it."

He digested all that she had said and finally proclaimed, "Those are all *great* ideas, Alona! I'll do it."

"Make her feel loved, like you did when you first married her."

The pastor smiled broadly. "Anything else?"

"I think that's enough suggestions from me, but I'll guarantee you one thing. She'll like this a whole lot better than she would a new vacuum cleaner!"

"I'll do it! I'll make it a surprise." Despite his height and broad shoulders, he seemed like a small boy. "I'll get her some little something and make her think that's the present. Maybe some perfume or something. And then I'll sweep her out of here before she can figure out what's happening."

"And your boys can come and stay with us while you're gone."

"That would be asking too much."

"Not a bit. They'll have a great time. You know how much our boys like to do things together."

"If you could do that, it would make things perfect. I've got to go," he said. "I've got to find out about reservations. Thank you so much. I'm going to let you handle all my anniversaries and birthdays from now on."

Alona was happy for Hazel as the minister turned and hurried out. She laughed when she saw him break into a run. "Hazel Sandifer, you're in for a big surprise!" She got into the car, and as she drove home, she thought about her own life. Just a week ago the pastor had said to her, *"Your life must be a lot better now, Alona."*

It's not better, she thought. *We just have more things and plenty of food on the table.* She remembered her honeymoon and how from the first moment she had understood that Oscar did not have the gentleness she longed for in a man, and he never would.

She also thought of the two occasions in the last two weeks when Oscar had suddenly been seized with a sharp pain in his chest. She had immediately moved to call the doctor, but he had grabbed her, saying, "No, just get me one of my pills." After he had taken it, he had lain still, not moving and his face pale. She had repeatedly urged him to go to the doctor, but he had refused. He seemed to believe that physical ailment was a weakness and it was best to simply ignore it.

Of one thing she was sure: she could not make Oscar into the kind of man Truman had been. She was trapped in a marriage that had no joy for her, and there was no exit. Pushing those things out of her mind as much as she could, Alona pulled up in front of the house and went in.

She was putting her purchases on the kitchen counter when Jason came into the room.

"We've got a little problem here, Alona."

"What is it? Something wrong with the boys?"

"In a way." He was chewing his lower lip as he always did whenever he was upset. "It's Mrs. Darrow. She made Tim tie Buddy up."

"Tie him up! Why, we've never needed to tie him up! What's wrong?"

"He was in the house and Mrs. Darrow didn't like it. The boys are pretty upset. She forbade them to untie him."

At that moment the housekeeper came in, her face set in an angry cast. "I suppose he's telling you about the dog."

"Yes, he is. What's this all about, Mrs. Darrow?"

"The boys brought that dog in, and he tracked muddy footprints all over my kitchen floor. And then Timothy took him into his bedroom. I won't have that dog in this house."

Alona stiffened. She was not argumentative by nature, but this woman had a way of setting her teeth on edge. Mrs. Darrow despised her and her boys and worshiped the first Mrs. Moran. Alona had not been in the house a week before she discovered that despite her best efforts, she and the housekeeper would never get along. Up until now she had simply given in to the woman's "suggestions," but now she suddenly understood that if she was ever to have any authority in her own house, she would have to draw a line.

"The dog will *not* be tied up, Mrs. Darrow." The woman stiffened her back and began to respond, but Alona interrupted. "This is my final word. I don't want to hear anything else about it. Do you understand?"

Mrs. Darrow glared at her, whirled, and marched out.

"Good for you! That woman's a witch," Jason said, a broad grin on his face. "You'll need to hold your ground, though when Oscar hears about this. He may take her side."

"I hope not, but if he does, we'll just have to resolve it."

"I'm taking the boys out to the river to do some fishing. Would you like to come?"

"Yes, I would," Alona said instantly. She was in an unhappy mood, and the very thought of staying in the house and doing battle with Leah Darrow was unappealing. "Let me put on some old clothes."

"The boys have been chomping at the bit to go. How about we take Buddy with us?"

"That'll be fine."

Alona quickly changed into a dress that she'd had for ages and then went downstairs and found the boys ready to go. Buddy was with them in the foyer, hopping up and down with excitement.

"Let's go, Mom!" Zac said. "I want to catch a lot of fish."

"All right. I wouldn't mind catching a few myself."

"Mrs. Moran!"

Alona turned to see Mrs. Darrow, who had come into the foyer. "You're not going out!"

"Yes I am."

"But . . . Mr. and Mrs. Black are coming to dinner!"

"I know, but we'll be back in time. Come on, boys."

Tim sat close to Alona on the grass back a ways from the riverbank, watching Jason as he moved along, throwing out his line, closely followed by Zac and Carl. Tim did not like fishing as much as the other boys did and had gotten his fill of it quickly. Alona cast a glance at him from time to time and noticed that he didn't look happy.

"How are things at school, Tim?"

"Okay."

The way he shrugged when he spoke alerted Alona. She put her arm around him and said, "I thought we were friends. Friends tell each other things."

Tim turned with a look on his face that made Alona very aware of how different he was from her other two sons. Both Carl and Zac were tough and hearty, loud and outgoing, while Tim was the opposite. "What is it?"

"I didn't do well in school this year. My grades are going to be pretty bad."

"Well, I'm sure you did your best."

He shook his head and watched as the trio laughed about something. Jason picked up Carl and pretended to throw him into the river, and Carl was laughing and protesting loudly.

"I . . . I wish they had painting classes at school."

"If they did, you'd make straight A's."

Tim looked up and watched a flock of birds as they wheeled and turned in the sky. He didn't speak for a long time. "He's not going to like it, Mom. He's already talked to me about my grades."

Oscar had insisted on seeing the boys' old report cards right after the honeymoon. *"The boys need to be encouraged, Alona,"* he had said. *"I'll see to that."* And in some ways he had been encouraging. He had talked to them each separately, and Zac and Carl had not been upset. But Tim had been.

"I'm not good with math and science. I think I'm going to fail math."

It grieved Alona to see the sadness in her boy's face. She loved all of her boys, but this one had a special place in her heart. He was more vulnerable than the other two, less able to handle the shocks that life handed young boys as they were growing up. Zac and Carl had a lot of their father in them. Truman had been able to handle anything that came along, but Tim seemed to be less resilient in general.

Squeezing his shoulders, she said, "Oscar will help you. He's very good at math." When he didn't answer, she said, "Don't worry about it, son. If we have to, we'll get a tutor to help you. It'll be all right."

Tim reached down and picked up a small stone and studied it for a moment. Then he threw it into the river as hard as he could. "I don't think so, Mom." He got up and walked toward the river but in the opposite direction from the other three. Alona got up to follow him but then realized that it would do little good to speak to him. *I'll have to talk to Oscar about this,* she thought. *He means well, but he doesn't know how sensitive Tim is.*

She sat back down as Jason came and sat down next to her. "I don't think you're going to catch enough fish to make a meal," she said.

"No, but the boys enjoy it." He looked over at Tim. "What's wrong with Tim?"

Alona hesitated but decided she really had no one else to talk to. "He's not doing well in some of his subjects. Math particularly, and he's afraid of what Oscar will say."

"He's afraid of Oscar," Jason said. His lips twisted wryly. "So am I."

"Not really."

"Yes, I guess I really am. I've failed him so often, and he's not an easy man to be around when you've disappointed him."

"Maybe you can talk to Oscar. Tim's got a gentle spirit. He needs gentle handling."

"Oscar wouldn't listen to anything I said."

The two fell silent, and for a while Alona sat there, occupied with the problem that her marriage had brought her family. She had already seen signs of difficulty with Oscar's strictness with the boys. He meant well, but he seemed to forget that they were not grown men.

"I'm worried about Tim. It's not a good thing to be afraid . . . and he is afraid."

"Yes, he is. I wish he weren't."

"I don't think Oscar's afraid of anything."

"What about you?"

"I've already told you. I'm afraid of flying, and I'm afraid of my brother."

Alona's heart went out to this tall man who had so many gifts and who wasted them all. She reached over and put her hand over his, and he looked up with surprise. "I think you need to work on those things. You have such gifts, Jason."

He sat absolutely still for a moment, then he said quietly, "My life might have been different if I'd had someone who believed in me and in what I wanted to do."

"Didn't Oscar encourage you?"

"No, and I can't blame him too much. I got off into so many foolish things, and then, of course, I cracked up and lost my nerve. He can't understand that at all." He covered her hand with his other hand. "You've been very kind to me. I'd about given up on myself."

Alona was highly conscious of his hands on hers. "You've got a long road ahead of you, Jason. I'm going to be praying that you will get over your fear."

Jason pulled his hand from hers. "You're a sweet woman, Alona. Gentle and tender, and yet at the same time, you're tough."

She sat absolutely still. He was watching her in a peculiar way, and she suddenly felt guilty. She got up quickly and said, "Well, I think it's time to go home. Mrs. Darrow will have my head if we don't get back soon."

Jason got to his feet too. "It's good to have you in the house, Alona. I was pretty lonely before, but you and the boys have made a big difference." Seeing that she was troubled by his remarks, he added quickly, "I'll get the boys. We'll get our stuff together and be on the way."

"I'll help you."

The two approached Carl and Zac. "All right, boys, we've got to go."

"Oh, not now, Mom!" Carl protested. "We haven't caught enough fish."

"You can come back some other day. I think you'd better put those fish back in the river. There's not enough to make a meal."

As usual, she had an argument over this with Carl, who would argue with a stump. Finally she leaned over to pick up the pole, but as she moved, her feet hit a wet, slippery spot. She flailed her arms, trying to regain her balance, but it was too late. She slipped over the bank and fell headlong into the river. The water closed over her head, and she came up spitting and sputtering.

Jason was there at once. He reached for her hand and pulled her ashore. "You all right?" he asked. His eyes were laughing, and Alona was so angry for a moment she couldn't speak.

"Gee, mom, you're all wet," Zac said.

"I *know* I'm all wet. What a mess! Come on. Let's go."
She headed for the car, feeling like an utter fool. She had
no towels in the car, of course, so she simply wrung out
her hair as best she could and then got in. When the boys
and Jason got in, she dared them to say a word, but
Jason, evidently, had spoken to the boys.

"We'll get you home as quick as we can, Alona," he
said. "I know you're uncomfortable."

Alona did not speak all the way home, nor did anyone else. They were all aware that she was furious. When
they reached the house, Alona turned and saw that Jason
was keeping his eyes straight ahead. Then she saw that
the boys were staring at her, and it suddenly struck her
as ridiculous. She began to laugh and said, "Well, now I
know how to get you boys quiet. All I have to do is fall
into the river."

Immediately the boys started laughing, and Zac said,
"You sure look funny, Mom."

"I'll bet I do. Maybe you'd better take me to the back
door, Jason."

"Might be best, but either way you're going to make
some wet tracks on Mrs. Darrow's floor."

Jason drove around to the back entrance. When the
group tromped into the kitchen, Oscar said, "What in the
world . . . ?"

"I fell in the river." Alona laughed and shook her
head. "No damage done."

But Oscar was not happy. "Do you know what time it
is? The Blacks will be here at any minute."

"I'll go get dressed at once."

She left, but she heard Oscar shouting at Jason.
"What in the world were you thinking, Jason? Can't you
do anything right?"

"It wasn't his fault, Oscar," Alona said, returning to
the kitchen. "I simply slipped and fell in."

"If he had any sense at all, he wouldn't have let you get near the river," Oscar said. "He'll never change."

Alona's gaiety flew out the window. "Oscar, look at me." She waited until he did. "Listen to me. It was *not* Jason's fault. It was my fault. There's no point shouting at him. If you want to shout at anybody, shout at me."

Oscar just stared. He started to open his mouth to respond but then evidently changed his mind and left the room.

Jason leaned over to her and said, "He doesn't like to be crossed like that."

"He had no right to blame you for something that was my fault."

"Well, maybe it was partially my fault."

"Don't be foolish," she said. "I can fall in the river without any help from you." She saw the boys were watching and made herself smile. "All right. You boys get cleaned up for dinner. Go now."

As they hurried off, Alona said, "I guess I'm a little afraid of Oscar myself."

"He's a stern man." Jason shrugged.

"We can't live with fear—any of us—so we'll have to stick together."

"All right. You be the captain, and we'll all do our best, Captain Alona."

As she made her way to the stairs, she passed Mrs. Darrow, who was glaring at her, and managed to say sweetly, "You should have been with us, Mrs. Darrow. We had a lovely time!"

CHAPTER FOURTEEN

"I'LL HAVE TO BE MORE CAREFUL"

★ ★ ★

Alona managed to get dressed and get the boys ready for dinner by the time the Blacks arrived. The dinner was less than comfortable, however, for Jason was on edge and Oscar was in a bad mood. He made little attempt to include Alona or the boys in the conversation, and she knew he was angry with her. She forced herself to speak cheerfully, and the Blacks didn't seem to notice Oscar's foul mood.

Vernon Black was a tall, distinguished-looking man who owned another large factory in town. Oscar and Vernon belonged to the same businessmen's club. This was the first time Alona had met the couple, but she found them very pleasant company.

After dinner was over, Oscar excused the boys while the adults went into the parlor. Alona and Genevieve sipped their coffee while the men talked about the war in Europe. Oscar commented that he was thrilled when he heard about the destruction of the *Bismarck*, the pride of the German navy. "I hope this teaches those Nazis a lesson," he spouted. "They've lost their best ship. I'm very proud of the British Royal Navy."

"I heard that the *Bismarck* sank England's battleship the *Hood* a few days ago," Vern commented. "That older ship just couldn't stand up to modern weapons. I think losing that ship really stirred up the British. They couldn't wait to get a good shot at the *Bismarck.*"

"I guess the *Bismarck* limped around for several days with some damage from the first battle. I'm glad they finally got it." Oscar sighed. "I sure wish the war would end."

"It won't end quickly," Jason said. "Did you hear President Roosevelt speak the other day?"

"Yes, I heard him. I think he's overreacting. All we have to do is sit quietly. We don't want to get involved in another European war."

President Roosevelt had stopped just short of declaring war when he spoke to the nation, saying, "An unlimited national emergency exists. The delivery of supplies to Britain is imperative. This can be done. It must be done. And it will be done."

"The president is a persuasive man," Vern asserted. "He'll declare war if he has to."

"Nonsense!" Oscar scoffed. "But even if he does declare war, we'll be safe here."

Alona noticed that Jason gave an almost imperceptible shake of his head, but she knew he wouldn't challenge Oscar's views.

"Perhaps we could talk about something less disturbing," Alona suggested. "Are your children happy that school is almost over for the year, Genevieve?"

Alona was grateful that the men willingly let her guide the discussion away from politics. When the Blacks left and the boys and Jason had gone to bed, she and Oscar were left alone in the parlor. Alona was doing

some hand sewing, and Oscar was reading the newspaper. She had wanted to go to bed, but she knew she
had to prepare Oscar for Tim's bad grades. It was something she dreaded, but it had to be done. "Oscar," she
said. "I need to talk with you."

He lowered the paper. "About what?"

"About Tim. His grades are going to be low in math
and maybe in science."

"I was afraid of that. The boy needs to apply himself.
He can do much better."

"I'm not sure that he can."

"Of course he can," Oscar declared. "It's just a matter
of discipline."

"Some people have better minds for that sort of
thing. Tim does better in artistic matters."

"You can't make a living in artistic matters." He
peered over the top of his glasses at her. "Are you telling
me he's going to fail these classes?"

"I think that's possible. He's worked very hard,
but—"

"We cannot have that, Alona. It's very important for
any young man to be well founded in arithmetic and the
sciences."

"Perhaps we could hire a tutor to help him."

"No need to do that. I've always been good at figures.
I'll take some time with him." He put the paper down
and folded his hands over his chest. "School's almost out,
but he's got all summer. I'll make out a schedule for
him."

"What kind of a schedule?"

"A tutoring schedule for the summer. Students who
are weak in an area have to study in the summer."

"How would you do that?"

"Why, I would get him extra books, and I could have
him stay inside each morning to study, and then in the
evenings I could go over what he's done."

Alona's heart sank. It was exactly the sort of thing she did not want to see happen. "I'm not sure that would be best."

For the first time Oscar showed the stubbornness and resistance that was in him when he was crossed. "Look, Alona, I know we both want what's best for Tim, but in this case I think I am the better judge."

"Tim doesn't take very well to being punished."

"Punishing him! I'm not punishing him!" Oscar exclaimed. "You should see that."

The argument became more tense, and Oscar was absolutely unbending.

"I'm not unreasonable," he persisted, "but you can surely see that Tim will have to have extra help." He got to his feet then, saying curtly, "I'm going to bed." He crossed the room but suddenly turned back around. "Oh, Mrs. Darrow told me about the problem with the dog."

"Yes, we did have a disagreement over that."

"She said the dog came in the house and tracked the floor up."

Alona knew there was trouble brewing. "We've always let Buddy come in the house. The boys are very fond of him and so am I."

"From now on we'll have to keep him outside and tied up, I'm afraid."

"No, Oscar. We won't."

His mouth drew into a tight line. "Alona, you're being very unreasonable."

"I don't think I am. I've done everything you've asked of me, Oscar, but Buddy is a beloved pet. I think it's cruel to tie up a large dog like that. If you insist, we will keep him out of the house. It's not what I want, but I'll agree to that. But I won't have him tied up."

A flush touched Oscar's cheeks, and Alona knew he was very angry. "I hope we don't have any more difficulties about this," she said. "I'll agree that Buddy can't come in the house if you agree that he doesn't have to be tied up."

For a moment, it seemed that Oscar would argue, but he finally nodded shortly. "Very well. We'll compromise on that, but Tim is going to have to do extra work this summer. I'm adamant about that."

Alona's hands were trembling by the time Oscar left the room. She hated confrontation. She went outside and walked down the block, allowing herself time to regain her composure. Overhead the stars were bright, and the night breeze was warm. It was a beautiful night, but she was not feeling peaceful. *I'll have to talk to Tim before Oscar does*, she thought. *He's not going to like this one bit!*

★ ★ ★

Tim threw himself down at the base of the huge magnolia tree that rose up from the back corner of Oscar's property. Buddy came up at once and tried to get onto his lap, but Tim pushed him away roughly. "Get away, Buddy! You're too big to be a lap dog." His tone of voice offended Buddy, who plopped down facing the other direction. Tim reached over and began to stroke his back. "I didn't mean to hurt your feelings," he said. "Don't be mad."

He closed his eyes and rested his head back against the rough surface of the tree trunk. He had left the house after lunch—which he had hardly touched. He just didn't feel like eating much these days. Carl and Zac had gone to explore the creek with the pastor's boys, but he had been forced to stay home all morning working on his math. On a Saturday! Oscar said he wouldn't have to do schoolwork every Saturday, but he wanted him to work extra hard these first couple of weeks so he could slack off a little later in the summer. On the first day of summer vacation, Oscar had lectured him about the importance of math and the sciences. He had bought several new textbooks and a supply of paper and pencils. Now as each summer day passed away, Tim was growing more and more unhappy.

A noise overhead caused him to open his eyes, and he looked up into the tree and saw a red squirrel perched on a limb, sitting up and staring straight at him. The animal's bright eyes were fixed, and he folded his paws as he considered the boy and the dog beneath him as if they were some exotic species.

"Hello, squirrel," Tim said. Buddy jumped up and broke into a furious symphony of wild barking at the squirrel. The squirrel did not move but just stared down at Buddy, who frantically ran around the base of the tree.

Tim had to smile, for Buddy had been chasing squirrels all of his life. He had never caught one, but he never seemed to understand that he never would.

"You're not going to catch any squirrels, and I'm not going to get this dumb old arithmetic, not *ever*!" Tim stood up and picked up a rock, then threw it at the squirrel, which scolded him and disappeared high up into the tree.

"Come on, Buddy. Let's go back to the house." Buddy reluctantly gave up his futile chase and looked up at Tim, who reached over and fondled his tulip-shaped ears, enjoying their velvety softness. As he did, he looked back and saw that the squirrel had reappeared. A thought came to him, and he reached into his shirt pocket and pulled out a small tablet and a pencil. Sitting down under the tree again, he then began to sketch the squirrel. The pencil moved rapidly and a sense of peace came over him. He had never analyzed it before, but he now realized that he always felt best when he was sketching or painting. When he finished the drawing, he said, "I can do better than that."

He stuffed the notebook and pencil back into his pocket and headed back toward the house. "I wish we lived back in our old place," he muttered. "Then I wouldn't have to waste all summer doing this old math."

His eyes brightened when he saw Jason's car parked out front. Jason was the one person he could talk to about art, and now he hurried into the house. He found Jason in the parlor with his mother.

"Hi, Jason," Tim said. "I just drew a picture of a squirrel. Look."

Jason took a good look at the drawing. "That's good, Tim. The head's not quite in proportion, but you've done the eyes real well. It's hard to make eyes seem alive."

"Let me see." Alona took the sketch and studied it. "It's a miracle to me how people can draw anything. I couldn't draw a realistic-looking picture if my life depended on it."

"Do you want to see some of the other sketches I've done this week, Jason? They're up in my room."

"I'd love to." The two left the parlor and went up to Tim's room. It was neat enough, with the bed made and most of the clothes hung up. The easel that Jason had given him stood in the corner by the window. It was old and they had had to reinforce it, but Tim loved it.

Jason examined the painting that was on the easel. It was the scene that Tim saw when he stood at the easel and looked out the window at the back yard. "I like what you've done with the texture of the grass here, Tim," he commented. "And the shadows from the tree are really nice."

"Thanks, Jason. Now I have to figure out how to do the bark on the tree."

"That's not easy, as you know." Jason gave him some pointers about how to get the texture right and then looked at the sketches Tim had done recently.

"I wish I could go to art school when I get out of high school."

"Maybe you can."

"Oscar would never let me do that. He wants all of us to go into business."

Jason was well acquainted with Oscar's views on the arts. "You know, I have a friend who's an artist. Jake lives about thirty miles from here. Maybe sometime this summer you and I could go over and see him. We could take some of your drawings and get his ideas."

"A real artist! Gosh, he wouldn't want to see my stuff."

"I think he might. He's not like some artists. He's a prizefighter too."

"A boxer?" Tim asked with astonishment. "And an artist at the same time?"

"Well, he doesn't paint when he's in the ring. He's a pretty tough fellow. He was in the navy with me. The boxing champion of the middleweight division. Even though he's a tough fellow, he likes to paint. But his painting is something you ought to see. He's even got a few of his pieces in museums now. Would you like to go?"

"Absolutely."

"Great. I'll see what I can arrange." He saw the boy's eyes shine with excitement and winked. "And maybe when you get rich and famous, you'll remember your old friend Jason. Okay?"

Tim stayed in his bedroom painting while Jason went down to the parlor to talk to Alona. He found her at the piano working out the descant part for Sunday's choir anthem. He told her about his idea of taking Jason to meet his artist friend.

"It would have to be some afternoon, Jason. Oscar

insists that Tim work on his studies most of the morning."

"And I'd have to get off work too. I'll see if I can arrange something."

"That would be great."

Jason looked at the music Alona had been working on. "That's a nice anthem. I still feel odd about going to church, but I do love singing in the choir."

"So do I," Alona said. She suddenly sensed that Jason's mood had changed. "Are you terribly unhappy, Jason?"

"I'm not sure about terribly, but I ought not to complain." He stuffed his hands into his pockets. "I'm not the only one who's unhappy."

Her eyes opened with surprise. "I hope that doesn't show on me too much."

"I think people like us who aren't really happy learn how to cover up pretty well."

"I really have no reason to be unhappy. The boys are being well taken care of. I've got a good home. I'm ashamed to complain."

"So am I," Jason said, a weariness in his voice. "Oscar pulled me out of the pit. I might even be dead now if he hadn't. I was on my way to something really bad."

"I know. I feel ungrateful. Oscar's my husband, and that's all there is to it."

Mrs. Darrow stepped into the parlor. "I'm going to the store," she said. "Do you need anything?"

"No, I don't think so, Mrs. Darrow. Thank you."

As the door closed Jason shrugged his shoulders. "Oscar will probably get a report about us."

"What do you mean, Jason?"

"Haven't you discovered yet that she tells Oscar about everything that goes on around here? She makes everything sound awful. She'll be telling him how we were all alone in here today."

"That's ridiculous. I was just playing the piano and you came in here to find me."

"I know that and you know that, but she'll make it sound like something else. She's got a tongue long enough to sit in here and lick the skillet in the kitchen."

Alona laughed at the image. "It'll be all right," she said. "By the way, I don't know how to thank you for the attention you've given to Tim. You know you're the only bright spot in his life these days. Thank you so much."

"Don't mention it. He's a good kid." He stood up. "Listen, I'll let you get back to your music."

"I'll see you at dinner tonight." Alona turned back to the piano as he left the room. As she played the descant part, she was thinking of Jason and what a tragic waste his life was. She was also aware that just talking honestly with him had brought a glow of pleasure to her. Startled at the thought, she closed the lid over the keys and sat quietly staring across the room. *I'll have to be more careful*, she thought.

CHAPTER FIFTEEN

TIM'S ADMIRER

★ ★ ★

The summer of 1941 was miserable for Tim Jennings. His stepfather relentlessly kept him at home every morning until eleven o'clock working on science and mathematics. The studying produced only one real result—Tim learned to hate the subjects even more than he had before! The tension between Tim and Oscar Moran grew all summer, for Oscar was convinced that Timothy could do the work but refused out of pure stubbornness.

Tim, in fact, had not spent his entire mornings on the books and problems Oscar laid out. He worked at it until his mind seemed to rebel, and then, despite Mrs. Darrow's frequent visits to assure that he was busy, Tim found other things to do. He kept sketch pads in the drawer of the big desk, and when his mind became too saturated in numbers to think, he would ease one out under his papers and draw sketches. He also kept novels handy, which he had learned to keep well hidden from Mrs. Darrow. He finished *They Shoot Horses, Don't They?* and *How Green Was My Valley*, both of which he loved, and even waded through *For Whom the Bell Tolls*, which he hated.

He also listened to popular music, keeping the radio turned down and shutting it off when he heard Mrs. Darrow's distinctive footsteps in the hallway. He learned to hum along with "I'll Never Smile Again," sung by a young man named Frank Sinatra; "When You Wish Upon a Star," from Walt Disney's film *Pinocchio*; and his favorite, "You Are My Sunshine," by Jimmie Davis.

Throughout the summer he kept close track of the war in Europe, listening to the newscasts on the radio. The big shock came on June twenty-second when Adolf Hitler, to the astonishment of the world, invaded the Soviet Union, despite a nonaggression pact signed with that country in 1939. The German army struck with all its force, and all summer long the two giants struggled. The Nazis circled Leningrad, and Hitler announced that he would starve the city to death. Hitler also announced that all Jews in Germany would be forced to wear the Star of David, and rumors had begun leaking out of Europe about terrible things happening to Jews confined to ghettos.

Despite Tim's secret activities, the summer was miserable for him. He had stopped speaking to Oscar except when spoken to, and the warfare between the two seemed unending. Alona tried to get Tim to modify his attitude toward his stepfather, but he found no reason to do so.

Once during the height of summer he was sitting with his mother in the back yard under the arbor when a large flock of crows flew over. "Mom, do you remember what Dad always said about crows?"

"Yes. He said when you see large numbers of crows in the summer it's a raincrow summer."

"And he said a raincrow summer meant something bad was going to happen."

"That's just an old superstition, Tim."

"I'm not so sure about that. It was a raincrow summer just before Dad died. Maybe something else bad is going to happen this year."

Alona leaned over and put her arm around Tim. "We're not going to believe that old wives' tale. Put it out of your mind." Despite her brave words, she could not watch the crows without a twinge of fear.

★　★　★

Finally the summer dragged itself out, and Tim was actually excited for school to start again. One day during the first week of school, he hurried home to read a new book about painting he had checked out of the library. His brothers had gone to play baseball in the park.

Tim walked along the broad street that led to Oscar's house. He never thought of it as his house or his mother's house but always Oscar's house. He was almost past a large brick house with an enormous yard, and even a barn out back, when he heard his name being called. Turning, he saw Helen Arnette inside the fenced yard, playing with a large German shepherd. Tim stopped and said, "Did you call me?"

"Yes. Come here."

He walked over to the gate opposite Helen. She was, without a doubt, the most popular girl in his school, and probably the prettiest as well, with pretty blond hair and blue eyes. Tim was surprised she even knew his name. There was a small group of students from well-to-do families that hung out together, and Tim never expected to be invited into that group.

"Hi, Tim." Helen smiled. "How do you like my dog? His name's Chip."

"He looks like Rin Tin Tin, the dog in the movies."

"He does, doesn't he? He's supposed to be a guard dog, but he's nothing but a pushover." She patted Chip's head, and he licked her hand, then reared up on the fence. Tim reached out his hand tentatively and stroked the big dog's head. "We've got a collie named Buddy."

"Does he look like Lassie?"

"Sure does. He's a beautiful dog, but he's a little sensitive."

"What do you mean sensitive?"

"I mean if you scold him, he goes off and pouts."

Helen laughed. She had a nice laugh, and her eyes sparkled. "It's hard to believe that a dog would pout. What does he do? How can you tell?"

"Oh, it's easy enough to tell. If he's in the house, he goes to a corner, flops down, and sticks his nose in the corner of the wall. He doesn't move until we go over and make a fuss over him."

"I think that's funny. I never knew a dog could be sensitive like that. You're not, are you, Chip?" She ruffled the dog's head. "Why don't you come in? Mom just made some cookies."

Tim was surprised at the invitation but quickly said, "That'd be keen! I love cookies. My mom makes the best in the world."

"No she doesn't. Mine does. When you have one, you'll see."

Tim followed Helen into the house. "You smell that?" she asked as they stepped inside.

"I sure do."

"Mom's probably still in the kitchen."

Tim followed Helen down a long hallway. It was a big house, and he couldn't believe the number of paintings on the walls. "You've got lots of paintings," he remarked.

"Oh, my mother loves art—especially paintings."

Tim paused to examine one of the paintings. "Why, this is an original—not a print."

"My mother won't have a print in the house. She likes the real thing. She painted that one herself."

Tim stared at her incredulously. "She did? That's wonderful!"

"You can tell her that." Helen smiled. "She goes to art shows all the time. Come on."

The large kitchen that Tim stepped into behind Helen was flooded with pale sunlight. The woman who stood at the counter removing warm cookies from a cookie sheet was very attractive. He had seen her before at school events.

"Mother, this is Tim Jennings."

"How are you, Tim?" Mrs. Arnette said. She had hair as blond as her daughter's and the same bright blue eyes. "I'll bet you don't like cookies."

"Oh yes, ma'am, I do!"

"Why don't you sit down and have a few. Are you in the same grade as Helen?"

"No, ma'am. Helen's a year ahead of me."

"I hear Tim makes straight A's in history. I'm going to get him to do my homework for me in exchange for all the cookies you're going to give him."

"But I didn't say that!" he protested.

"You be careful, Tim," Mrs. Arnette said. "She'll wrap you around her little finger just like she does her dad. Here, try a couple of these." Tim took the plate of chocolate chip cookies and bit off half of one. "Hey, this is really good, Mrs. Arnette."

"Thanks, but anybody can make chocolate chip cookies." She checked on the cookies still in the oven. "I met your mother at a PTA meeting. I see where you get your good looks from."

Tim flushed and could not think of an answer.

"Look, Mom, he's blushing!" Helen laughed.

"I think that's a good sign. It shows modesty—of which you could use some, young lady."

Tim shoved the rest of the cookie into his mouth to keep from having to speak. He was almost tongue-tied in the presence of this beautiful and intimidating girl. Tim's poverty-stricken background still made him very uneasy in an affluent home like this, and he felt self-conscious around wealthy people. He knew that Mr. Arnette was president of the First National Bank, so money was obviously no problem for this family.

Tim ate so many cookies he was ashamed of himself, but Mrs. Arnette only laughed at him. "You'll have to take some of them home with you if you like them that much, Tim. I made way too many."

"Tim liked your painting," Helen told her mother, sipping her milk and leaving a thin white mustache on her upper lip.

"Wipe your lip, Helen," Mrs. Arnette said, then turned to Tim. "I thought I'd be a professional painter at one time, but it didn't work out that way."

"Gosh, that painting I saw in the hall is just beautiful!" He took a sip of milk. "I wish I could learn to paint like that."

"Do you do some painting?" Mrs. Arnette asked.

"I try. I've never had a class, but Jason, my stepfather's brother, has helped me a lot."

"I never knew Jason was a painter."

"He told me he gave it up. He said he didn't have the talent, but I saw some of his things, and I thought they were good."

"Would you like to see some of the other paintings in my collection?"

"I sure would." To his delight, Tim discovered that Mrs. Arnette had a great many paintings she had bought that were not on display. She talked about them, explaining the schools and the techniques, and Tim was enthralled. He fired question after question about them.

"Would you like to see my studio?"

"Aw, Mom, he doesn't want to see your old paintings."

"Yes I do!" Tim said quickly.

"Maybe you'd better go do your homework while Tim and I talk about painting," Mrs. Arnette said, winking at Tim.

Helen rolled her eyes and followed the two as they went upstairs to a room with skylights that let sunlight flood the room. It was a messy room, and the walls were covered with paintings. There were canvases stacked against the wall, and she showed him the painting she was presently working on. It was a watercolor painting of the city hall, and Tim was awed. "It looks exactly like city hall!"

"Well, not exactly like it. Paintings shouldn't be identical to the object."

"Really?"

"No, of course not. If you want it to be exactly the same, you take a picture of it. You'll notice that this one is painted a little after sundown. I wanted to paint it at dusk, because the lighting is so interesting then. You'll notice I've got several bats up here flitting around. I think they roost in the top of the old courthouse."

Tim listened entranced. "I've never met a real artist before, Mrs. Arnette. Jason was going to take me to meet a friend of his who's an artist, but it turned out the man was in Canada all summer."

"That's too bad. I know you would have enjoyed that. Anyway, I like to dabble with paints, but I don't consider myself a real artist. I chose to get married instead, and now I've got three children. But I still paint quite a bit when I can get to it." She gave Tim an odd look and said, "Do your parents encourage you in your painting?"

He could not think clearly for a moment and tried to frame an answer. "My mom does, but my stepfather doesn't think painting is something worth spending my time on. He wants me to study science and math and stuff like that."

"Well, stuff like that is useful. But so is painting. I'll tell you what," she said. "Why don't you come by some afternoon after school and bring some of the things you've done? Maybe I can give you a few pointers, although I'm not a teacher."

"Gosh, that would be wonderful, Mrs. Arnette!" Tim exclaimed. "But it would be too much trouble."

"No it wouldn't be. I think it would be fun."

Tim smiled broadly. "I'd really like that."

Helen had been trailing behind the two, not saying anything. Now she spoke up. "Come on, Tim. I've got some homework you can help me with. You and Mom can talk about painting anytime."

He followed Helen down to the dining room table, where her books were spread out, and for the next half hour he helped her with her history lesson. His thoughts were not on history, though, but on the paintings and drawings he would bring over to let Helen's mother see.

★   ★   ★

After the ball game Zac and Carl headed toward the foundry, where Oscar was waiting to show the boys around. "Come on, Carl," he said when he saw his brother hanging back.

Carl kicked the dirt and stood his ground. "I don't wanna see the stupid ol' foundry again. I'm goin' home."

Zac shrugged. "Suit yourself. Mr. Oscar promised to show us around the whole place this time."

"Sounds boring to me. I got better things to do."

"Go on home, then. Mind your own taters."

Carl went on his way and Zac went into the foundry and to Oscar's office.

Oscar smiled broadly at his stepson. "Well, Zac, did you win the ball game?"

"Nah, we lost. But I don't care."

"Where's your brother? I thought he was coming too."

"He said he had other stuff to do."

Oscar chuckled. "I can understand that, but I'm sure glad you made it. I'll show you the whole business."

It turned out to be a long tour because Zac fired question after question at his stepfather. Oscar was immensely pleased at this and explained everything slowly and carefully, introducing Zac to some of the workers and showing him exactly how the work was done.

When the two got back to the office, Zac said, "Gee, Mr. Oscar, that was great! You sure have to be smart to run a foundry."

"Well, it takes years to get a feel for the whole process. I think you may have a knack for it, Zac."

"I like to do stuff with my hands. Maybe next summer I'll be old enough for you to let me have a job."

"You certainly will. And in the meantime, anytime you want, you come by. You can learn an awful lot just by watching."

"Thank you, sir. I'll do that."

"You don't mind the noise and the dirt?"

"No, I don't mind it a bit. It looks like fun to run some of those machines."

Oscar laid his hand on the boy's shoulder. "I'll teach you the whole business, son. It'll be fun for both of us."

★　★　★

Later that night Oscar returned home from the deacons' meeting and found Alona in the living room.

"That was a long meeting," she remarked. "It's nearly ten o'clock."

He threw himself into a chair and shook his head. "We're facing a serious problem."

"Some kind of trouble at the church?"

Oscar sighed. "Well, I suppose you'll hear about it sooner or later. It's Leland Short."

"What's the problem with him?"

"He's been having an affair with a woman in town—a low-class woman, I might add."

"Why, that's terrible! Are you sure?"

"Oh yes, it's all out in the open. The woman's husband caught them together and is making quite a stink. Of course we're going to have to do something with Leland."

Alona put down her book and asked quietly, "What will happen, Oscar?"

"He's already been taken off the board of deacons. The question is what to do about him as a church member."

"I feel so sorry for him. He seems like such a nice man. . . . And his poor wife."

"We had a long discussion about it. It's pretty certain he'll be asked to leave the church."

"Leave the church! Did the pastor make that suggestion?"

"No, as a matter of fact, he was against it. And the board of deacons was split almost down the middle."

"What did you say, Oscar?"

"Why, I think you know. We can't have an adulterer in our church, Alona. I'm surprised you would even ask."

"But surely there's got to be a better way. The poor man needs the church right now more than ever."

"He should have thought of that before he took up with that woman," Oscar said shortly. "I don't like it, but we've got to have discipline in the church."

Alona felt a twinge of anger. She wanted to speak but knew how sensitive Oscar was about being crossed.

"But the deacons can't decide a thing like that, can they? Wouldn't the whole church have to vote on it?"

"Yes, you're right about that, but I feel sure the church will do the right thing."

When she didn't comment, Oscar asked, "What's the matter?"

"I think we need to show kindness. Has Leland repented—apologized?"

"Oh yes . . . he broke it off with the woman, and he told the deacons he was contrite about it, but the fact is there. He's guilty."

"I don't think we agree about this, Oscar."

"What do you mean?" he demanded.

"I think when someone has a fall like this, that's the time for the church to show compassion."

"But it would be a bad example! Can't you see that, Alona?"

"I don't think so. Most of us have fallen short of what we ought to be."

"This is a bit different from gossip or some minor failing."

Alona knew it would be impossible to change her husband's mind, so she slowly got up. "I think I'll go to bed. Good night, Oscar."

"She's too tenderhearted," he muttered. "You have to be firm about things like this."

★　★　★

"I love this squirrel." The next afternoon Mrs. Arnette was looking at the painting Tim had done from his sketch. "You caught the mischievous look all squirrels seem to have. You managed to make his eyes gleam— like he's up to no good! I really like it."

"I had problems getting the proportion of the head to the body right at first, but I think it's pretty good now."

"That's always so difficult. No matter how good you get, getting the proportions right is one of the hardest things. If you look carefully, every painting has some flaw in it. And sometimes the flaws don't matter."

"Really? I thought they did."

"There was an Italian painter called Andrea Del Sarto. He was called the perfect painter, but many critics have said he wasn't a great painter because his paintings didn't really have any life in them. Lots of poets have written about this kind of thing . . . that the finest art sometimes has glaring faults."

"My mom reads Charles Dickens novels. She says he's got enough faults to sink ten novelists, but that doesn't matter because of the good things he does."

"That's exactly the way it is with painting. Now, what are you going to do with this gift you have?"

Tim stared up at her dumbfounded. "Do with it? What do you mean, Mrs. Arnette?"

"God gives all of us gifts. We either use them or we don't. My motto has always been 'Use it or lose it.'"

"Well, I can't do much with it because my stepfather doesn't like it."

"How old are you, Tim?"

"I'm thirteen."

"You've got plenty of time to develop your gift. You're not even in high school yet. If you are serious about painting—and I think you are—I'll help you all I can."

His eyes were shining. "Gee, Mrs. Arnette, that would be neat!"

At that moment Helen stuck her head in the door and said, "Come on! You two have been talking about painting for an hour. I want to show you my new horse, Tim."

"You two run along," Mrs. Arnette said. "Don't fall off the horse, though, Tim."

"Thanks, Mrs. Arnette." He hesitated for a moment but then looked her straight in the eye. "Nobody but Jason has ever encouraged me. Thank you so much."

"You're so welcome. It's fun to help a young fellow like you. Go on, now. The next time you come by, I'll show you a few things I had to learn the hard way."

Helen grabbed Tim's arm and dragged him outside. "You never come here to see me. You just come to see my mom."

"That's not true . . . but you don't know how lucky you are to have a mom like that. She really understands how much I like painting and drawing."

"Oh, Mom's great, but I'm no artist. I'm more interested in horses. I plan to ride in a rodeo someday."

Tim could hardly believe his eyes when he discovered that besides the small barn on their property, they also had a fenced-in ring. Helen's passion was horses, and her father had bought her a fine chestnut filly. Tim watched as she saddled the animal and rode her around the ring.

"Isn't she beautiful, Tim?" Helen asked as she got off the horse.

"She sure is. About the prettiest horse I ever saw." He reached up to stroke her velvet nose. "I bet you'll be in a rodeo someday, Helen, or maybe riding in one of the horse races you see in the movies."

"Oh no, I'm gonna be too big for that! I already am, I think."

"Too big? What do you mean?"

"Those jockeys have to be tiny. I think the rodeo is where I'll be."

Helen told him all about her filly as she unsaddled

the horse and turned her loose. "You can carry the saddle to the stable."

"Okay." Tim picked up the saddle and carried it inside the stable. It was dark inside except for the light coming in the open doors at each end. "Where should I put it?"

"Right there on that rail."

Tim put it on the rail and then turned around and bumped into Helen, who had moved closer. "Excuse me," he said.

"Tim, you're a funny boy." Helen smiled.

"What do you mean funny?"

"You never try to kiss me or hold my hand or anything."

He suddenly felt tremendously uncomfortable. She was the most popular girl in school, and he had absolutely no experience at romance. "I guess . . . I don't know how."

She laughed and reached out and ruffled his hair. "You need to read a good romantic novel. I'll give you one. I've got dozens in my room."

"I don't want to read any old romance novels!"

"Yes you do." She took his arm and pulled him outside, saying, "I'll find you a good one."

★   ★   ★

The First Baptist Church was buzzing over the matter of Leland Short's infidelity. The gossip mills ran at full speed, and of course, it wasn't the Baptists alone. Other churches were watching closely to see what they could do. So far there had been no action, but everyone knew that Pastor Sandifer was against making the offender leave the church. Many agreed with him, but there was also a large group, led by Oscar, that strongly felt the opposite way.

A special meeting was called, open only to members of the First Baptist Church.

Alona had stopped talking to Oscar about the matter, for they were at opposite ends of the spectrum. She went to the meeting, though, and took a seat midway toward the front. The deacons were all seated together up on the front bench, and the church was packed. Some members who hadn't been to church in months or even years were there as well.

Alona's eyes were fixed on Leland Short and his wife, Mary Beth. They were seated alone in the front pew on the right side of the church. She could see that Mary Beth was holding her husband's hand and that her face was pale and her lips were unsteady.

That poor woman—and that poor man! This is wrong. The thought raced through her mind as the pastor rose and went to the pulpit. "I'm calling this meeting to order with great reluctance. I think I have made my point to the deacons that I'm against this proceeding, but I'll serve as moderator."

Alona could see that Brother Byron was having a very hard time. His face was stern as he read the charges that had been made. When he finished, he said, "Leland has asked to say a word to the church. There will be no objections, I'm sure. Leland, you may say what you'd like."

Leland Short owned the dry-cleaning establishment in town and had been a faithful church member for many years. His wife stood by him as he stood in front of the congregation. He had to struggle for composure. "I have committed a great wrong. . . . I've confessed it to my wife, and now I confess it to the church. I have no excuse. I have failed the Lord. I've failed my church and I've failed my family, but my wife has forgiven me, and so has the Lord. Now I am asking the church to forgive me. Thank you." He collapsed into his seat and put his face in his hands. His wife put her arm around his shoulders and held him tightly.

Pastor Sandifer cleared his throat. "I would entertain a motion, and I think you know what I would like that motion to be."

Oscar stood up immediately. "We would all like to be compassionate, but I feel that we're setting a precedent here. If we allow this unspeakable sin to go without any action, what would be the result? It would encourage other wrongdoers to do the same. I move that the name of Leland Short be removed from the roles of the First Baptist Church."

The motion got a second from Allen Grimes.

"The motion is made and is seconded and now is open for discussion," the pastor said heavily.

There was much discussion, with several people speaking in favor of excluding Leland from the church. Others were dead set against it. Alona hesitated to speak out because of Oscar's strong views, but she finally could no longer remain silent. "Brother Byron, I would like to speak for Brother Leland and for his wife and family."

Oscar swiveled around, and his mouth dropped open in astonishment. His face grew flushed, and he set his lips in a stubborn line, but Alona was past caring.

"The Bible seems to be very clear about one thing," she said. "That forgiveness is a part of being a Christian. I can't help but think of the woman taken in adultery, and Jesus said, 'He that is without sin among you, let him first cast a stone at her.' I am not without sin." She paused and took the time to catch several of the members by the eye. "Maybe some of you feel that you are, but as for me, I can't belong to a church that doesn't have a forgiving spirit."

Alona walked to the front pew and embraced Mary

Beth, who was crying. She released her and said, "Brother Leland, I know the Lord has forgiven you, and I can't do any less."

Alona was shocked when people from all over the church suddenly came out of their pews. She stepped back as the Shorts were enveloped by a crowd of men and women all trying to put their arms around them. She moved back and looked up at Byron, who was smiling at her with tears in his eyes.

A man spoke up from the crowd. "Take the vote, Preacher."

Immediately Byron Sandifer said, "Those in favor of removing Leland Short's name, raise your hand."

Alona looked straight at Oscar, who raised his hand, but she saw that he had little support. No more than half a dozen hands were up, most of them raised very tentatively and then lowered.

"Those in favor of letting Leland stay, let it be known by saying amen."

A rousing cry of *amen*s filled the sanctuary. "The Lord's will has been done tonight," the pastor declared. "Tonight I think we have seen God's mercy in action."

"You are not loyal to me!" Oscar shouted. He had barely waited to get alone with Alona before he had started in on her, his face red. "A woman should stand beside her husband!"

"I couldn't stand with you on this because I thought you were wrong, Oscar. The church thought so too. Didn't you see the joy in people's faces?"

"Then they're foolish! They have no responsibility!"

"They have mercy, though. It was the right thing to do."

Oscar glared at her, and Alona saw the side of him she had heard about from others.

"You're not a proper wife! Do you think I don't know about you and Jason?"

"Me and Jason! What about me and Jason?" she asked sharply.

"You think I don't know how you get together when you're alone here?"

"I see Mrs. Darrow has been telling stories."

"Yes, she has, and I won't have it anymore! You understand me?"

Alona stood very still. "Oscar, I'm your wife. I have done nothing improper. If you are wise, you won't make an issue of this."

Oscar stared at her. He was accustomed to having his own way, but something in Alona's stance and the steadiness of her pose warned him. He stiffened and said, "I'm disappointed in you!" and stormed out of the room.

Alona felt weak—so weak she had to sit down. She was trembling but filled with indignation. "How can he say such a thing? How could he?"

★ ★ ★

Alona saw to it that she and Jason were never alone in the drawing room again after that. She did see him at choir practice, and one night as they were leaving at the same time, he said, "I can't help but tell you how I admire you for standing up for Leland and his wife. It was heroic."

"Oh, it was hardly that!" she protested.

"I didn't have the courage to say anything, but you did."

She felt a surge of pity. "Jason, why don't you leave this town? Go somewhere and start fresh. You're wasted here."

"Where would I go, Alona? I left once and made a wreck of my life."

"You crashed a plane, but that's all. You could do anything you please. You've got greatness in you."

He laughed harshly. "You're the only one who sees it. Don't worry about me, Alona." When he left to hang out with a friend, she worried about the trouble that she saw lying ahead for this man for whom she felt such compassion.

CHAPTER SIXTEEN

A Season of Turmoil

★ ★ ★

"You can put your shirt on, Oscar."

Dr. Roberts stood back and watched as Oscar donned his shirt again. He was a cautious medical man, not quick to give opinions, and Oscar had been his patient for many years. As Oscar buttoned his shirt, the doctor said, "I expect you'd like me to give you some good word, but I can't do it."

Oscar knew Dr. Roberts was a blunt, straightforward individual like Oscar himself. He buttoned the last button, tucked his shirt in, and pulled up his suspenders. He picked up his tie from the chair and began to knot it. "It's the same old trouble, isn't it?"

"Yes it is, only worse."

"You said that the last time I was here."

"It *was* worse the last time you were here, Oscar. You wouldn't listen to me then, but you've got to listen to me now."

"All right, I'm listening. What's your verdict?"

"You're going to die if you don't take some precautions."

The man's harsh words struck Oscar hard. "That's pretty blunt, Doctor."

"I never had much of a bedside manner. You know that. But I'm telling you, Oscar, you've ignored this problem for years now, and I've seen too many people like you who thought they were immortal. I'm telling you the truth. Your heart is like a time bomb. You know what a time bomb is?"

"Certainly I know what a time bomb is! You think I'm a fool?"

"I *do* think you're a fool," he said calmly. "Because only a fool would run the risk you've been taking for the past five years or longer. Sit down. We've got to talk."

Slowly Oscar lowered himself into a chair. He fumbled for his pocket watch, which hung suspended by a thick gold chain, and frowned at it. "I've got to be back at the foundry, so get on with what you have to say."

Roberts sighed heavily. He leaned back against the wall and shook his head. "Has it ever occurred to you that you might not get back to the foundry?"

"What are you talking about?"

"I'm telling you, you could die before you get there."

"Don't try to scare me, Ed."

"I wish I *could* scare you! You're in bad shape, Oscar. Terrible shape, in fact. If you don't listen to me, you won't live six months."

"You can't know that."

"No, I don't know it, but I can make an educated guess."

"All right. Let's have the sermon. I know what's coming."

Dr. Roberts shrugged his beefy shoulders. "You know what I'm going to say. You're overweight, you never get any exercise, your diet is terrible, you drink too much wine, and your life is in a constant state of stress. Those are the things that could kill you."

Oscar's shoulders twitched restlessly. He had heard all this before, but now there was an ominous glare in his doctor's face. "Well, I'll try to do better." He rose to his feet, anxious to get away from this conversation.

"You're a foolish man, Oscar. You've got everything that most men want, and you're throwing it out the window. You've got a fine wife now and three boys who need guidance—it's everything you've always wanted. But you've got to take care of yourself or you won't live to enjoy it."

"I'm almost out of those pills you gave me. Give me a prescription for some more."

"These aren't vitamin pills. They're nitroglycerine—the same stuff that blows up buildings. What it does is open up your arteries. I'd hate to see the condition of your arteries with the way you like to eat. They're bound to be closed up tight. Now, you can't just gobble these pills like popcorn." He pulled his prescription pad out of his pocket, scribbled on it, and handed the sheet to Oscar. "I'll give you the prescription, but these won't solve your problems long-term. I'm your friend, Oscar. I'm telling you for your own good that you need to make some serious changes—starting right now."

Oscar took the prescription, fumbling with it as he stuck it in his shirt pocket. "Thanks, Ed. I really will amend my ways."

"I hope so. I'd hate to see you go like so many others I've seen."

Oscar nodded and left the office. As he stepped out into the bright sunlight, he paused and looked down the street. It was an ordinary day with people walking along the sidewalks going into shops. Cars and trucks were making their way along at a leisurely pace. Just an ordinary day, but suddenly he had a touch of fear. The doctor's words had cut deep, and he thought with chilling certainty, *Tomorrow I might not be here to see this street. I've got to be more careful!*

★ ★ ★

"I don't think you'll ever get the hang of it, Tim."

Helen had been trying to teach Tim how to ride a horse, but he just couldn't get comfortable in the saddle. By the end of their lesson, he felt as if he'd been bumped up and down like a pumpkin in a sack. And to top it off, he fell off the gelding when the horse made an abrupt turn. "Well, I never did claim to be a horseman."

Helen slipped off her filly. "That's enough for today. Let's get these animals unsaddled."

The two led their horses to the barn, where Tim proved more adept at unsaddling his mount than he had at riding him. After turning the horses out to pasture, Helen smiled at him. "Did you read that novel I gave you?"

"Yes, I did. It was pretty soupy. Nothing in it but hugging and kissing."

"Um-hmm. Doesn't that give you any ideas?"

Tim had steeled himself for this moment and now boldly took Helen by the upper arms and kissed her, almost missing her mouth in his nervousness. After a brief kiss, he stepped back. Then to his horror she giggled!

He glared at her, then whirled and started to walk stiffly away. Helen ran after him and caught his arm.

"Wait, Tim. I'm sorry. I didn't mean to hurt your feelings."

His face was rigid, for he knew he was out of his league. He knew Helen had gone out with some older, more experienced boys, and he was very nervous about what she expected of him. He said almost hoarsely, "I just don't know how to act around girls."

Helen had gotten to know Tim very well, for he was coming to her house on a regular basis now to see her mother. It amused her that he was more interested in art than in her. She was used to having boys flock to see her. "You're so funny, Tim. So different from other boys. I have to fight them off sometimes, but all you want to do is talk to Mom about art."

"I'm sorry if I'm not what you want me to be."

"Don't be mad." She smiled. "You remind me of Buddy. You pout just like he does when you get your feelings hurt."

"I do not!"

"Come on. Let's go in the house."

"No, I should be getting home."

"Mom said to bring you in after we got through riding. She wants to talk to ask you about your latest painting."

He hesitated. "Well . . . all right."

As they moved toward the house, Helen studied the lean young man. He was still very boyish looking but was starting to fill out and grow taller. She was a year older than Tim and was already quite womanly in appearance. She could have her pick of older boys, but Tim's innocence and naïveté appealed to her.

"Tim, why haven't you ever asked me out on a date?"

"Why, you're the most popular girl in our school, Helen. The important guys want to go out with you—the athletes and all."

"That doesn't mean I wouldn't like to have you ask me."

"Would you really?"

"Of course I would. I thought you would have guessed that by now."

"All right. I will." He thought hard about where he might ask her to go. "Would you like to go squirrel hunting with me next Saturday morning?"

Helen wanted to laugh at his innocence. "I've never been squirrel hunting. I don't think I could kill a nice little squirrel."

"I'm not a very good shot. I probably won't hit any, but it's nice to be out in the woods."

"All right. What time?"

"I'll come by about eight o'clock. That ought to give us plenty of time."

"It'll be my first date going squirrel hunting," Helen said. "I can hardly wait," she said with a giggle.

★ ★ ★

Tim made the final brush stroke on his latest painting, then stepped back. "What do you think, Jason?"

"It's not your best, but I like the way you've got that light coming through the trees. Light's a tough thing to handle."

"I know it. I struggled with that."

"You seem a bit disturbed today. Anything wrong?" Jason asked, studying the boy's face.

"I had a run-in with Oscar early this morning. He doesn't like me *wasting* my time painting. That's what he calls it!" Tim said bitterly.

"I know. I had the same argument with him when I was about your age. I lost the argument too. But I don't want you to."

"It makes it real hard. He gets along better with Carl and Zac than he does with me. Especially Zac."

"That's because Zac does what Oscar wants. He gets along with everybody who does what he wants."

"He doesn't get along with Mom."

Jason did not answer for a moment. "It's probably better if you and I don't talk about that. It's a very private matter between Oscar and your mom."

"All right. I won't talk about it." He put his paint-brush down. "I gotta talk to you about something, Jason."

"Okay. I'm listening."

"Umm, there's this girl that I like a lot."

Jason smiled. "Does she like you?"

"I think she does, but Jason, she's the most popular girl in the school. She can go with anybody she wants to."

"But if she likes you, what's the problem?"

"I don't know how to act around her. I tried to kiss her, and I made a mess out of it. You gotta tell me what to do."

Jason laughed. "You want me to give you kissing lessons?"

"Oh, come on, Jason, you know that's not what I mean! I just don't know how to act around girls. I feel awkward and embarrassed."

"So do I."

"Aw, you don't either."

"I do sometimes." He shrugged. "Women are complicated, and I hate to tell you this, Tim, but it doesn't get much easier as you get older. Let's sit down and you can tell me all about this girl."

Jason listened while Tim told him how the two had become friends and had started spending a fair amount of time together. Jason made no comment until Tim finally said nervously, "I like her a lot, Jason."

"The only advice I can tell you is to respect that girl and be yourself. You can't be another guy. You want her to like you for yourself. And she already does, right?" He smiled and clapped Tim on the shoulder. "A fine, upstanding artist like you that's going to be world famous, handsome, and charming."

"Aw, Jason, don't kid me like that!"

"I'm not kidding. You're a great kid. Just be yourself. She's lucky to have a boy like you interested in her."

★ ★ ★

For months now Alona's life had been divided into two distinct parts. One was the pleasure of seeing her boys well clothed and well fed and living in a comfortable fashion. This meant less to her than it did to them, however. Even though she was now surrounded by luxury she had never known before and could buy anything she wanted, it mattered little.

The luxuries that at one time might have made her happy and excited now left her cold, for the other side of her life was miserable. She'd had an exceptionally happy marriage to Truman. He had been a man of great wit, and until he was gone, she had never realized how much his humor had meant in their marriage. He had always been able to keep her spirits up by with his joking and teasing, and she missed it more than she had ever thought she would. She also missed the tenderness he showed her—the little things he did. She missed his habit of writing short messages on pieces of paper and putting them where she least expected them. He had hidden them inside the coffee can so that when she went to get the coffee in the morning, there was a little note from Truman saying, "I love you, sweetheart." He had been unafraid to express his affection to her alone or in company, something she now realized was very rare in a man.

As for the matter of the marriage bed, Oscar had practically terminated this aspect of their relationship— which gave her tremendous relief. There had been no pleasure at all in his embraces, for he was rough and demanding and insensitive. Ever since the church meeting concerning Leland Short, Oscar had kept his hands off her. It was obvious he still resented her actions in going against his wishes that night.

It was on a bright chilly November afternoon when she sat thinking of these things that Jason unexpectedly came home from work. She assumed he had forgotten something when he went straight downstairs to his bedroom.

"Jason, do you have a minute?" she asked, intercepting his path as he came up the stairs.

"Oh, hello, Alona. Yes, I had to come home and get some papers for the office that I forgot." He shook his head and a rueful expression crossed his face. "Oscar wasn't too happy about that."

"I've been wanting to talk to you. Is now a good time?"

"Sure." They went into the parlor and sat in matching armchairs. "What is it?"

"I'm worried about you, Jason."

He blinked with surprise. "What about?"

"About your drinking." He had been coming home drunk with some frequency, and even now she could see that he had been drinking the night before by the redness of his eyes.

He dropped his head, unable to meet her gaze. "I'm worried about it too. It gets the best of me sometimes. Nobody hates me worse than I do for that."

"You shouldn't hate yourself. I certainly don't hate you, Jason." She leaned closer and put her hand on his arm. "You've done so much for the boys, and I've become very fond of you." Alona, in all honesty, knew she had strong feelings for this man. But being a woman of strict morals, she had gone to great lengths to conceal this from Jason. She was usually careful to not even think about her attraction to him. "And the boys love you," she continued. "I've asked you this before, but don't you think it might be better if you left this place? It's not good for you to work for Oscar. I know he did a lot for you when you were younger, and he pulled you out of trouble after your crash. But he's not the kind of man who can sympathize with weakness."

"You're right about that." Jason was very conscious of her hand on his arm and started to speak, but at that moment Mrs. Darrow stuck her head into the room.

"There's a phone call for you, Mrs. Moran."

Instantly Alona dropped her hand. "I'll be right there. Thank you, Jason. Do what you can about the matter."

"I'll see what I can do."

As he left, Alona saw Mrs. Darrow watch him. Without a doubt, she would be telling Oscar the two had been caught alone in the parlor again.

★   ★   ★

As soon as Jason stepped into Oscar's office, he knew a storm was brewing. Oscar had been silent all day, but he had summoned Jason to his office and now he sat at his desk, his eyes as hard as flint.

"You wanted to see me, Oscar?"

"Yes, I wanted to see you." The words were flat and hard. "I've tried to be a help to you, Jason, but evidently that doesn't mean much to you."

Jason tried to think what could have stirred up Oscar this time. "You have been a help to me. I've never denied that."

"You don't act like it."

"What have I done now?" The words came out more bitterly than Jason intended. He had been through this scene many times, and he had no desire to go through it again.

"I've overlooked your drinking and your being unable to carry out your duties here at the foundry, but I can't overlook what you've been doing in my home."

An alarm went off in Jason's mind. "I don't know what you're talking about," he said flatly.

"I'm talking about the attention you pay to Alona."

"Why, that's crazy! I've nothing but respect for her."

"Is that why you meet with her in private every chance you get?"

"I don't go out of my way and neither does she."

"That's not true. Mrs. Darrow tells me you two are together all the time. You're an ingrate, Jason, and I'm not going to put up with it any longer."

"What does that mean?" he asked, although he knew Oscar was not a man given to idle threats.

"I mean I want you out of my house."

"All right. I'll get out today."

"And I don't want you in this foundry. I want you out of my life."

Jason stood staring at his half brother, and suddenly he was so tired of his own problems that he could hardly speak. He said in the sparest of tones, "All right. I'll be out of the house tonight, and you won't see me around here again. Thanks for all you've done for me, Oscar." He left the office, his mouth dry and his stomach in turmoil. All of his life he had been afraid of Oscar, and now it had come to this. "If that's what he wants," he mumbled, "then he can have it."

★   ★   ★

"What do you mean you fired him?"

"I was sick of his pestering you. I asked him to get out of the house, and I don't want him in the foundry."

"Oscar, you shouldn't have done that! He needs your help."

"I've given him my help, but he's broken trust with me. You think I don't see how you two look at each other?"

"Well, it's finally out in the open. You actually said it," Alona said.

"Yes. Can you deny it?"

"Of course I can deny it! I'm your wife, and I've been faithful to you in every way. You've made a mistake, Oscar, a bad mistake. It's not too late. Go to him and tell him you're sorry."

"Never."

"I feel sorry for you, Oscar," she said quietly. "You have no mercy for anyone who disagrees with your thinking."

As she left the room, Oscar felt an urge to go after her, to tell her he'd changed his mind, for he was already having second thoughts, but his pride prevented him from doing that. He slowly left the house, not knowing where he was going, only that he needed to get away.

CHAPTER SEVENTEEN

REDEMPTION OF A MAN

★ ★ ★

As soon as Tim stepped into the parlor, Alona knew that something was bothering him. She had learned to read this sensitive son of hers very well. He always had certain telltale signs when he was disturbed, and she read every one of them now as he halted irresolutely in the middle of the room.

"Come and sit by me, Tim. We haven't talked in a long time."

Tim came over to the couch and sat down slowly. Alona knew she would have to pull out whatever it was that was bothering him.

"You've done so much better in school this year," she started. "I'm very proud of you."

"At least I'm passing math this year. That ought to make Oscar happy."

"I'm sure it will." When he didn't say anything else, she said, "You haven't mentioned Helen much lately. Do you still like her?"

"Yeah. I still like her." He grinned and color filled his

cheeks. "She's real good with horses, Mom. You should see her ride."

"I'd like to do that sometime."

He fell silent again.

"Anything else going on?"

His lips drew together in a tight line. "Mom, why did Oscar make Jason leave the house? Why did he fire him at the foundry?"

Alona had been dreading this question but up until now had managed to say nothing to anyone. She wasn't sure how much of the truth she should give her son. "They had a disagreement. I think it was the wrong thing to do, and I said so."

"But what did Jason do?"

"You know, Tim, it's not a good idea to get involved with other people's arguments."

"Well, I don't think it's fair! Do you know that Jason's living in a ratty old room and that he's drinking all the time?"

"No, I didn't know that. How did you hear it?"

"Everybody knows it. They just don't tell you. Mom, I . . . I went to see him. As soon as I heard about it, I went to see him. I've been back three times. It's awful, Mom. That place is a dump."

"I'm not sure that was wise for you to do."

"You stood up for Mr. Short in church. Everybody knows about that, so why wouldn't it be the right thing for me to stand up for my friend?"

Alona had absolutely no answer for that. As a matter of fact, she felt proud of Tim, but she was walking a narrow line. "It's a tricky situation. We're living under Oscar's roof. He's my husband, and now he's in the place of your father."

"But he's wrong, Mom."

"I think it was a mistake, but Oscar doesn't think so."

"Well, I think it's terrible! He's his only brother, pretty

much his only kin, and he kicked him out like he was a bum. I know Jason has problems, but he's a good man."

"Yes, he is. A very good man. And yes, he does have problems, so we've got to pray for him, Tim."

Tim hesitated, fidgeting with his fingers.

"Is there something else bothering you?"

"Well, no not something else. Jason is sick. I went to see him this morning, and he was so sick he didn't even want to get out of bed, and he won't call a doctor. I tried to get him to let me go get Dr. Roberts, and he refused. It's awful, Mom. It's terrible!"

Alona's mind was racing. "Tim, I don't want you to go back."

"But, Mom!"

"You don't need to make a bigger rift between you and your stepfather. I'll go see him. If he's still sick, I'll get Dr. Roberts to stop by."

"Will you, Mom?" Tim asked, his eyes shining.

"Yes, I will, but this is just between you and me. Don't even talk to the other boys about it."

"Okay, Mom. I won't."

★　★　★

The note tacked to the outside door said "Come in," so Alona opened the door cautiously. The rooming house was in the worst area of town. Now she could smell the odor of cabbage and other more unsavory smells. She noticed the list of tenants' names, along with their room numbers, and she quickly spotted Jason's name.

She went up the stairs and found room two and knocked on the door. When there was no answer, she knocked again and said, "Jason, are you there?" She put her ear against the door and thought she heard a sound. Tentatively she tried the knob. The door was not locked, so she opened it and stepped inside. A single bulb hung from an overhead fixture, illuminating the squalor of the room. Jason was lying on a single bed, his eyes closed, and he had evidently not shaved for days. The room smelled terrible, and Jason looked terrible. His cheeks were sunken, and his face was flushed.

"Jason," Alona said and stepped closer. "Are you all right?" He twitched and then his head moved from side to side. His eyes opened slowly.

"Who . . . who is it?" he whispered hoarsely.

"It's me, Jason. Alona." She pulled a chair up to the bed and sat down beside him. "How long have you been sick?"

"Don't know." He coughed several times. "Four days . . . five."

She put her hand on his forehead. "You're burning up with fever. Have you seen a doctor?"

"No. Don't want a doctor."

Alona did not argue. "I'll be back."

"What for?" he asked bitterly. "Don't bother."

She did not answer but left the rooming house and immediately went to Dr. Roberts's office. She had to wait for half an hour before she got in to see him.

"My brother-in-law is very sick, Doctor," she told him, "and he won't come in to see you. Can you come with me to see him?"

"I'll get my bag," he responded without hesitation.

"Tell me how you're feeling, Jason." The doctor pulled a chair up close to the bedside while Alona watched from the far side of the room.

"I'm feeling pretty lousy," he responded.

"I figured that much, but give me some specifics. Start from the beginning.

"At first I thought I had a cold. But then it got worse and—" He started coughing. "I guess you noticed I have a cough," he said when he could speak again. "I'm hot. And my chest hurts—right here." He laid his hand on his chest.

"All right. Let's have a listen." He put his stethoscope on Jason's chest and then helped him sit up so he could listen from the back.

"Um-hmm. I think you've got a touch of pneumonia. You're going to need to get plenty of rest and drink lots of water and juice. You should start to feel better in a couple days."

Alona moved closer to the bedside. "I'll take good care of you, Jason."

"Excellent," the doctor said. "I'll come back and check on you tomorrow. Don't die on me."

"I will if I want to."

The doctor laughed. "I don't think you will."

When he left, Alona asked, "Are you hungry?"

"I don't know. I guess not much."

"I'm going to get you something from the café—some soup, a drink, and some ice."

"The ice would be good," Jason said, adjusting the sheet over himself. "You shouldn't be here, Alona. I've caused enough trouble between you and Oscar."

"I'll be back shortly," she said, ignoring his comment.

When the door closed, Jason lay staring at the ceiling. "Here I go again," he mumbled, "making more trouble for people."

★ ★ ★

Oscar was waiting for Alona when she got home that afternoon. "Is it true what I've heard?" he demanded.

"What have you heard?" she asked coolly.

"That you're nursing Jason in a run-down rooming house in the worst part of town."

"No, it's not true, although I do intend to do whatever I can to help him get better."

"So you've been there."

"Yes, I've been there, and I'm going back again."

"I forbid you to go!"

"You can forbid it all you want to, Oscar, but I think you're wrong again. You should be helping Jason. You're his brother."

"I won't have it."

"Then you'll have to do what you want to do. Throw me out if that's what you want, but I'm going to continue to do the right thing."

"You've always cared for him!"

"That's nonsense, Oscar. You're not thinking clearly." She saw his face was turning redder, and she said, "This stress isn't good for your heart. Look, I can't convince you that Jason and I are nothing more than good friends. You ought to believe it because it's true."

Oscar stared at her, a vein throbbing in his forehead. "I'm sorry I married you," he whispered.

Alona almost said, *I'm sorry too*, but instead she said, "Go lie down. This stress isn't good for you. I'm taking the spare bedroom."

"That will be up to you," he said evenly as he left the room.

She watched him leave, then shook her head in a swift denial of the way things were turning out. But there was nothing she could do about it.

★ ★ ★

Jason was feeling a little better the next day. Dr. Roberts was pleasantly surprised, and he told Alona, "He may feel like getting back to his normal activities in a couple days. Make sure he takes it easy until he's completely better."

"I wish you wouldn't talk about me as if I weren't here," he said grumpily.

"You just concentrate on taking care of yourself and getting healthy."

As soon as Dr. Roberts left, Jason said, "Why don't you go on home? I'm as grumpy as an old bear. It couldn't be any fun for you to be here."

"I'm going to stay until you drink that big glass of orange juice."

"That's going to take a few minutes, so you might as well take a seat."

Alona sat down and the conversation turned to her boys. "Carl is getting so tall," she commented. "I think he's grown an inch just since school started."

When Jason made no response, she said, "Jason?" Still no response. He was clasping his hands tightly together. "What's bothering you, Jason?"

He jerked his head toward her. "Sorry. I guess I wasn't listening." He ran his fingers through his hair. "You know, for a time there, I wasn't sure I was gonna make it. I thought I might die."

"But you didn't, and the doctor says you're going to be fine."

"Yes, thanks to you. I had some pretty vivid dreams while I was feverish. Scary ones." He looked down at his hands. "I'm tired of the way I've been living, Alona."

His statement made her ears perk up. She had been praying to hear him say this. "Then you can change, Jason."

"I'm not sure I can."

"You can with God's help."

"It's hard to believe that God still cares for me after the way I've lived."

"Jesus is the friend of sinners. That means He's *our*

friend, for we're all sinners." She quoted some Scriptures and spoke from her heart about how God had always provided for her and her family. She related the story of Paul and his amazing conversion from going out of his way to persecute believers to turning his life over to Christ completely.

"I know all about Paul," Jason reminded her. "But sometimes his story seems like something that happened so long ago. It's hard to believe that God can forgive me in the same way now—in modern times."

"Would you like me to pray with you, Jason?"

He looked up, and she saw tears in his eyes.

She folded her hands and closed her eyes. "Lord, I ask that you would receive Jason. Forgive his sins. Take him as your own and deliver him from all of the difficulties that have beset him. I pray especially that you would give him strength, that he might become a strong man of God. I know it will be hard for him, but walk beside him every step of the way as he grows in grace." She continued praying fervently for this friend and finally concluded with an enthusiastic amen.

Tears were running down his cheeks. She got out her handkerchief and handed it to him.

"I don't know how I'm going to make it, Alona, but I know that God did something to me while you were praying."

"I know he did. And I'm so glad." She took her handkerchief back. "I'll be praying for you and others will be too."

CHAPTER EIGHTEEN

A DISTANT THUNDER

★ ★ ★

Alona rose to her feet with the rest of the congregation after Brother Byron's sermon.

"I have presented unto you the Lord Jesus Christ," he was saying, "as the one who can save you from your sins, and now I want to give you an opportunity. If you want to follow Jesus Christ as your personal savior, as we sing this invitational hymn, I ask you to come forward and give your life to Him publicly.

The congregation joined together in singing "Just As I Am." Alona closed her eyes and prayed as she sang from the choir loft:

"Just as I am, without one plea
But that thy blood was shed for me.
And that thou bidst me come to thee
O Lamb of God, I come, I come."

She opened her eyes before the second verse started and saw Jason striding purposefully down the aisle. His head was up, and his eyes were bright as he came forward. Brother Byron had moved down in front of the podium, and the two men embraced each other. Tears came to her eyes, and her throat grew thick, making it impossible to sing. She gave a fervent prayer of thanksgiving to God for what was happening.

She looked at Oscar, who was sitting with the boys in his usual seat—four rows back on the inner aisle—watching Jason with a blank expression. *Oh, Oscar,* she thought. *Don't close your heart to your brother.*

Even as she watched the scene before her, she was thinking about what had happened to Jason since his illness. He had recovered fully and had taken a job selling furniture. She had not seen him since, but she kept hearing reports that he had quit drinking. He was such a dedicated worker at the furniture store that Fred Gibbons, the owner, was enthusiastically singing his praises. "Why, he's a fool for work," he had told Alona when they had met by chance at the bakery, "and he doesn't mind getting his hands dirty. He'll help the guys load the furniture on the truck and even deliver it. He's a good salesman too, and I'm lucky to have him."

Alona had expected Jason to come see her, but he had not. She suspected it was because he wanted to avoid Oscar at all costs. She wanted to tell Jason how proud she was of him, but she realized it was probably best that they not have too much contact. Strangely enough he had not been back to church since his illness three weeks earlier, but she had heard that he was visiting other churches. As much as she had wanted to see him, she knew he was being sensitive to Oscar's feelings by staying away, and ultimately she knew that was the right thing for him to do. Now it gave her great joy to see him in their church publicly giving his life to God.

"We will all rejoice together, for Jason Moran has given his heart to Jesus."

A chorus of *amen*s and *hallelujah*s arose, and Byron

smiled radiantly. "Jason has asked to say a word to you, so let's hear what he has to say."

"Most of you here today know that I have not been a godly man," he started. "I have been a slave to alcohol, and it almost took my life. Three weeks ago on a bed of sickness when one of the saints of God came to help me, I found the Lord Jesus Christ. I have long known that I was a sinner, but on that day I finally confessed it to God—" his voice broke and he took a moment to regain his composure—"and asked Him to save me in the name of Jesus. Since that moment, life has been different. I want to apologize to any of you who I have offended with my behavior. I would like to join this part of the body of Christ and follow Jesus in baptism."

Immediately Byron said, "Those in favor of accepting this dear brother into the fellowship of our church by baptism, let it be known by saying loudly amen."

The *amens* rocked the room. Alona joined them. She glanced down at her boys in the fourth row, and all of them were grinning broadly. Zac held his thumb and forefinger together and waved it at her. She wanted to do the same but just smiled instead.

Brother Byron was speaking now, but she heard little of what he said, for she was filled with joy. The only thing that troubled her was the uncaring expression on Oscar's face.

"After the benediction, I want you all to come and welcome Jason into our family," the pastor said. He pronounced the blessing and then many people made their way to the front of the church.

Oscar shouldered his way out through the crowd. Alona joined the other choir members who were forming a line to greet Jason. When it was her turn, she took his hand and whispered, "I'm so happy for you, Jason."

"I'll never forget you, Alona. As long as I live, I'll

remember how you prayed for me. And I hope you'll keep on praying for me."

"I will, Jason," she said and then moved quickly on.

The boys surrounded her, and Tim's eyes were especially bright. "Isn't it great, Mom? Isn't it just great!"

"Yes, it's great, Tim."

"You think he'll come back and live at Mr. Oscar's house?" Carl said.

"I . . . don't know. We'll just have to see."

"I hope he does," Zac said. "I miss shootin' pool with him and other stuff."

Alona had little hope that Oscar would open his home to Jason, but she could not dampen the boys' enthusiasm. "Let's go home. I've got a nice lunch planned."

Oscar did not say a word on their way home, although the boys chattered on about Jason's new status within the church. Alona was apprehensive that one of them might bring up the subject of Jason being invited back into the house, but they said nothing of that. They knew that Oscar made all those decisions.

When they got home Oscar said, "I'm not hungry. Don't fix me any lunch."

"Don't you feel well?" Alona asked, studying his face.

"I'm all right. Just not hungry."

Alona went to the kitchen and threw herself into making a good lunch for herself and the boys. Mrs. Darrow had Sundays off, and Alona always enjoyed cooking the meal after church.

She was making the topping for the blackberry cobbler the boys all loved when the three of them came rushing in.

"Mom," Zac cried, "come and listen to the radio!" His eyes were wild with excitement.

"What's on the radio?"

"The Japanese have bombed Hawaii! Come on and listen."

Wiping her hands on her apron, Alona went at once into the parlor. The radio announcer was obviously shaken. "We have no reports of how many have died," he was saying, "but we do know that our navy, which was stationed in Hawaii at Pearl Harbor has been attacked by Japanese planes. The attack comes after the Japanese representatives had been in Washington speaking of peace. Stay tuned as we bring you the late-breaking bulletins as they come in."

"Golly, that means we're at war!" Tim exclaimed.

"We'll have to fight those Japanese, won't we, Mom?" Carl piped up.

"I don't know. Maybe it's all a mistake," she said.

"No, they've been talking about it, Mom. They're dropping bombs on our ships there."

Alona sank down on the couch in disbelief and listened. The announcer kept breaking in with new bulletins, but it was obvious that the United States was now at war.

A smothering fear came over her as she sat between her oldest and her youngest son. She was thankful that Tim was still too young to fight, but she thought of all the thousands of mothers who would have to let their sons go to war. She put her arms around Tim and Carl and looked down at Zac, who was sitting on the floor staring at the radio. *Oh, God, I'm so afraid,* she prayed. *Please take care of all those families that have lost sons and fathers and brothers on this terrible day.*

★ ★ ★

The day after the deadly and explosive assault, President Roosevelt addressed the nation. "America was suddenly and deliberately attacked by naval and air forces of the empire of Japan," he said. "We will gain the inevitable triumph, so help us God."

War was declared immediately, with only one dissenting vote in Congress: that of Jeannette Rankin, Republican representative from Montana. In his address, the president declared December 7, 1941, a date "which will live in infamy." America was stunned, and no one who was alive in America on that particular day would ever forget what they were doing when they got the news that the United States was now thrown into a terrible world war.

★ ★ ★

In the days following the declaration of war against Japan, Jason listened to newscasts while he studied maps, following the progress of the war. He took long walks when he wasn't working and spent many hours praying. He talked to no one about this, but he finally made an important decision and knew that he had to tell two people—Oscar and Alona.

He waited until most of the workers at the foundry were gone, knowing that Oscar was usually one of the last ones to leave. He walked into the foundry, where he had spent so many years, uncertain of what kind of reception he would get. He knocked on Oscar's office door, and when he heard his brother's gruff "Come in," he stepped inside.

Oscar was standing at a filing cabinet, and he turned at once and stared at Jason. "What is it?" he demanded.

"I won't be around much longer, Oscar, and I just wanted to come before I left and tell you I'm sorry that

I've given you such grief. I know I've been a bad brother, and you've done so much to help me. You've been a good father to me—a good brother too—and I care for you deeply. I'd like to ask you to forgive me for all the trouble I've caused you."

Oscar stood stock-still. His face was hard, and he said gruffly, "I suppose you can't help being the kind of man you are." He seemed to brush aside Jason's plea for forgiveness and asked instead, "Where are you going?"

"I'm going to sign up with the army. My country needs me."

Oscar seemed to struggle with himself, then asked brusquely, "Do you need anything?"

"No, thank you. I'm all right." Jason took a step forward and put out his hand. "This is good-bye for a while. Will you shake hands with me?"

"I don't believe in sentimentalism. I doubt you'll make it in the army any better than you did in the navy."

Jason dropped his hand. "I'm sorry you feel that way, Oscar. I know I've failed in the past, but I've got hope for my future. Good-bye."

Oscar watched his half brother leave, then when the door closed, he went quickly to the door and grabbed the handle. He started to turn it but then stopped and stood frozen. He finally released the handle. *He'll either be back or I'll have to go pull him out of a hole again. It's always been that way.*

★ ★ ★

"Why, Jason, I wasn't—" Alona started.

"You weren't expecting me," he said. "I know, but I need to see you for a few moments."

"Please come in."

Jason stepped inside the house and saw that she was

feeling awkward. "I won't be but a minute, Alona."

"Come into the parlor," she said as she led the way. "Won't you sit down?" she offered.

"Yes, but I won't be here long. I've just been to see Oscar at the foundry."

Alona was instantly alert. "What did you say to him, Jason?"

"I asked him to forgive me for all the trouble I've been in his life and told him that I cared for him."

"What did he say?" Alona asked, her eyes fixed on Jason's.

"He still has some hard feelings, I'm afraid, but I hope he'll get over them."

"I hope so too. You've really turned your life around. Mr. Gibbons says you'll be running the store if you keep on doing as well as you have."

He shook his head and smiled. "I won't be doing that, Alona."

"Why not?"

"Because I won't be here. This war has changed everything."

At that moment Alona knew exactly what Jason was going to say. "You're going to join the service, aren't you?"

"Yes, I am. I'll be joining the army today, and I hope to be leaving immediately."

"You mean the Army Air Corps?"

Jason looked surprised. "Why, no. Just the army. I'll be a foot soldier in the infantry, I expect."

"Jason, you mustn't do that."

"I've got to do my part!"

"I know that, but there are many young men who can serve in the infantry. You've had special training. You could go into the Army Air Corps or you could join up with the navy again and do what you do best, which is flying. How many young men are there out there who already know how to land a plane on an aircraft carrier?"

"That's what I used to do best, but you know I can't go back."

"Jason, I don't believe that." Her eyes were flashing. "You've got to give your very best. Not just for your country but for the Lord. The Bible says, 'Whatsoever thy hand findeth to do, do it with all thy might.'"

"But I can do that carrying a rifle."

"I feel very strongly about this, Jason. I have for a long time. If all this hadn't come up, I was going to beg you to go back to the navy and try again."

"I never even thought of such a thing," he said.

"Think about this. When you failed before, you were not God's man, but you are now. You're a servant of the Lord Jesus Christ. You can call upon Him, and He will give you the strength to do whatever you need to do. Please, Jason, don't throw this opportunity away. I think a door has been put before you, and if you don't go through it, you'll regret it for the rest of your life."

He passed his hand across his face. "You just don't know what I went through—how awful it was to be filled with fear. When I got in the plane for the first time after the accident, it was as if everything inside me crumbled."

"The Bible says that God has not given us a spirit of fear but of power, love, and a sound mind. You've got all of that, Jason—power, love, and a sound mind. Jesus is your Savior. I feel strongly that God would have you do this."

Jason didn't know what to say, and Alona went on, "I prayed with you once. Will you let me pray with you again about this?"

"Sure, Alona. Go ahead."

She began to pray, not only for Jason but for all the other young men and women who would be going into

harm's way. "Lord, Jason has a new heart now. He's not
the man he was when he failed before. I know that you
can give him the courage and strength to do this job, and
I ask you right now to lay it upon his heart to do it. In
Jesus' name. Amen."

Jason opened his eyes, and she saw a startled look on
his face. "It's happened again," he said, a grin pulling at
his mouth.

"What's happened?"

"When you prayed for me back in the rooming house,
I sensed the immediate presence of God. And it's happened again." He took her hands in his and gave them a
quick squeeze. "Alona, I'm going to try."

"That's wonderful, Jason. I know God will be with
you."

"I'll join the navy if they'll give me another chance,
but I'll join the army as a regular soldier if they won't."

"The boys and I will be praying for you every day."

"I'll need it." He stood and said, "Well, this is good-
bye for a while."

"Good-bye, Jason, and God keep you."

She followed him to the front door, and when he
opened it he turned around and studied her, memorizing
her features. As far as he knew, this might be the last
time he'd see this woman. He took in the self-possessed
curve of her mouth, her fair complexion, and the smooth
ivory of her throat.

He had loved her for a long time but had never said
so because of her marriage to Oscar. Now he couldn't
leave her without letting her know his true feelings.
"Alona, I know it won't ever come to anything—there
are too many things against it—but I want you to
know . . . I love you. I've loved you for a long time."
Without another word he left, walking away at a rapid
gait. He got into his car and drove off without even a
wave.

Alona stood there shocked and shaken. She felt tears flood her eyes and she began to sob. "O God, forgive me, but I love him too. Take care of him, Lord, and keep him safe."

PART FOUR

December 1941–December 1942

★ ★ ★

CHAPTER NINETEEN

"HE CAN'T CUT IT!"

★ ★ ★

Staring out the window from his desk in Pensacola, Florida, Commander Lloyd Baker should have been happy, for the weather was beautiful. Having grown up in Boston, he was accustomed to heavy snows, freezing weather, and generally miserable conditions. Miserable for flying, that is, which pretty much consumed his life. Now the sun shone bright and brilliant, even in mid-December. He noticed a group of his pilots throwing a baseball around laughing, most of them wearing shorts and T-shirts.

"They'd better enjoy that," Commander Baker growled deep in his throat. "Where they're going, they won't be tossing a baseball around very much." Glancing up at the calendar on the wall, he noted the date: December 15, 1941. Only eight days since Japan had opened the door to an all-out war for the United States of America. The bright sunshine outside made a stark contrast with the dark gloominess that filled Lloyd Baker's mind. He, along with other pilots who flew for the U.S. Navy, had foreseen the situation coming. It had infuriated Baker, but he had been unable to convince any of the higher-ups of the military world, and certainly not of the political world, that Japan was not going to lie down and roll over.

Getting up from his chair, Baker walked over and looked out the window at the landing field. He counted the Douglas SBD-3 Dauntless dive bombers and the Douglas TBD Devastator torpedo bombers and shook his head. "Too few," he said loudly. "Not near enough."

A knock interrupted his thoughts, and he barked, "Come in!" Baker had the habit of speaking sharply even when he gave a cheery good morning to the men in his command. As he expected, Captain Hack Odom came through the door and saluted sloppily. *Odom does everything sloppily,* the commander thought as he returned the salute crisply. Everything, that is, except fly the Dauntless aircraft. That he did with precision, speed, accuracy, and a deadly attitude toward the enemy. But the man's uniform, as always, looked as if he had slept in it, and he seemed to have a perpetual problem with standing at attention. The commander had to laugh. "You look like you just got out of the drunk tank in Boston, Hack."

"I'm disappointed you should say that, sir. I paid a lot of attention to my personal appearance this morning."

Hack Odom was a short man built like a beer keg. He had bristly black hair that he kept cut short and always needed a shave—or seemed to. His face, which reminded Lloyd of a bulldog, was broad, tough, and scarred—a broken nose and a cauliflower ear testifying to a violent past. He had played football for the navy and could have gone into the pros, but he was a navy man to the bone.

"Sit down, Hack. I've got a problem."

"You've got more than one, Commander." Hack grinned. "You've got the whole Japanese Navy to get rid of."

"You're right about that, and not enough manpower or equipment to do it with. How is your squadron looking?"

"A bit spotty. The boys are all hopped up about the Japs, but they think the way to answer that is to pour on the coal. Don't think that'll work too well."

"I'm afraid you're right about that, Hack. They've got us outgunned."

"But they didn't get our carriers at Pearl," Hack said quickly. "That's the good news."

"They're the only thing that can save our bacon. We both know that. We're going to meet up with them sooner or later. This will be a carrier war in the Pacific. Battleships don't count anymore."

Hack laughed. "I know some admirals who would have you busted for saying a thing like that, sir."

"Old fossils! Should have been put on the beach years ago."

"Well, General Billy Mitchell tried to reform the navy. You know what happened to him."

The two men sat silently for a moment, thinking about the man who had had the right idea but was too early for the brass above him.

"I wish we had Billy back with us now," Lloyd Baker said wistfully. "We could use him."

"Sure could. But we've got some good boys coming up. They just need the whip. It's funny. I see these young guys coming in, and it's like when I go to a doctor now. I put my life in a kid's hand who looks like he ought to be taking up tickets at a movie theater."

"It takes young fellows to fly the Dauntless. You know that better than I do, Hack."

The two men reminisced for a time, and all the while Hack Odom was aware that his commanding officer was holding something back. Finally he grinned and said, "You're trying to give me some bad news, sir. Why don't you just give it to me and be done with it?"

Baker returned the grin. "Am I that easy to read? Remind me never to play poker with you." He rocked back and forth in his chair a few times and then stopped himself. "I've got a problem, but it's not necessarily a bad problem."

"It's a good problem, then."

"It could be good. Have you ever heard of Jason Moran?"

"Don't believe I have. Who is he?"

"He was a pilot. He flew under me when I was a squadron commander just like you are now. He sailed through our whole program at the top of his class. Best flier I ever saw, Hack."

"Better than me?"

"Nobody's better than you, but he could have been."

"What happened?"

"He had some tough luck. That fellow could put the bomb on the target better than any flier I've ever seen. It was almost like magic. Give Jason a plane and a bomb, and he could put it right down a smoke stack no more than two feet wide."

"It sounds like the kind of fellow we need. Where is he?"

"He's here on the base. He wants to join up again."

"So what's the problem? If he can put the bomb on the target—"

"There's more to it than that. He crashed his plane, Hack. Mechanical failure. It wasn't his fault, but after that he lost his nerve."

Odom frowned. "Lots of fellows have problems with that, especially after a bad crash."

"It really wasn't that bad. He walked out of the wreckage with a couple bruises and scratches. I was with him the next day when we put him in a new plane. He couldn't do it."

"What do you mean he couldn't do it?"

"He couldn't even take off, Hack. The rest of us went on our mission, and Moran just sat there on the ground. When I came back, I saw he was a mess. His hands were shaking, and I'd never seen that before. He had always been real cool. Never nervous. I asked him what was the matter."

"What did he say?"

"He couldn't say anything except, 'I can't do it.'"

"What? That's all?"

"Yep. But we kept him around. I talked to him. We had the shrinks talk to him. He was fine until he got into the cockpit, and then he would begin to tremble. Couldn't do a thing."

"What did you do with him?"

"What could I do? He washed out, of course. He only had a few months to serve. He left. I lost track of him—that is, until he walked into my office yesterday. He wants to join up again."

"Has he been up since his problem started?"

"He says not. Of course I told him we couldn't use a pilot that couldn't take off."

"What'd he say?"

"He didn't argue. He said, 'I'd like another chance, but if you won't take me, I'll go into the infantry.'"

"I guess Pearl Harbor changed his mind. Changed a lot of minds."

"I suppose so. I told him he'd have to prove himself before I'd take him."

"And you want me to check him out. Is that right, sir?"

"That's right."

"That shouldn't be any trouble. He either can take off or he can't. Where is he?"

"He's out on the field. I got him geared up, and he's waiting."

"Okay. I'll go see if he can get off the ground."

"I hope he makes it. He's a likable fellow, Hack. But more important than that, we need every man we can get, and we need them right now! The old Moran I knew would be ready to go. So go put him in a plane."

"Yes, sir, I will, and I'll report back. It may not take long."

"I hope he makes it. We need men like that, at least men like he was. I'll be anxious to hear your report, Hack."

Jason had donned his flight suit and waited in the shade of the building. The pilots were laughing and joking; some of them glanced at him curiously but said nothing.

"Moran?"

He got up at once and saluted the short, stocky officer who was wearing flight gear. "Jason Moran, sir."

"I'm Captain Hack Odom, the squadron leader. I've been talking to Commander Baker. He tells me you have a problem."

"Yes, sir, I've had a problem."

"What makes you think you can fly now? You couldn't the last time you were in a plane."

"I don't know that I can."

Odom stared at the young man. Moran was pale and obviously tense. "What's that supposed to mean?"

"I won't know if I can fly until I get in an airplane."

"We don't have time for psychological treatment here, Moran. We're going on a training mission. We'll be dropping our bombs on a target. You've been through all that before."

"Yes, sir."

"No sense talking, then. You either can or you can't. Let's go."

Jason walked across the field. The concrete was blisteringly hot under his feet, and the sun was blazing down. They approached one of the planes, and Captain Odom said, "Turner, take a break."

Lieutenant Turner looked surprised but merely nodded. "Yes, sir," he said. "If you want to eat something, tell me what it is and I'll go eat it for you."

"Get out of here." Odom laughed shortly and then addressed Jason. "You take this ship and fly on my right wing." He went on to show him a photo of the training area and showed him where he should drop his bomb.

As Odom went to his own plane, something like an invisible cloud settled over Jason. He was aware of the planes, of the roar of engines, of the shouts of the men to their mechanics, of the white clouds drifting lazily across the sky, but he felt almost detached from the situation. His mind kept trying to go back to the moment before impact when he had crashed. He half expected his hands to begin to tremble and perspiration to break out all over his face, but somehow that did not happen. A sergeant was at his side and asked, "Are you ready, sir?"

Jason glanced around to see that the other pilots were climbing into their planes. He said, "Yes, sergeant." He got into the plane, and the sergeant checked his harness. He was conscious of the parachute pressing against him, of the controls and the stick. He automatically checked the instruments and throttled up the engine.

"Good luck, sir!" the sergeant yelled and disappeared. Suddenly a voice blasted into his ear through the radio in his helmet. "Ready for takeoff!"

Jason gripped the throttle and waited for the mindless terror to overtake him as it had the last time he had sat in the cockpit of a Dauntless.

But it did not come! Expertly he advanced the throttle, and the Dauntless stirred under his touch. He glanced out and saw the squadron leader, Hack Odom, watching from another plane. He nodded, and Odom returned the nod. Then Jason moved his aircraft forward.

As Jason taxied into position to begin his takeoff, he kept waiting for the old fear to paralyze him. He expected it. He was going through this mainly because he had promised Alona he would, but now as the plane began to gain speed, he felt an emotion he had not felt since he had flown before the accident. It was joy and exhilaration.

"It's all gone! I'm not afraid!" he said aloud, forgetting that his radio was open.

Hack Odom's voice came crackling into his ear. "Keep off the radio, Moran! Nobody cares whether you're afraid or not. Now, follow me."

The Dauntless was obedient in his hands. Jason took off smoothly and jammed himself immediately under the right wing of the squadron leader.

"Get out of my pocket, will you!" Odom snapped. "We're not flying closed formations."

"Yes, sir."

The sky was large and spacious, and as Jason rose up along with his squadron, following the formations Captain Odom was putting them through, he began to praise God. *I know this is you, O Lord, and I thank you for it. I know it was the prayers of others that brought me here. Thank you for taking away the fear. Help me to serve with honor and to always remember that you have not given us the spirit of fear.*

He gunned the engine, and ten minutes later dropped his bomb right on target. He held it until the last possible moment, pulled out with a screaming of engines, and felt the lightness of his head as he was pulled back into the seat. He resumed his formation, and he saw Hack Odom give him a thumbs-up.

"How did he do, Hack?"

"Why, there was nothin' to it. He got in that airplane

and stayed right with us as we went through some pretty rough formations. And then when we dropped the bombs, he was right on target."

"Did you talk to him?"

"Sure did. As soon as we landed. I never saw a fellow so happy. He kept saying that he wasn't afraid. I think he's some kind of religious nut. He said God took away all his fear."

"He's probably right."

"Maybe so. Anyway, I checked him out every way I can think of. He may be the best pilot I've got right now."

"Good. We're going to need him."

"You think it'll be soon?"

"I think the Japs will move across the Pacific with everything they've got, and we're all this country's got to stop them."

★　★　★

When Alona picked up the phone and said hello, the person on the other end didn't bother with greetings.

"Alona, it worked! I can fly!"

"Jason, that's wonderful!" she exclaimed. "Tell me all about it."

She listened as the words tumbled out of him. He could hardly speak fast enough. "It was all your prayers that did it. I know it was."

"And others were praying for you too, Jason."

"But you were the first. You were the one who talked me into it. I'm so happy, Alona. Everything's different now."

She felt a sudden twinge. "What will happen now, Jason?"

"Well, since I've already had my training, I won't be here at the base very long."

"You'll be . . . you'll be leaving?"

"Oh, sure. But don't worry. I'm with a good squadron. Got a good squadron leader. There are good men here. It's exactly what I needed to do. I don't think I'll ever be the same again."

Fear gripped Alona as she realized she had put him in harm's way. *If something should happen* . . . "Be careful, Jason. Please promise that you will."

He laughed. "Okay. I promise. Now, tell me what's going on at home."

She told him about the boys. "Tim painted a picture of Helen on her filly. It's very good. Mrs. Arnette has entered it into a national contest. She thinks it has a good chance to win."

"I hope so. What about . . . what about Oscar?"

"Well, he's doing all right. His heart is still not very strong, and he got a huge order from the army for the foundry. They've started working double shifts now and may put on a third."

"Oscar never knew how to do anything halfway. Try to make him take care of himself."

"I try, but you know your brother."

"Alona, I'm going to write him a letter and tell him again how much I appreciate him. He's done a lot for me. Do you think it'll be all right if I write to you?"

She hesitated. "I don't know, Jason."

"I just thought it would be nice to tell somebody what's happening to me, and I'd like to hear about the boys."

"I . . . I suppose that would be all right."

"Alona, I know I shouldn't have told you how I felt about you. I wasn't thinking. But I don't want it to be a burden to you. I'll never mention it again."

"No, you mustn't, Jason."

"I promise. But do write to me and tell me all about

what's happening."

There was a moment of silence then, both of them very much aware of the dangerous world into which Jason Moran was moving.

"I'll pray for you every day," she said quietly.

"Thank you, Alona. Good-bye for now."

"Good-bye." She hung up the phone, and a heavy spirit settled on her. She realized it was not going to leave until the war was over and Jason was safely back home.

CHAPTER TWENTY

"I Never Gave Death a Thought"

★ ★ ★

"I'm sorry, Mrs. Moran. You don't have enough coupons left to get all of your groceries."

Alona picked up her ration book and frantically thumbed through it. "I was sure I had enough."

The grocer shook his head regretfully. "I'd like to help you out, but you know how it is with the government these days. They're watching over these ration stamps like they were money."

Alona had not yet become accustomed to the new rationing system the government had imposed. Each person in a household was given a book with stamps in it, and now it was necessary at the grocery store not only to have money, but also the stamps. She was fortunate with her three boys to have enough of the stamps, as a rule, but she had left two of the books at home.

"Couldn't you let me give you the stamps the next time I come?"

"I'd like to, ma'am, but they're pretty strict. There's a war on, you know."

Alona gave Stevens a hard look. "Yes, I know," she said curtly. "But somehow I don't think it's going to make a great difference in the outcome if you let me bring you the stamps next time."

"But if I let you get by, I'd have to let everybody else. I'm sure sorry, but rules are rules."

"Very well. Take all the groceries out that I don't have stamps for," Alona said in a resigned tone. She watched as the clerk removed several items. "Will that make you happy?"

"Really it ain't me, Mrs. Moran."

"Oh, I know it. I'm sorry. I guess the war news has made me gloomy."

"It ain't good, is it? I thought our boys would do better."

"Well, you have to remember that we weren't pre-pared for this. Our troops were ill armed and not ready for what the Japanese are throwing at them."

Gathering her purchases, Alona left the store. She put the groceries in the car, then drove directly to the church. When she got there, she went inside and found Pastor Sandifer in his office.

When he looked up, his eyes grew bright, and he got to his feet. "Alona, I'm glad to see you. Come in and sit down. I was going to come by and visit with you later today."

"As you know, I've been directing the choir now that Brother Paul has joined the army," she said as she sat down. "I was wondering if you've had any success in finding a permanent replacement for him."

"I've got a lead on a young woman who might do very well for us, although she's reluctant to leave the church where she directs now until the end of the school year."

"She's probably right that April isn't a good time to take a new position. I'd be happy to work with the choir until we go on break for the summer."

"That would be excellent, Alona. I appreciate your willingness to do that."

The two chatted about the affairs of the church, and eventually their conversation turned to the war. "Things look pretty grim in the Pacific," Brother Byron said. "Have you heard from Jason?"

"Yes, I have. Just a V-mail. You can't say much on that little sheet of paper. Several of his sentences were scratched out by the censor."

"He wrote me too. Thanked me for what the church had meant to him. He sure sounds like a different man, doesn't he?"

"I believe he *is* a different man. He was always so beaten down and cowed, and now when I read in the papers about all the fierce fighting that's going on, I can't help being afraid for him."

"It is hard," Sandifer said, nodding. "Nobody knows exactly what's happening, but one thing for sure, there's going to be a big battle someday when our carriers meet up with those Jap carriers."

Alona stood up, not wanting to say more. Indeed, she had been burdened with concern for Jason and for several other young men from their town who had signed up to serve immediately after Pearl Harbor was bombed. Many of the others, however, were still in training camps, while she had the feeling that Jason was in the very heart of the battle.

"One other thing," the pastor said as he got up as well. "Would you mind going by and seeing Julie Donaldson? She just got word yesterday that her husband was killed in Corregidor. She's got two small children, and she's pretty devastated."

"I'd be glad to, although I don't know what I can say."

"There's really not much that we can say. Nothing can ever heal the wound of losing a husband. She just needs someone to be with her, listen to her. I was there yesterday and again this morning, but women do this sort of thing much better than men, I think."

"I'd be glad to go."

"You know where she lives, don't you?"

Alona nodded. "I'll go straight there."

★ ★ ★

Jason approached the carrier, and as always, experienced a moment of fear. To put a Dauntless dive bomber down on the heaving deck of a carrier that looked no bigger than a postage stamp from the air was always a challenge. Already three pilots had misjudged their landing. One of them had been killed, and two others had been fished out of the sea. Jason had a natural gift for this sort of thing, however, and expertly came in with the nose high, and he felt the cable grab. The impact threw him forward as the plane was halted abruptly. He sat there for a moment while the men who cared for the planes swarmed over it. He undid his safety belt and climbed out, finding that his legs were so stiff they felt weak.

"You feeling okay, Lieutenant?" Jim Abraham was a neat young man from New Mexico. He took care of the plane as if it were his own private property and at times even scolded Jason for treating it roughly.

"I'm all right, Jimmy. Just stiff."

"That was a long flight. You see anything?"

"Lots of ocean."

"No carriers, huh?"

"Not yet."

"We'll see 'em one day, and when we do, you and *The Daisy* here will sink one of them carriers." Jimmy had called the aircraft *The Daisy* ever since he had started working on it. The two men worked closely together, and nobody knew better than Jason how important it was that the airplane be in tip-top shape. He knew it would be, as Jimmy always took care of it.

Jason joined Tommy Edwards and the other pilots who were walking wearily across to the island.

"I'm gonna give you some more lessons on landing on a carrier," Tommy told Jason teasingly.

"Why, I'd appreciate that, Tommy." In fact, Tommy had wrecked two planes already and was the most inept pilot in the squadron at landing a plane. He was, however, an expert at everything else. It was only the landings that gave him problems.

Captain Hack Odom, the squadron leader, overheard the two and said, "We're gonna run out of airplanes if you don't stop crashing them, Edwards."

"Oh, I reckon I've broken the habit, Captain. When are you going to find us some of them Jap carriers? I want to get a medal. Plan to sink two or three by myself."

Odom liked to see cockiness in a pilot and possessed some of that quality himself. "I'll see what I can do. I don't guess the rest of us even need to bother going if you're going to handle it all."

"That's all right. You fellows can come along," Edwards said airily, waving his hand in an eloquent gesture. "You can confirm all my kills."

A laugh went up from the other pilots. Everybody liked Tommy, even though he wasn't the best pilot.

The men made their way to the mess hall, joking all the way. Jason grinned at the tall black man who was putting food on the plates. "What do you have for us today, Tall Boy?" Jason asked. "Something fit to eat, I hope."

"Now, Lieutenant, don't you be bad mouthin' my cookin'."

"I won't. You're a great cook. When I get rich and famous, I'm going to hire you to cook for me."

"Didn't know you was that rich, Lieutenant." Tall Boy grinned.

"Well, I'm not yet, but I may be someday. When the war is over, then I'll get rich."

A great deal of howling and gyration arose from Jeff Tombs. "I bet you own one of them big cotton plantations, Moran. Have folks waitin' on you hand and foot."

"That's me. Just like *Gone With the Wind*."

"You got a Miss Scarlett waitin' for you back there on that plantation?" Tombs asked.

Jason's face suddenly lost its grin. "No, not me." A silence fell on the room, for at one time or another, all of them had tried to find out what kind of life Jason had led. Most of the others had been willing to talk about their family and their background, but Jason had said almost nothing. He was the crack flier of the squadron, surpassing even Hack Odom, which many had sworn could never be done.

Jason ate methodically. He had almost become a machine. Eat, sleep, get up, fly. Come back, eat, sleep, get up, fly. So far the men had seen absolutely no action, but still every flight was a nerve-wracking experience. They flew long sweeps, and fuel consumption became a problem. Finding a carrier in the middle of a trackless ocean was a feat that was difficult for most people to conceive. On each flight the men were wary, for rumors were circulating that the Japanese were on the prowl in the Pacific. They had some huge carriers, and their pilots were good. The Americans knew this much.

When Jason finished his meal, he complimented Tall

Boy and then went to his bunk, which he shared with Tommy Edwards and Jimmy Abraham. They had stayed at the mess hall to play poker, but that particular vice had little appeal for Jason. He lay down, picked up his Bible, and began to read. Something had happened to him when he had completely given himself to God back in Jonesboro. Before that time, the Bible had been pretty much a dead book to him, but now it was living indeed! He was finding the book of John and the Psalms to be his favorite books. He began reading now in the Psalms. He read aloud in a soft whisper and after a time put the Bible down and turned his heart to prayer. He prayed for the members of his squadron, for Alona and her boys, and finally for Oscar. . . .

★　★　★

Alona heard the boys shouting and went outside. They had gathered a wagonload of what appeared to be junk. "What on earth have you boys got?"

"Aluminum, Mom. Haven't you heard about the aluminum drive? It's to build airplanes with," Zac said. His eyes were bright as he added, "Look at all we got!"

"Yeah, we need some of your pans, Mom," Carl said.

"Or whatever else you have that's made of metal," Tim put in.

"All right. Let's see if Mrs. Darrow has some extra things she can part with." She and the boys went into the kitchen and started looking through the cupboards. They would have taken every pan in the house if she had not kept them from it.

Leah Darrow came scurrying in, her eyes wide. "Mrs. Moran," she said, "you have to come quick."

"What is it, Mrs. Darrow?"

"It's Mr. Oscar. He's in the hospital."

"Did he have an accident?"

"No, ma'am, the doctors say it's his heart, and they say for you to come right now."

"I'll go right away."

"We want to go with you, Mom!" Zac insisted.

"No. You boys stay here. I'll call as soon as I find out how serious it is."

Alona left the house and drove at once to the hospital. When she got there, she ran inside to the reception desk. "I believe Mr. Oscar Moran was just brought in?"

"Yes. He's in intensive care. It's on the second floor."

When she reached the intensive care ward, she encountered Dr. Roberts coming out. "What is it, Doctor?"

"He had a heart attack, Alona. It doesn't look good."

"But he seemed to be doing better lately. He hasn't had any chest pains for a few weeks, at least."

"That's the way these things are." Dr. Roberts shook his head. "I've been warning him for years. He works too many hours, and he hasn't lost weight."

"He'll be all right, won't he?"

"I hope so. But his heart is in bad shape. I can't hide that from you."

"Can I see him?"

"Yes. He's awake. Try to give him all the encouragement you can, Alona."

"I will." She went through the door and searched the beds until she found Oscar. He had an oxygen mask on his face, and his eyes were closed.

"Oscar, are you asleep?" she asked gently. His eyes opened, and she saw his lips move. "Don't try to talk," she said. "I got here as quick as I could." She reached out and took his hand and held it in both of hers. His skin was clammy, and she felt a tremor in it. He had strong hands and had never shown any weakness, but now she knew that this had shaken him deeply. "I'll pray for you," she whispered and began to pray aloud softly. She felt his hand close on hers tightly.

CHAPTER TWENTY-ONE

BATTLE IN THE CORAL SEA

★ ★ ★

After the bombing of Pearl Harbor, it seemed that the Japanese empire did not need to worry about a long war as they swept through the Pacific, unstoppable in their assault. In the central Pacific, Admiral Isoroku Yamamoto's carriers aided the Japanese marines as they took Wake Island after a terrific defense by American marines. The Japanese took the Netherlands East Indies in March 1942, with its wealth of rubber so desperately needed by Japan.

The Japanese were hoping to isolate Australia, which would prevent American forces from using that country as a basis for counterattacks. An aura of invincibility seemed to surround the Japanese forces, but Japan's supremacy was about to be challenged by the United States. The United States had only four aircraft carriers in the Pacific: the *Yorktown,* the *Hornet,* the *Lexington,* and the *Enterprise.* Opposing them was Yamamoto's carrier fleet, comprised of six massive carriers. Altogether the Japanese had ten carriers with which to carry out its attack. Up to this point nothing had been able to stand before the Japanese onslaught, but now in order to keep Australia from falling into the hands of the Japanese, the United States naval carrier force stood as the only hope of achieving that end.

★ ★ ★

"What do you think, Lieutenant?" Mack Morrison asked. "We gonna get us a carrier today?"

Jason was leaning against the side of *The Daisy*, grinning at his gunner. Morrison was a tall, gangling Texan who chewed gum nonstop, his jaw slowing down only when he was asleep. He chomped now like one of the Texas longhorns he often spoke of, but Jason shrugged his shoulders. "That would be nice, Mack. You just keep those Zeros off our tail when they come after us."

"Aw, shucks, Lieutenant! It'll be nothin' but a turkey shoot." Morrison was apparently one of those men born without fear. In the recent battles off the northeast coast of Australia, he had flown seven missions with Jason, shooting down three Zeros. The man was now smiling broadly. "I aim for us to get a couple of medals, then when I go back to Texas and go to a dance, the gals will line right up to have their turn with me."

"I thought they already did that."

"Well, shoot, Lieutenant, they do, of course, and that's why I gotta come through this war. If anything happened to me, there'd be women all over Texas wearin' black mournin' outfits."

Morrison had a soothing effect on Jason's nerves. Even though Jason had miraculously overcome his fear of flying, to dive straight into the fire that flew up from Japanese warships was something else again. He always functioned fine when he needed to, but after the action was over, it was not unusual for him to get worked up over what could have happened. He had kept it hidden from his fellow pilots, and he was strangely comforted to know that most of them had the same problem.

"I'll be glad when we get a better fighter to take care of us," he mumbled as an F4F Wildcat fighter shot off the deck.

"You don't like them Wildcats, sir? Why, I think they're plumb nifty." As a matter of fact, the Wildcat was a little beer bottle of a plane with four .50-caliber wing-mounted machine guns. It was a close match for the Zero but slower. It was, however, heavily armored and harder to shoot down, though it could not climb as quickly or turn as sharply as the Zero.

"The plane's all right, but most of our pilots haven't seen real combat, and those Japs have. Most of them were in on the Pearl Harbor attack."

"Well, scuttlebutt says there's gonna be a fight," Morrison said. He popped his gum, a habit that irritated Jason to no end, although he never mentioned it. "As long as we got *The Daisy,* them Japs better watch out."

The two men stood on the deck, for the fighter escorts were all circling overhead, then the signal came for the Devastator torpedo bombers to begin launching. The two men watched, and Morrison shook his head. "I'd hate to be on one of them torpedo bombers. Why, I can run about as fast as they can fly." In truth, the Devastator was already obsolete. Its maximum speed was 206 miles per hour, and it had a cruising speed of a 128 miles an hour, which made it a perfect target for the enemy. As it came in slowly, the enemy gunners could not miss. One of the pilots in the squadron called it the coffin squadron.

"Those fellows have more nerve than anybody I've ever known," Jason said.

"Yeah, they're nervy all right, but they shoot a pretty good stick with that torpedo."

Jason did not tell Morrison that the torpedoes used by the Devastators were highly inferior. Half of them did not even explode when they did make impact, but there was no sense in telling the Texan that.

As the last of the dive bombers were being launched, Captain Hack Odom came by. "It's the real thing this time," he told the pilots. "We got word that two Jap carriers are out there, and we know where they are."

Mack Morrison said innocently, "Well, shucks, Captain Odom, there ain't no sense in the rest of you boys goin'. Me and Lieutenant Moran here can take care of them fellows."

"You gonna sink both of them with your one bomb?"

"We'll make it ricochet." Morrison grinned.

Odom didn't smile often, but the tall Texan always amused him. "You watch out for Moran here," he told Morrison. "I can't afford to lose him, or you either."

"No problem, sir."

"We need to wipe out those two flat tops, Moran," the captain said. "America needs a victory of some kind. If we don't stop this Japanese drive to bottle up Australia, it's going to be a blow for the folks at home."

"Yes, sir. We'll do our best."

"And take care of yourself up there."

"I'll do that, Captain."

Odom nodded and jogged across the deck. He got into his plane, and Jason said, "Well, let's go, Tex."

"Yes, sir!"

The duo scrambled to their plane, Jason climbing into the front cockpit and Morrison in the rear. In no time Jason was looking down from the sky to the sea. It always seemed to Jason that the sea was crawling. The motor throbbed, vibrating the plane as he corrected his course. He checked out the position of the rest of the squadron, knowing they would be wide ranging, not in perfect formation, for Hack Odom felt that flying in formation was for demonstrations at air shows back home. "Scatter out," he always said. "If you're flying a foot from my wing tip, you've got to think about not wrecking me. Just stay close enough where you can pull back, but every man looks for those flat tops."

"Right down below us" came a voice over the radio. "There's that flat top!" Instantly both Jason and Morrison craned their necks to look down. "There she is, sir—and there come them pesky Zeros. They've seen us!"

"Where's our fighter cover, I wonder?" Jason shouted over the roar of the engine.

"I reckon they've got to someplace else. What are we waitin' for?"

The squadron leader had radioed back to the carrier for more dive bombers. He had urged every bomber to come at once, for he had identified the ship as the *Shoho*, and shortly afterward they sited another one, the *Zuikaku*.

Another squadron quickly arrived on the scene and immediately joined the attack on the two carriers.

"Why don't we go in, Lieutenant?" Morrison yelled.

"I don't know, but keep your eye out."

Odom's squadron had to dodge the Japanese Zeros that came swarming after them. Morrison's gun rattled, and almost immediately he sent one Zero in a twisting, spiraling dive toward the earth, black smoke rising from his engine. "I got him!"

"You sure did, Tex."

There was no time for more talk. The battle was fierce. The Zeros were absolutely determined that the bombers would not drop down, and two of Odom's squadron were hit hard. One of them lost control and went down.

It was one of those days when it seemed the dive bombers could not hit the target. Bomb after bomb fell to the port or the starboard side of the twisting Japanese carrier. Odom's bomb missed, and they could hear him cursing over the radio.

"Moran, can you hear me?" he asked over the radio.

"Yes, sir."

"I kept you until last. You're the best shot. You've got to put your egg right down the stack of that carrier. You're the only hope we've got, son."

"Yes, sir."

Even as Jason spoke, suddenly a blinding flash of pain rushed through him. His Plexiglas canopy was shattered, and he got a brief glimpse of a Zero as it zipped by.

"Get him, Tex!" he yelled. His own blood was splattered all over the cockpit. He was hit in the torso and in the leg. He twisted around and saw Mack Morrison slumped lifelessly behind him, riddled by bullets. "Mack!" he cried out, but he knew it was hopeless.

"Are you okay?" Odom's voice crackled over the radio.

"They got Tex, and I've taken a couple of bullets, but I'm able to fly."

"You can't do it. All the Zeros have swarmed over the *Shoho*. Go on home. We'll send another squadron," Odom directed.

"I hate to disobey orders, but that's the way it is, Captain."

A red haze seemed to fill Jason's eyes, but he could fly. He shoved the throttle forward and put the Dauntless into a steep dive. Pain was raging through his body, but he held it steady. The Zeros indeed were swarming around like hornets, and more than once he felt his plane rattle and shake. But he was focused on the *Shoho* below him, which was turning and wheeling, trying to avoid taking a bomb. Jason set his sights on the big stack and gritted his teeth.

Closer . . . closer . . . closer. The *Shoho* seemed to swell up before him, and when he was no more than three hundred feet up, he released his bomb and jerked back on the throttle. The force of gravity forced him back, and he passed out.

It was only for a few seconds, but when he came to, his plane was rising straight into the air. Glancing out, he saw that his bomb had made a terrific impact. Evidently it went right down the stack and set off some munitions deep in the bowels of the carrier. He rolled the plane over, and the engine was running roughly. Weakness washed over him, and he could only manage to keep the plane level.

He heard Hack Odom shouting, "You got him, Jason! You got him! It's breaking in two!"

Jason did not even have the strength to rejoice. The loss of blood had weakened him, and he could only mutter, "That's good, Captain."

"Can you get back to the carrier?"

"I don't know. Shot up pretty bad."

"We got some more help here. Follow me in."

He saw two flights of Wildcats come, and they drove the Zeros away. Hack Odom maneuvered his dive bomber until he was in front of Jason and led him back to the carrier. Hack shepherded him like a wounded lamb, but Jason's plane coughed and the engine stopped when the carrier was in sight. "I'm going down, Cap."

"Hang on. You can do it. You can land that thing."

"No. The engine's quit."

Jason kept as much control as he could as his wounded plane headed down toward the sea. He took a second to glance back at his partner once, and sorrow filled him as he saw the lifeless body of Mack Morrison. "A good man," he whispered as the sea rushed up to meet him.

* ★ *

Oscar pushed the eggs in his tray around listlessly with his fork. Tentatively he lifted a fork full and stared at it for a moment before putting it in his mouth and chewing it slowly. He put the fork down and stared out the hospital window. Outside a gray squirrel was perched on the limb of a hickory tree, nibbling furiously at a nut. Oscar watched as the animal turned the nut around rapidly, its teeth moving so fast it was hard to see them. When the squirrel finished its delicacy, it licked its paw and then scampered off out of Oscar's sight.

Wearily Oscar picked up the newspaper and read the front page. The war was going bad for the Allies as usual, and he tossed the paper down with a discouraged gesture. As he did, the door opened, and Alona came in carrying a small wicker basket of fruit. She was wearing a soft blue dress, and the summer sun had laid a light tan on her face. Health seemed to glow from her as she came over to the bed and said, "Good morning, Oscar. How are you feeling?"

"All right."

"I brought you some fresh fruit. Look, aren't these apples beautiful?" Alona picked one up and admired it. "Do you want one now?"

"Maybe later."

"All right. I'll put them here on the table." She put the fruit down and sat in the chair beside his bed, keeping the smile on her face. She always found it difficult when she looked at him not to reveal her dismay. He had lost some weight during the two weeks he'd been in the hospital, so that the skin of his neck hung in limp folds, and his eyes seemed to be sunken back in his head. He had been such a strong, vigorous man that the change in him was alarming. "I talked to Dr. Roberts. He was seeing another patient down the hall. He says you're doing better."

"That's doctor talk," Oscar said. He held up a hand and stared at it. It seemed thin and frail. "I'm not doing better, Alona."

"But the fluid is all gone from your lungs now. He said you can get up soon and walk a little."

"I doubt if that will ever happen." The sickness had drained Oscar's will, and Alona felt a sudden touch of compassion. She reached out and picked up his hand and held it in both of hers. "Oscar," she said softly, "would you like to come home?"

"Come home?" he asked. "Did Dr. Roberts say I could?"

"He didn't say, but I think I could care for you at home. I think Mrs. Darrow and I could do as well for you as they do here." Alona saw something change in his eyes, and she realized that Oscar had longed to get out of the hospital. She knew how he hated it, but he had been so ill, there had been no question of leaving. Even now she was not sure Dr. Roberts would permit it. "I'll go ask him if that's what you want."

"I . . . I would like it very much."

Alona saw that the admission was hard for her husband. She put his hand down and said firmly, "All right. I'll go ask him right now."

When she was gone, Oscar lay there thinking over the past weeks. He had had peaks and valleys in his illness, but the valleys always seemed to be deeper than the peaks were high. The fluid in his lungs had been a constant concern, and pneumonia was always a threat. Alona had been more faithful than he had dreamed she would be. Much of the time he was too sick to talk, but she had come and sat beside his bed day after day, telling him what the boys were up to. She had even gone by the factory and talked to the manager who was in charge in his absence. Alona had reported back to Oscar that everything was fine at the foundry.

Alona was gone for what seemed like a long time. As he lay there trying to keep his hopes from rising, he realized how far the two of them had drifted apart. He was filled with regret over the way their marriage had turned out. He longed to say something to Alona but didn't know how to start. He had no practice in the art of reconciliation. His strength had always been a wall of separation from others. He did not allow any gaps in it that would allow others to come too close.

Alona came back, her eyes bright, with Dr. Roberts in tow. "The doctor says we can take you home tomorrow, Oscar."

"Now, wait a minute. I said it was a bad idea. You didn't add that."

Dr. Roberts looked weary, for he carried a heavy load. It seemed that the war had brought more sickness even here at home, although there was no obvious connection. "This woman ought to be a salesman. She doesn't know what the word *no* means."

Oscar grinned briefly. "I understand that well enough."

"She's convinced me that she and Mrs. Darrow can handle the job, and I've insisted that she have a nurse to help at least part time. And, Oscar, if you get worse, you'll have to come back."

"Thanks, Ed."

He reached down and patted Oscar on the shoulder. "I hope you get better," he said gruffly.

"He will, Doctor," Alona said. "I'll take such good care of him."

When Dr. Roberts had left the room, she said, "We'll keep you in the guest bedroom downstairs. It'll be close to the kitchen, and the boys can come in and visit with you." She brushed his hair back off his forehead. "I need to run some errands now, but I'll be back for a longer visit this afternoon."

She started to move her hand, but he held it. "What is it, Oscar?"

He tried to say what was on his heart but couldn't make the words get past his lips. "Thanks. . . . It'll be good to be home."

Alona gave his hand a squeeze. "You'll feel better when you're at home. I know you'll improve just being away from here." She smiled and left the room abruptly when she saw tears gather in Oscar's eyes. She knew he would hate it if anyone saw him so weak. Leaving the hospital, her mind was filled with plans for caring for an invalid.

★   ★   ★

". . . and so Oscar will be coming home tomorrow morning. He'll stay in the guest room on the first floor, and Mrs. Darrow and I will take care of him."

"Is he better?" Zac demanded. "He must be if he's gettin' out of the hospital."

"He's well enough to come home, but he's still very sick. You boys will have to work on being quiet."

Carl wrinkled his nose. "Aw, Mom . . ."

"You can't yell like wild animals when you're outside, and we'll have to keep the volume down on the radio. We're going to have to be careful to let him get his rest. I'll be very strict about this."

"That's all right, Mom," Zac said. "I'll keep 'em quiet."

"You couldn't keep anybody quiet!" Carl argued. "Besides, you're the noisiest one of all of us!"

"We'll all work together on being quiet. He's a very

sick man, but he loves you boys, and I want you to visit quietly with him and let him see that you care for him."

"Sure, Mom," Carl said, "we can do that."

"I also wanted to warn you that he looks different than he used to. But don't let that scare you."

Tim stared at his mother. "Is he ... is he going to die?"

"We've all got to do that someday, Tim, but I think Oscar is going to be fine. He'll be his old self before long."

"Can we go play now, Mom?" Carl asked.

"Sure. Mrs. Darrow and I have a lot of work to do."

When the boys started to leave, she held her oldest son back. "Tim, I know you and Oscar have had difficulties in the past, but you must put all that behind you now."

He flushed guiltily. "Sure, Mom. It won't be hard."

"That's my good boy." Alona smiled and hugged him.

★　★　★

A few days later, Alona finished her shopping late in the afternoon. She pulled into the garage and greeted Tim, who was already there to help her carry in the groceries. He picked up two of the sacks while she got the third.

They went into the kitchen, where Leah was cutting up a piece of meat. "We ran out of ration stamps for some of the items," Alona told her. "We'll just have to make do."

"Did you get the butter?"

"No, but I was able to get something that looks like butter. A little bit, anyway. It's funny stuff," she said, prowling through the packages. She pulled out an item. "Look, it's white."

"White butter?" Tim said. "I never heard of such a thing."

"That's because it's not real butter. It's called margarine."

Buddy was following all the action with his eyes, even though Alona couldn't imagine that a dog would be interested in margarine *or* butter.

"Ugh, I don't think I could spread that white stuff on a biscuit!" Tim said.

"It comes with this little capsule of dye," she said, holding it up. "You mix it in, and it makes the margarine yellow."

"Well, I never . . ." Mrs. Darrow said. She took it and examined it. "I'm glad it's yellow instead of green or blue," she said with a grin.

Alona laughed. Leah Darrow had undergone a transformation since Oscar's heart attack. She was an excellent nurse, and with the aid of Bea McCulloch, who came for a couple hours every morning, she had become almost cheerful.

"Well, it's not going to be polka dot butter, anyhow," Alona said. "How's Oscar?"

"He hasn't had much to say today."

"We played checkers after school, Mom," Tim said. "And I beat him two games out of three."

"I think he let you win." Leah smiled. "I never heard of anyone ever beating him at checkers."

"Yeah, I think he probably did, but I didn't say anything."

"I'll help put the groceries away and then help with supper," Alona said as she started pulling more items out of the bags.

"No. You go sit with Oscar. I don't mind doing this."

Buddy was sitting there looking at the two, and suddenly Mrs. Darrow laughed. "That dog has become a beggar!"

"You spoil him, Leah, always giving him things to eat. He's going to get fat." It had been a shock to everyone that Leah had become very attached to Buddy. The big dog, always affectionate and hungry for attention, took all he could get.

Mrs. Darrow cut a chunk of meat for Buddy. She held it above his nose until he sat up and begged.

"Good boy, Buddy." She dropped the meat into his mouth. "There. That's all you get. Now, go lie down and get out from under my feet."

Obediently Buddy went over and flopped down on the rug by the wall.

"I had a dog like him when I was a girl," the housekeeper commented, "but my mother made me get rid of him."

Alona patted the older woman on the shoulder. "I'll go sit with Oscar for a while. Get the boys to set the table for you."

"All right. You go now."

Alona went at once to Oscar's room and found him sitting up in the chair they kept beside his bed. He loved to sit there and look out the window. She spoke to him cheerfully and drew up a chair, but when he didn't speak, she said, "I hear you've been playing checkers."

"Yes."

The reply was short, and Leah was suddenly concerned. "Don't you feel well, Oscar?"

"I feel all right, but I've got some bad news. A telegram came this afternoon. I've been waiting for you to get home to tell you."

"A telegram?"

"It's about Jason." Oscar took the yellow envelope from his bedside table.

A chill slid over Alona, and she could not move. She knew well what a telegram usually meant. She reached out slowly and took the envelope. Feeling Oscar's eyes on her, she opened it and took out the single sheet. "We regret to inform you that your brother, Jason Moran, has been wounded in action." She read the rest of the telegram silently. "It doesn't say how badly he was wounded."

"No, but he's alive, Alona."

"Yes, thank God he's alive."

She sat there unable to think clearly, aware that Oscar was waiting for her to speak. "We'll have to pray that it's minor."

"Yes. We'll do that." He cleared his throat and then said, "I've been wanting to talk to you, Alona, but this isn't the right time. Maybe tomorrow."

"No, let's do it now." She put the telegram back in the envelope and put it back on the table. "What is it?"

Oscar Moran was good at giving commands but not at other kinds of conversation. He was clearly struggling for words, and Alona thought she knew what was coming.

"I . . . I've been wrong about so many things," he started. "Lying in that hospital bed, and then the days here at home, I've been reflecting on my whole life. I've always been one to *do* things, but that's been taken away from me. Now all I can do is think, and I've been thinking about the past." He lifted his eyes and said quietly, "I was wrong about you and Jason. I ask you to forgive me."

Alona knew what it had cost him to say this. She took his hand and held it. "Of course I do."

"Thank you. That's like you." She kept his hand in hers, and he began to tell her about the early days of how he had tried to help Jason, how he had tried to be a father for the boy the best way he knew how. "I thought I was being a good father figure, but I know now I wasn't understanding enough. I was so busy keeping the foundry going I didn't have time to think. Jason's not like me. You know that very well. He's more sensitive. As a matter of fact, he's like Tim."

"Why, yes, he is like Tim." Alona was surprised that Oscar had the insight to notice that. She knew then that he had been spending a lot of time thinking.

"I should have encouraged Jason when he wanted to be an artist. Maybe it's not too late yet."

"Maybe not."

"When he gets home I'm going to try to make it up to him."

Alona couldn't believe her ears as her husband shared his feelings with her. He seemed to have become a completely different man.

"I wish I had done things differently," he said with a sigh, "so many things. . . ."

She could see that he was getting tired. "Why don't we get you back into bed. You may be pushing yourself a little with sitting up for so long."

Oscar allowed her to help him make the transfer from the chair to the bed. After she had made sure he was comfortable, she said, "I'm going to go help Leah with supper. I'll bring your tray in as soon as it's ready."

"I know it'll be good. I've got the two best cooks in Jonesboro right here waiting on me." Oscar managed to smile.

How he's changed, she thought as she left the room. *It's been a terrible experience, but I see something in his heart now that I never saw before, and I think he sees it too.* As she walked down the hall, her thoughts turned to Jason and she wondered how she would tell the boys that he had been wounded. There was no easy way to break news like that, especially since they didn't even know how badly he had been hurt. But it had to be done.

CHAPTER TWENTY-TWO

FRONT PAGE NEWS

★ ★ ★

Jason couldn't figure out what the buzzing sound was. At first it sounded like bees and then eventually the buzzing sounded more like voices. But the words did not make any sense. He might have been listening to a foreign language. A sharp pain in his side caught his attention and then another in his right leg jerked him further out of the dim world where he had been dreaming of green fields and blue skies and into the harsh reality.

He smelled something acidic, sharp and biting, and he was aware that he was lying in a bed. Suddenly he remembered what had happened in his last moments of consciousness ... the blue-green water rushing up to meet him as his plane dove straight at it.

"He's doing better than I expected, Captain Odom. He had a little water in his lungs, but I think your men got him out just in time."

Jason's eyes opened almost involuntarily, and he saw a man standing to his left with a long face and a shock of stiff black hair. The sight of Captain Hack Odom brought him a great surge of relief. Odom was a known factor, something he could relate to.

"Look, his eyes are open!" Odom said, leaning over until his face filled Jason's view. "Hey, are you awake, Moran?"

"Yes," Jason managed to say. Odom's face disappeared, and another man appeared, a stethoscope around his neck.

"How do you feel?" the man asked.

"Just . . . peachy."

"Bullets from a Zero and crashing a plane into the ocean didn't take the devilment out of you, I see," Odom said as his face joined the doctor's. "You're gonna be okay. I guarantee it."

"You're not the doctor here, Captain. I am. Now, will you please leave so I can examine the man?"

"No, I won't."

The doctor laughed. "You military types are all alike. Think you can shoot your way out of anything. Okay, you can have five minutes. I'll be right back."

"Thanks, Doc."

Odom's face seemed to grow more distinct instead of having a slightly fuzzy outline. "Where am I?" Jason whispered.

"You're in the hospital, of course. Where did you think—this was heaven and I was Saint Peter?"

"My leg hurts . . . and my side."

"Yep, I think you should be a little sore. You took a bullet in your side—that one just gouged a little trench in you—and another one in your thigh. But the doc says the bigger problem is your leg. You broke your thigh bone and both bones in your lower leg."

"How'd you get me out?"

"One of our destroyers was no more than a half mile away from where you hit. The sailor boys saw you coming down and made for you. They did a good job getting you out just before your plane sank. You owe them one for that."

"How . . . are the rest of the boys?"

"Most of them made it back."

"Mack's gone. The Zeros got him the same time they winged me."

"I know. I'm sorry about that. He was a good man."

A pain raced up and down Jason's leg, and he couldn't speak. He closed his eyes and heard Hack Odom say, "I'll get the doc to give you a shot for that. You do whatever he says."

Jason felt his hand being squeezed and managed to whisper, "What about the flat top?"

Odom was grinning broadly. "Scratch one flat top," he announced. "You put your bomb right down the stack. It broke in two. You're a hero, boy. But don't get bigheaded."

Jason thought about that moment when he had released the bomb, and then he could stay awake no longer and slipped back into the warm, pleasant darkness.

★　★　★

"Look, Oscar, it's a letter from Jason!" Alona shook his shoulder gently. "See, it's his handwriting."

Oscar had been dozing in a chaise longue on the front porch, but he instantly came awake. "From Jason? What does it say?"

"It's addressed to you," she said, excitement in her voice. "And there's another one addressed to the boys. He must be better if he can write."

"Open it up."

"Let me take this to the boys and then I'll be right back."

She found the three boys playing marbles out back behind the house. They argued about who should get to read the letter first and then finally agreed they would each read two sentences aloud to the others. She waited while they took turns reading it. You would hardly know Jason was lying in a hospital bed. His letter was full of teasing and references to some of the goofy things the four of them had done together during Alona and Oscar's honeymoon.

Alona returned to the front porch and told Oscar about the boys' letter. Then she carefully tore into Oscar's envelope, took out the single sheet of paper, and read aloud.

"Dear Oscar,

"I am feeling much better now than I was when I wrote you the first time. I was pretty dizzy, although my captain, Hack Odom, says it's hard to tell about me—that I'm dizzy most of the time.

"They have treated me very well here in the hospital. My side is doing much better, but my leg is still pretty useless. The doctors keep warning me not to hope for too much, and I keep telling them that Dr. Jesus is going to get me on my feet again."

"He told them that!" Oscar exclaimed. "I think that's great!"

"So do I. I'm sure he'll be all right." She began to read again.

"The doctors are right about one thing, though. I'm going to be out of things for some time. I don't know exactly how long, but I won't be flying for quite a while.

"I want to thank you, Oscar, once again, for the way you've stood by me all my life. A father could not have been better to me. I know I gave you all kinds of problems, and I'm sorry for all of them, and I hope you'll put those out of your mind and just remember the good things.

"I hope you're taking care of yourself. I'm praying every day for your recovery. When you're flat on your back, there's nothing much to do but pray, so I've been catching up.

"Your loving brother,

"Jason"

She handed him the letter and he scanned it. "That's the best letter I ever got in my life, Alona," he said in a husky voice.

"I'm so glad you're willing to start fresh with Jason."

"Would you write a letter for me?"

"Of course. Let me get a pen and paper."

Alona was back in a moment, and Oscar spoke haltingly.

"Dear Jason,

"I thank God that you are alive, and I will pray for your recovery.

"We all talk about you every day here. The boys appreciate the letters you've sent to the three of them. They have the first one on the bulletin board in Tim's room, and I think they've all got it memorized. It gave them a great thrill to get a letter from a real war hero. I think they all three want to go into naval aviation now. I pray, of course, as you do, that they won't have to. That this war will be over long before they're old enough to enlist.

"I have great pain when I look back over my life and realize how badly I handled some things—and especially you. I wasn't the kind of dad you needed. I should have been much gentler and much kinder. I made the mistake of throwing all my energy into making money. It seemed like the right thing to do at the time, but I ask you to forgive me for the harshness with you.

"We are all longing for the day when you come

home. Please write again, and once again, I hope you can forget the bad things that I did and try to remember the good things.

"Your brother,

"Oscar"

"That's nice, Oscar." Alona reached over and put her hand on Oscar's. "It will make Jason very happy."

"Do you think so?"

"Oh yes, I know it will. I'll stamp it and get it mailed right away."

★ ★ ★

Tim stepped hesitantly into Oscar's bedroom. Oscar was sitting in his chair beside the window looking out. "You wanted to see me, sir?"

"Yes, I did. Did you bring those drawings of yours?"

"I brought a few of them."

"Come over here and show them to me in this good light and tell me about them."

Tim swallowed. "Tell you about them?"

"Yes." Oscar smiled. "Tell me if you had any particular thing in mind while you were drawing or if you had trouble with some part of it. I don't know anything about art. It's almost like magic to me when someone can do what you do. I can't even draw a straight line."

"Well, they're just sketches," Tim said tentatively as he sat on a chair near Oscar. He put the sketches down on the table, holding up one of them. "I had a lot of trouble with this one. I'm still not happy with it."

Oscar took the sketch and slanted it to get the best light. It was a sketch of the back part of their property where three tall pecan trees were in full flower. "This is great, Tim. I love those trees."

"I didn't draw in the house we can see on the other

side of the property. I wanted to make it look like it was way out in the country. But I'm not very good at drawing the flowers."

"I might disagree with that. They look very realistic."

The two talked for some time about the sketch, and then Oscar asked to see another. For thirty minutes Oscar listened as Tim told him about his drawings, and finally Oscar handed the last one back and said, "You have real talent, son."

"Oh, I don't know. But I'm going to keep working on it."

"I've been thinking a lot about you and your desire to be an artist. Now that I'm pretty well unable to do anything, I've been trying to think of things I can do. And here's what I've decided. If you're interested, I'd like you to pursue your career in art. When it comes time for you to go to college, you should pick out one that has a good art program. If you want to go to Europe to study, I'll provide the funds for that."

Oscar wasn't sure what to make of Tim's expression. His lips were parted and he looked frozen in his chair. "Would you like that, Tim?"

"I'd be crazy if I didn't like that, sir, but it would cost a lot of money."

"If it's what you want, it might be the best money I've ever spent. In a decade or two most of the things we make at the foundry will be junk—rusted and thrown away. But some of your paintings may be hanging on the walls of museums long after you're gone. I'd like to see you do your best at this. I think Zac will want to do something with his hands—maybe even work at the foundry—and as for Carl, well, it's too early to tell what he might like to do. But I've made a will out, and none of you will have to worry about funding your dreams. Whatever happens to me, you'll be able to become an artist."

Tim swallowed hard, and Oscar saw that the boy had tears in his eyes. "Let me look at this last sketch," Oscar started but was interrupted when Zac's voice filled the house.

"He's on the front page! He's on the front page!" he yelled.

"What's he yelling about?" Tim asked. "Mom told him to be quiet."

But there was no quieting Zac Jennings down, and even as Tim stood up to go tell him to hush, Zac came flying into the room, waving a newspaper in the air. "Look, Mr. Oscar, it's Jason! It's him with the president!"

Oscar took the page from Zac, who continued to talk excitedly.

"Look, it's Jason," Zac repeated, pointing at the picture. "He's getting a medal from the president!"

Alona and Carl came into the room. "What is it?" Alona asked. "Is something wrong?"

"Mom, it's Jason. His picture is on the front page with President Roosevelt. Show it to her, Mr. Oscar!"

Alona went to Oscar's side and bent over the paper. She could hardly believe her eyes when she saw Jason sitting in a wheelchair across from President Roosevelt. You could not mistake Roosevelt. He was grinning at Jason, and the headline said, "Naval flier wins Medal of Honor for sinking flat top."

"The Medal of Honor!" Oscar exclaimed. "Jason has won the Medal of Honor!"

"What's that?" Carl demanded.

"It's the highest honor a soldier or sailor can get," Oscar said. "They don't give these away to just anybody."

The boys were all talking excitedly, and Alona went over and squatted beside Oscar. "You must be very proud, Oscar."

"I am, and all of us are, aren't we, boys?"

"We need to buy about fifty papers so we can give them to our friends."

"I expect everybody in Jonesboro will keep this one." Alona smiled. She looked down at the picture of Jason again and shook her head. "He looks so thin."

"Yes, but he's smiling," Oscar said. "I hope he can come home soon."

Alona instantly knew why he had said that. Oscar had never talked about the possibility that he could die before he saw Jason again, but she knew that it was on his mind. "I'm sure he will as soon as he can."

"I'd love to see him and that medal," Oscar said quietly. Then he smiled and said, "Put that in your prayers, Alona."

CHAPTER TWENTY-THREE

"TELL JASON I LOVE HIM"

★ ★ ★

August had come with all of its heat, and Alona felt stretched thin. For a time it had seemed that Oscar was getting stronger, but that had been short-lived. He now was becoming steadily weaker and was unable to get out of bed. Even with the nurse, who came in every afternoon, Alona had her hands full taking care of the boys and her sick husband.

The war had taken a turn for the better when the Battle of the Coral Sea had halted the Japanese, and then in June, the Allies had destroyed, for all practical purposes, the naval strength of the Japanese empire during the Battle of Midway. General Eisenhower had assumed command of the United States forces in the European theater, and Americans were beginning to feel better about the war. Even the news from Russia was good, for the Germans had been stopped at Sevastopol.

Each day Alona took the paper into Oscar's room and read the headlines and some of the news stories to him. He listened with interest but was obviously growing weaker.

She went in to check on Oscar and saw that he was lying flat on his back but his eyes were open. "I'll have your lunch ready soon."

"I'm not very hungry."

"You've got to eat."

"Alona, come here."

Surprised, she walked over. He held up his hand, and she took it and held it in both of hers. "What is it, Oscar? Do you want something?"

"Yes, I do. I want you to forgive me."

"Forgive you for what?"

"I had to get sick before I realized how badly I behaved toward you, but—"

"Don't worry about that," Alona said quickly. "That's all in the past. You've already asked for my forgiveness and I've given it to you. When you get better—"

"I want to write a letter to Jason."

"Of course, Oscar." She went over to the table and picked up some paper and a pen. Even as she did so, Tim came running through the door. "Mom—Mr. Oscar!"

"What is it, Tim?" Alona said. "Is something wrong?"

"No. Look what just came in the mail."

He handed her the letter with trembling fingers. She read it quickly and then gave him a big hug. "I'm so proud of you!" Still holding onto Tim, she handed the letter to Oscar. He took it and read it to himself.

Mr. Timothy Jennings,

The committee is pleased to inform you that your sketches have won first place in the Columbia Art Contest. Our congratulations to you, young man. Your sketches will be exhibited in the Atlanta Museum of Art. Please find a check enclosed, and we will be in touch with you in the near future.

Oscar looked up, his face wreathed in a smile. "Tim, congratulations."

"I couldn't have done it if it hadn't been for you, Mr. Oscar." Tim went over and when Oscar put out his hand, Tim ignored it. Instead he put his arms around Oscar and said, "Thanks . . . Dad."

Alona felt tears come to her eyes. Tim pulled out of the embrace and before he ran from the room, she saw tears in his eyes as well.

"That was wonderful, Oscar." She took a handkerchief out of her pocket and used it first on her tears and then on Oscar's.

"Your son is a fine boy, Alona, and I'm so proud of him."

"Do you want me to write your letter now?"

"I'd like to write it myself this time."

"Are you sure you feel like it?"

"Help me sit up and then bring me that board to write on."

Alona pulled Oscar into a semi-upright position, stuffing pillows behind his back, and gave him the board he used when he felt like writing himself. She put an envelope and paper and pen on the board and said, "I'll come back later." She leaned over and kissed his cheek. "It's a wonderful thing you've done for Tim and for all the boys."

"I wish I'd had more time with them."

"You will," she said. "You'll have plenty of time with them."

He did not answer for a moment; then he reached out and took her hand again. He squeezed it gently and said, "I want you to take care of those boys, Alona, and I know you will. And I want to thank you for being in my life."

"Why, Oscar, you've done so much for us. I need to thank you for all you've done for the boys and for me."

She leaned over and kissed him on the cheek. "I'll be back in half an hour with your lunch."

"All right, Alona."

She left the room and went to the kitchen.

"How is he feeling today?" Leah asked.

"Physically, about the same, I guess. Emotionally, I'd say he's feeling very well. Better than ever."

She told Leah about what had happened.

"I'm so glad that Tim called him Dad," Leah said. "That must have been one of the best moments of his life."

"I think it was."

Carrying a lunch tray carefully in one hand, Alona opened the door of Oscar's room. The board was still on Oscar's lap, but his head hung down at an awkward angle, and fear swept through her.

"Oscar!" she cried. She quickly put the tray down on the bedside table. "Oscar, are you all right?"

But when she touched him, she knew he was not all right. She felt for his pulse as the nurse had taught her and knew he was gone.

She took a deep breath and tried to compose herself. The envelope she had given Oscar had fallen to the floor. She picked it up and noticed that it was sealed. She read the unsteady handwriting: *For my beloved brother, Jason— when he comes home.*

She gazed down at this man who had so changed her life and the lives of her sons. She smoothed his hair and caressed his cheek. "Thank you, Oscar, for all the good things."

Closing the door quietly, she left the room and found the boys listening to the radio. She turned the radio off. "Boys, I have something to tell you. . . ."

★   ★   ★

Jason was navigating down the hall of the hospital, swinging along on his crutches, when Chaplain Barnes came around the corner. "Hello, Padre, you out spreading the gospel today?"

Chaplain Barnes ordinarily had a cheerful face, but today he was looking quite somber. "I've got something for you, Jason."

"What is it?"

"Let's go to your room."

Jason reversed and the two moved back down the hallway into Jason's room. He sat down and leaned the crutches against the wall while the chaplain pulled a chair up next to his. "What is it? It's got to be bad news."

"I'm afraid it is. I got this letter from your brother's wife, Mrs. Alona Moran. She asked me to speak with you."

"Someone is sick," Jason said. "Who is it? One of the boys?"

"No. It's your brother, Oscar."

Instantly Jason knew the worst. "He's gone, isn't he, Chaplain?"

The man nodded slowly. "She enclosed a letter here for you in which she'll tell you the details, but she wanted me to break the news to you. I'm sorry, Jason. She says he slipped away peacefully."

Jason took the envelope the chaplain handed to him, feeling empty inside. "We had our differences, but those are long forgotten. If you have a few minutes, let me tell you what a good man he was to me."

The chaplain leaned forward in his chair.

"He wasn't a gentle man, but he took care of me just like he was my father. There were some hard times during the Depression, and he saw to it that I never lacked for anything. Since I've been here I've tried to tell him in letters how much I appreciated that, but I was hoping to see him again."

Chaplain Barnes patted Jason's good knee. "You will, son. You will. Christians never say good-bye!"

CHAPTER TWENTY-FOUR

RETURN OF THE WARRIOR

★ ★ ★

Alona put her hat on but was so nervous that it slipped off and fell to the floor. Quickly she bent over, picked it up, and fastened it with a hatpin. She heard the boys talking in Carl's room, and taking one more quick look at herself in her dresser mirror, she went to his room. The three boys were talking excitedly, and as usual, Zac's voice rose above the other two.

"Everybody in town is gonna be at the station to meet Jason, Mom!"

"That's right," Carl said, his eyes shining. "The high school band's gonna be there and the mayor."

"Hey, Mom," Tim put in, "I heard there's going to be a reporter and a photographer from Atlanta. Maybe Jason will get on the cover of *Life* magazine."

"Come on, Mom, we're going to be late!" Zac said.

"All right. I'm ready."

The group went downstairs, and Leah was waiting at the door. "I've got his room all ready." Alona could see that the woman was nervous and she looked worried. "I wasn't very kind to Jason when he was here. I hope he won't hold it against me."

Alona reached out and embraced the woman. "He won't," she said cheerfully. "He's not that kind of man."

"Let's go, Mom," Carl said as he opened the door.

The group went out and piled into the car. "When we come back, I get to ride in the front with Jason," Zac announced.

"No you don't. I'm the oldest. I do!" Tim said.

"You boys hush. You all three are going to ride in the back. Jason's leg is still stiff. He needs the extra room." She backed the car out and drove toward the train station. *What will he be like?* she wondered. She could not forget that he had told her he loved her the last time she saw him. *He's probably forgotten all that,* she thought and pressed the accelerator.

★ ★ ★

Old memories came rushing back to Jason as he peered out the window at the familiar scene. He had thought about this town so often, and now as he passed by the football stadium where he had thrown many a forward pass, he shifted to see better but then winced as his leg protested.

"Say, Jason, we're glad to have you back again." Sam Freeman, the conductor, had paused by Jason's seat, swaying with the movement of the train. Jason could hardly believe it when he got on the train earlier and saw someone he knew from the First Baptist Church. "I guess you're gonna get tired of hearing it, but I can't help telling you before we get into town how proud I am of you, Jason."

"Thanks, Sam, but the men we need to be proud of are those who didn't make it back."

"Of course that's true, but still you did a great job." He hesitated and then said, "I'm real sorry about Oscar."

"Yes. I wish I could have made it home before he was taken."

"You know he changed a lot after his heart attack. Everybody talked about it. People who went to visit him said he talked about you a lot, son. Said he was so sorry he wasn't a good father to you."

"Well, he was a good father and a good man. I'll miss him."

Freeman bent down to look out the window. "Almost to the station." He stood up and tilted his head. "You know it's real strange. You was the one gettin' shot at, but it was Oscar that the Lord saw fit to take."

"You never know about those things."

He bent down to look out the window again. "My land, I believe everybody in town's there! Look at all the banners and streamers. And there's Miss Alona. You know she took over the music program at church." He smiled and added, "I guess you two will be making music again like the old times."

Jason was humbled by the size of the crowd but his focus kept returning to Alona. When the train jerked to a stop, Jason got to his feet. Sam handed him his crutches and followed him as he swung down the aisle.

"Wait a minute. Let me go first. I'll help you down." Sam jumped down and the porter was already there with the portable step.

"You be careful gettin' down, Lieutenant," the porter told him over the cheering of the crowd and the blaring of the band. He grinned broadly, his white teeth flashing.

"I will," Jason yelled. "I'd hate to break my neck just when I finally got home."

"They shouldn't be making such a fuss," he said to Sam.

"Of course they should. You're a war hero. Now, boy,

you've got to show 'em you're glad to see 'em."

Jason did manage to smile. He made his way to the spot where the mayor stood with Alona and the boys. Suddenly a bright light flashed in his face and a photographer shouted, "What was it like? Give our readers something, Lieutenant."

The mayor, a giant of a man, seized the reporter by the upper arms and moved him and the photographer out of the way. "You fellows will have your chance later. Right now, this celebration is for us hometown folks."

He reached for Jason's hand and shook it firmly. "Welcome home, Jason."

"Thank you, Mayor."

As soon as Jason released the mayor's hand, Carl ran forward, crying, "Jason—Jason!" He nearly knocked Jason off of his crutches, and then the other two boys were there as well, hanging on to him. Jason dropped one of his crutches and put his arms around them. "It's so good to see you fellows," he said, his eyes misty.

"Welcome home, Jason," Alona said over Carl's head.

She's as beautiful as ever, he thought, and he saw that she was weeping. He put his free hand out and she latched onto it, but he couldn't say a word. He had been looking forward to this moment for many weeks now. Her hand was warm and strong in his, and he wished they were alone on the platform.

"Lieutenant, would you care to say a word to the townspeople?" the mayor asked. He held up his hand and caught the band conductor's eye. The band stopped, and Jason turned, releasing Alona's hand.

His heart was full and his throat was thick, but he managed to say, "I'm so thankful to be here. I've thought about you all so much. This town and you good people, my fellow church members, my friends, and my family are what kept me going. I know many of you prayed for me. I thank you for your prayers, and I urge you to keep praying for the men and women who are still in harm's way."

Jason couldn't wait to get out of the crowd and have a moment alone with Alona, but instead he shook many hands and spoke to the reporter and had his picture taken with the mayor. Finally he grew weary, and the mayor said, "That's enough for today. You take him home, Miss Alona."

She was at his side at once. The boys gathered around him, forming a half-circle. "Yes," Jason said, "take me home, Alona."

★ ★ ★

Jason's first week at home flew by quickly, as the boys and everyone else he knew wanted to have some time to get reacquainted and hear about his first-hand experiences in the war. But there was an uncomfortable awkwardness when he was alone with Alona. They'd had many private conversations, catching up on all that had happened, including Oscar's last months and Jason's experiences in the war.

Early in the week she had shown him the will, explaining that Oscar had designated enough funds to cover college expenses for all three boys and had left the house, the foundry, and most of his other assets to both Jason and her.

"He shouldn't have done that!"

"It's what he wanted. He had it all planned out. If you like, we can sell the foundry. I know you've always hated it."

They had agreed to talk about it later, and as the days passed, Jason felt even more awkward and ill at ease around Alona. The boys were unchanged, but Alona seemed reserved and uncomfortable, and he felt the same way.

On a Monday morning when he was sitting in the backyard enjoying the perfect day, Alona came outside, holding an envelope. "I have something for you."

He took it and read, " 'For my beloved brother, Jason—when he comes home.' You haven't read this?"

"No. I wanted to wait and give it to you after all the other business was settled. It was the last thing he wrote . . . on the day he died." She told him exactly what had happened that day. "When I came back with his lunch he was gone, but he had managed to write this letter. It was sealed. So it will be your last word from him on this earth."

Alona watched as Jason opened the envelope. He took out the sheet of paper and read it. And then he appeared to reread it another time or two, nodding as he read. He folded it, put it back in the envelope, and then stuffed it into his pocket, making no comment.

★ ★ ★

As the weeks passed and winter approached, Alona and Jason spent evenings talking in the parlor. On this particular night, they sat by a crackling fire, sipping on some hot chocolate after the boys had gone to bed.

"It's almost Christmastime," Alona said. "What do you want?"

He smiled. "I guess I got what I wanted. To get home. But if you want to get me a present, you could always get me a pair of socks."

"If it wouldn't be too much bother, I'd like you to go shopping for the boys with me."

"Sure, I'm hobbling around pretty well with a cane now."

"You still mustn't rush, Jason. You were very badly hurt."

"When would you like to go?"

"Maybe in a couple of days."

★   ★   ★

The first snow fell the day before Christmas, and the boys were busy building a snowman. Buddy was barking and rolling in the snow and digging at it, and Jason was watching from off to the side, leaning on his cane. "That's the ugliest snowman I ever saw," he declared.

"Aw, Jason, it's hard to build a pretty snowman," Tim protested.

"Snowmen aren't supposed to be pretty. They're supposed to be big and round," Carl said as he patted some more snow onto the snowman's belly.

Zac had grown tired of the snowman and was shuffling through the yard, making tracks in the snow. He bent down and scooped up a handful of snow. After shaping it into a ball, he sent it flying through the air. It caught Tim right on the ear.

"Hey, who did that? I'll get you for that!"

Immediately snowballs began flying in all directions. Jason packed one and threw it at Zac. It missed, and then at the same time he heard Alona, who had come out of the house. "You're doing too much, Jason! Don't be foolish!"

"Oh, come on, Alona. It's only a snowball fight."

"You come in the house right now. Boys, you stop that."

There were protests, but she said, "You can build snowmen all you want to, but I don't want you throwing those icy snowballs. Somebody's going to get hurt. Now,

Jason, you come in the house. You're putting too much pressure on your leg."

"You sound like a top sergeant," Jason said, but he was grinning. They went into the house and she hung up his coat and hat. They went into the parlor, and Jason stood in front of the crackling fire, warming his hands.

"After the boys go to bed tonight, I'm going to get the gifts out that we bought for them," she told him.

"Good. I'll help you wrap them."

"You can watch," she said firmly.

"You're treating me like an invalid."

Alona laughed. "Well, that's what you are, for heaven's sake!"

Jason sank down into the couch with a satisfied sigh. "It's been good to be home."

Alona sat on the opposite end of the couch. "And it's been good to have you here, Jason."

"I thought about you all the time I was gone—and the boys too."

She didn't know how to respond. Although they had been alone a number of times since he'd returned from the war, he hadn't opened up to her about whether his feelings had changed. She couldn't assume that he still loved her. When the silence in the room started to feel uncomfortable, she made an excuse about checking on the boys and quickly left the room.

★ ★ ★

Alona put two more logs on the fire, and it was now burning brightly. After she was sure the boys were asleep, she had gotten the presents out and wrapped them. Now they were all under the tree, and she and Jason were sitting in silence, enjoying the setting.

Alona didn't think she could bear the tension

between them for one more minute, so she took a deep breath and said, "I've got to tell you something, Jason."

"What is it?"

"I did the wrong thing to marry Oscar. I didn't make him happy."

"Don't ever think that. You know the letter I got from him—the last one?"

"Yes. You never told me what was in it."

"You can read it now. Just give me a minute to get it."

She waited while he went downstairs to his room and returned with the letter in hand. He gave it to her and sat down next to her on the couch. She unfolded the letter, her hands not quite steady, and read it silently.

Dear Jason,

I will not be here when you get back, but I want to ask you to do me one last favor. You and I have grown closer together than we ever have been, thanks to the mail. I feel like we are true brothers at last. But I am ready to go and be with the Lord. Instead of getting stronger with every passing day, I'm getting weaker. I know that my time here is short.

Jason, I beg you to take care of Alona and the boys. It's my last request. Our marriage was not right, but she made me happy during these last months. She's the finest woman I've ever known. If you two could ever learn to love each other and care for each other, I can think of nothing that would make me happier. And the boys couldn't do better than having parents like you two. I am very tired now. God bless you, dear brother.

Oscar

She lowered the letter and brushed the tears from her eyes. "He changed so much in his last few months. I wish you could have been here."

"Alona, do you remember the last thing I said to you before I left to go to back into the service?"

Her throat was thick. "Yes," she whispered, "I remember."

He reached forward and took her in his arms. She looked up at him and knew that he was going to kiss her. When she did not protest, he put his lips against hers. After a nice gentle kiss, and then another one, he drew back. His voice was husky as he said, "My feelings haven't changed, Alona. I still love you. I want to be with you forever. I want to do what Oscar said, to take care of you and the boys."

She put her arms around his neck and kissed him firmly. All tension was gone from the room, and she was filled with joy. "When do you think you can start taking care of us?" she asked, a huge smile on her face.

He laughed. "Why don't you just learn to come out and say what you mean, Alona? I'll tell you what. Tomorrow morning, after the boys have opened all their presents from under the tree, you can say, 'I have one more present for you.'" He laughed then and squeezed her. "Then you can say, 'Here it is. Your new dad . . . ta-daaa!'"

Alona found herself laughing, but she stopped when a thought came to her. "Do you think it's too soon . . . I mean, after losing Oscar?"

"I've lost too much time, Alona. I want to marry you as soon as I can and start taking care of you and the boys right away."

"I've lost too much time too. So the boys get a new dad—and I get a new husband for Christmas."

Looking for More
Good Books to Read?

F